DELILAH

DELILAH

By: C.R. Hanover

Published by: Bite Me Publishing LLC

Delilah by C.R.Hanover

Cover Design: Shashika2

Published by Bite Me Publishing LLC

Interior Design:
C.R. Hanover and Bite Me Publishing LLC
Library of Congress Control Number: 2019918187
ISBN: 9781734232417 (Ebook)
ISBN: 9781734232400 (Hard Cover)
ISBN: 9781723232424 (Paperback)

First Edition 2019
Printed in The United States

Dedicated to Colin, Mia, Kyle, Nicholas, Alexis, Tarajanae, Perriona, Talaija and little Jalysia

Always work hard for the things you want most. It might not happen right away but fight for it, push yourself and one day it will. You deserve the very best this world has to offer. I love you all.

"A journey of a thousand miles begins with a single step." (Lao Tzu)

Acknowledgments

I would like to take this opportunity to thank the small fraction of family that knew I was writing a book.

You might not think you contributed much but in a world of darkness you were the little specs of light I needed to find my way.

Writing this book was by far the most challenging thing I've ever done and your encouragement, tips and advice mean more to me than you know.

Mom I wanted to list you separately, not just because you're my mom but because you listened and never judged me.

You stuck it out with me over this last decade reading and re- reading the jumble of half assed papers I kept giving you while I grew as a writer and you gave me the feedback I so desperately needed. I know I still have a long way to go but with your encouragement I have definitely come a long way from where I started.

THANK YOU a million times over. You are amazing and appreciated in too many ways to count.

I would also like to shout out my cousin and fellow Author Rhonda Dennis. Even though you didn't know me well you answered all of my questions anyway. You are an awesome person and from the bottom of my heart I thank you.

Table of Contents

Prologue..VI
Chapter 1..1
Chapter 2..20
Chapter 3..33
Chapter 4..46
Chapter 5..54
Chapter 6..63
Chapter 7..77
Chapter 8..83
Chapter 9..114
Chapter 10..132
Chapter 11..144
Chapter 12..153
Chapter 13..160
Chapter 14..170
Chapter 15..180
Chapter 16..185
Chapter 17..196
Chapter 18. 212
Chapter 19..224
Chapter 20..235
Chapter 21..244
Chapter 22..254
Chapter 23..270
Chapter 24..281
Chapter 25..286
Chapter 26..295
Chapter 27..300
Chapter 28..302
About the Author..307

This is a work of fiction. Names, characters, businesses, places, events, locals and incidents are either the product of the author's imagination or used in a fictitious manner. Any resemblance to actual persons, living or dead or actual events is purely coincidental.

Prologue

I stood there on the Bridge looking out at the River. The reflection of the full moon sparkled on black water as the snow silently fell all around me.

I watched the little white flakes descend from the cloud-covered sky, marveling as they twirled in the wind like tiny ballerinas before disappearing, one by one into the awaiting black abyss below.

I grabbed the Ruby droplet that hung around my neck as memories slowly flowed back in like the tide. The memories of how it all began those many years ago.

How my life had started out so boringly normal. How that first night at the Bakery would lead me here to this very Bridge and how one kiss would ultimately change my life forever…

Chapter 1

I was born Delilah Waters to William and Charlotte Waters on November 19th 1909. We lived in Detroit Michigan in a small 3 bedroom, red brick, row house on a little dead end street that led to a Cemetery.

I had to admit life had moved boringly smooth throughout my younger years and before I knew what happened it was 1929 and the world was alive! Cars were crowding the streets. Women were celebrating finally being able to have their opinions and voices heard and it was obvious that nothing was ever going to be the same.

I was 19 and should have been having the time of my life, wearing the hottest new fashion trends and dancing away the night with all of my friends. I should have had a hard working man on my arm and been on the short road to being a full time mother. Should have.

Instead I was single, didn't have many friends and worked as long as I could everyday at the family Bakery. I was more old fashioned when it came to my clothing choices. I liked to look nice but I didn't have the means to buy a new wardrobe, plus my mother hated everything about the new era and the modern woman. She was completely against anything that suggested women do more with their lives than take care of their families and I was against anything she viewed as "natural."

Don't get me wrong, the thought of marriage was nice and all but I wasn't the kind of girl that would settle and the guys left to choose from were… let's just leave it as, less than appealing. So I chose to stay single and earned the nickname of the "old maid" from the older generation that lived on our block.

Either they were all really worried I would die a lonely old lady. Or… they were just hoping I'd throw myself off a tall building soon. With their persistence lately I was willing to bet it was the latter.

The night he walked into my life had started just like any other day. The smell of cakes and pies met me as I opened the glass and wood door to Willies Wheat and Rye (named after my father of course.)

I walked the short distance to the white marble counter, setting my things down so I could switch on the lights. The bakery was empty and always seemed a little bit lonely until I got everything going. I always tried to make it as inviting as possible though. I kept pretty cakes in the glass display cases on both sides of the counter. Placed pies and pastries on glass pedestals and headed to the back to start the bread and cookie dough for the day.

Working at the Bakery was hard but I liked the work. Kneading the dough helped me work out my frustrations and the cakes let out my creative side. It was a good balance and added with my writing kept my mind and body busy.

Some days were slow but others were extremely busy. Pay day was usually my busiest day of the week. Bread was a cheap filler so even the families on a tight budget would come in to buy it from me. The morning seemed to have rushed by that day, it being Friday and all. It was now late afternoon, and I was sitting there jotting in my journal, when Mrs. Helen Herbert walked through my door.

She was younger than me by a year and was already married to Mr. Sherman Herbert. He was a plump little man and older than her by more than just a couple years. He had light brown hair he kept neat and one of those faces that were easy to talk to. If he didn't already work with my father at the Ford Plant my guess is he would have made a great Kirby salesman.

The couple had only been married for ten months and Mrs. Herbert was already eight and a half months pregnant with their first child. She was a sweet girl that stopped in often and whenever I saw her I always got the feeling that she came by more for the sake of company then baked goods. She had wondrous big brown eyes and looked a lot like a porcelain doll. There were no signs of age anywhere under her honey colored bangs and I wondered how long she would keep that innocence now that she was a wife and a soon to be mother?

"How are you doing today Mrs. Herbert?" I asked after the small golden bell on the door announced her arrival.

"Helen, please?" She reminded me with a smile. "And today's been a good day; hardly any morning sickness. Ya know, I always thought there were only a few months of that, but boy was I *wrong*!"

She answered shaking her head. Her laughter was contagious and I couldn't help joining in.

"I'm sorry, that has to be miserable." I said still chuckling.

"It is. But he's worth it." She sighed, affectionately patting her belly. "I'm sure you'll know all about it in no time." She added with a smile and a wink.

"Yeah, sure." I remarked dryly.

"Oh come on Delilah, you're a very pretty girl. I'd kill for those curly red locks. At the very least I know there's someone that can appreciate those *eyes*!"

I just kind of shrugged. I didn't think there was going to be women standing in line to acquire my long, ruby curls any time soon. Especially considering almost every woman had very short hair to go with the fashion trend. As for my eyes? Well, I did always love those. They were a jade green with brown, gray and even blue mixed in. I had never seen another pair like them.

"Hmm?... I've got it!" she snapped her fingers. "How about Steve Miller?"

"Steven, who?"

"Steve Miller? Sherman's friend."

I looked at her puzzled trying to remember him, until…

"He's forty!" I blurted.

"He's nice." She argued.

"He has gray hair, well what hasn't already fallen out." I continued.

"So what?!"

"Okay then," I shot back. "How about the fact that he has brown teeth in the front of his mouth? Lord only knows what's going on in the back?" I finished with a grimace.

She thought for a second, then shivered.

"See?!" I said hand gesturing toward her.

"Okay, okay." Helen laughed, putting her hands up in surrender. "Not Steve Miller, but you're going to have to stop being so picky ya know?"

"Well if men like Steven Miller are my only option then I'm content with *this*," I gestured around the room.

"Don't worry Delilah, I'm sure we can find you someone."

"I forgot about his teeth. Imagine kissing that?" She asked and shivered again.

"Yeah, thanks for the mental image Helen. That's just been burned into my mind forever. No thank you, I think I'll pass. If you don't mind?

She giggled. "Deal!"

"Thank you. What can I get you now that you're done trying to set me up with rusty old men?" I asked smiling.

"Well, I originally came in for some bread but what've you got today that's sweet? She pried searching the glass cases already excited.

"I made oatmeal raisin cookies about an hour ago if you're interested?" I answered grabbing the pedestal and removing the lid.

"Mm… that sounds great! We'll take two," she said caressing her large round belly.

"Do you still want the bread?"

"Yeah, I guess I'd better for dinner tonight."

I nodded and slid the bread and cookies into the brown paper bag.

"Just put it on Sherman's tab." She said taking the bag.

"No problem, and make sure you keep me posted about the baby. You did say *he* earlier right?" I asked curiously.

"Well, no way to know for sure. I just have a feeling it's a boy." She answered happily.

"Oh, well good luck."

"Thanks, and I'll be sure to send news if anything exciting happens."

"Alright." I yelled. And just like that she was out the door, already searching the bag for her cookies.

The day continued to run right on by me and it was getting late, only a few more minutes until I could close up for the night. I started doing the little things that wouldn't matter if I suddenly needed to place another order, just so I could get done faster.

As I wiped down the counters the bell rang and I looked up to see *Percival*.

Percival was a fourteen year old, blonde boy that had a squeaky voice that liked to go in and out as he spoke, and bad acne. His parents had moved down the street from me a year ago and ever since, Percy had high hopes of us dating. Unfortunately for me he liked to stop by the Bakery. Personally I think he used it to his advantage that I couldn't leave, and for that he was a sick and cruel little boy.

"Oh, hello Percy." I said already annoyed that he was here.

"Hi Delilah!" He answered. Beaming.

I sighed. "What can I do for you?"

"I was in the neighborhood and thought I would stop by and see you."

"That was nice." I lied. What I really wanted to say was "*You live in the neighborhood, idiot*!" But I'm supposed to be a lady and as I've been constantly reminded, ladies don't insult people. So I smiled and then stood there waiting for him to speak again. I knew of course, that it was inevitable.

"So… I was uh… I was wondering if maybe you'd like to go to dinner?" He rushed out the last part of the question in one squeaky breath as he stood in front of the door, conveniently blocking my escape.

"Dinner huh? It's pretty late Percy. Don't you have to be getting home?" I asked trying to avoid the question.

He looked back out through the glass of my big window at the darkness and sighed.

"Yeah, I guess you're right. I can't wait until spring's here again. See you around?"

Not if I can help it. I smiled at him by way of answering then said "Goodnight Percy."

I mentally cringed as he smiled back and with a sigh he walked back out the door.

I didn't feel too bad about blowing him off. I was, after all, too old for him, plus after he was out of his awkward years I was sure he'd have plenty of other girls to take to dinner. So I shrugged it off and went back to my cleaning. I had just walked in to the back room to finish up for the night when I heard the bell on the door chime.

"Oh! Now what? I swear if someone else is here to fix me up I'm going to… "

That's when I saw him. He was just standing in the middle of the room, staring at me.

He was a taller man, I'd say a little more than a half foot taller than my 5.6". Soft looking glossy, black hair, slicked to the left side sat just a few inches above the most piercing blue eyes I had ever seen in my life. The tint they gave was so blue they almost looked purple causing the whites of his eyes to have a blue tint too. His skin was pale in contrast with such dark hair and his face was masculine with a defined jaw line and high cheek bones. Nice full lips parted to reveal the beautiful white teeth that made up his dazzling smile.

His broad shoulders were draped nicely with a long, black dress coat that was no doubt put in place to protect the expensive looking gray double breasted suit peeking out at me from beneath its folds. My eyes continued to follow the suit down, past a set of long legs finally stopping just above a pair of shiny, black dress shoes that rested on the black and white tile floor.

"Wow." Wait, did I just say that out loud? I mentally cringed at the thought as I continued to take in every beautiful feature he had to give. Wow actually didn't seem like a big enough word but I couldn't do any better at the moment. He was just so different from anyone I had ever seen. In my assessment I decided he was *definitely* not from around here. I wanted to say more but I was completely dumbfounded and frozen in mid stride; unable to do anything but continue to stare at this delicious man, like an idiot.

"Hello." he said in a friendly but low tone.

My brain was screaming at me, *say something!* But I just nodded and continued to stand there and stare… like a moron.

"And you are? He prompted.

Damn! Those eyes, so beautiful… Wait, what's my name? I thought as I sorted through all the files in my head… Ah ha!

"Delilah!" I burst out sounding like an even bigger moron. He smiled at my exuberance and I could see he wanted to laugh at me. I mentally groaned in embarrassment and at that moment I just wished the floor would open up and swallow me whole.

"My name is Vincent; Vincent Vanhorne. It's nice to meet you Delilah."

"C— can I help you with something?" I stammered when I woke up enough to realize he was probably just stopping in to buy something on his way to somewhere else.

"It does smell delicious in here." he answered with a smirk. "But perhaps another time. Actually I saw you through the window a moment ago and I was wondering if you had plans for this evening? When you've finished up here, of course."

I looked at him confused at first then I looked behind me just to make sure he was talking to me.

"Me?" I asked pointing to myself.

"There's no one else here; at least I don't think so anyway?" He said with a quick glance around the room.

"No, there's no one else here." Wait, should I have told him that? My subconscious was such a mixture of feelings. I mean, is it the best idea to tell a large powerful looking man that you're alone? What if he wanted to rob me? Or worse? My palms were starting to sweat.

"I normally just walk home when I finish work here. I have people waiting on me there." I thought it would be a good idea to add in that someone would miss me, just in case.

"Perhaps I could accompany you on your walk?" He insisted.

I paused. Should I let him walk with me? I did have to walk through Patton Park. I didn't know this man. This could be very dangerous. Alone with a strange man I've never seen before in a big park, at night.

"Yeah, I don't kno—"

He walked to me and put his hand on my shoulder.

"Shh… I mean you no harm." He smiled and suddenly, my worries melted away like butter on a hot skillet.

If he didn't want to hurt me then what would be the harm of walking with someone else?

"Yeah, I guess that would be alright. It's going to take me a minute to finish up here; do you mind waiting?"

"Not at all. Take all the time you need."

I know he said he didn't mind waiting but I hurried through the rest of my chores as quick as I could. I figured I needed to hurry before my brain came back to tell me this was a horrible idea. I had never did anything like this before and I knew she was bound to snap back to reality at any moment to stop me.

Afterwards I grabbed my light blue jacket off the metal coat rack in the back room and headed back towards the front of the Bakery with it hung over my arm. I got my keys from the cash drawer and set them on the counter so I could put on my coat.

"Allow me?" Vincent said lifting his hand to help me.

"Thank you."

"Ready?" he asked enthusiastically after I finished with the last button.

"Almost." I paused and reached for my journal on the other side of the counter and mentally checked for my badgering conscience… Nope, seems she had taken the night off for a change so I was free to go.

"Alright, now we can go." I announced smiling and waving the journal in the air. I tucked it under my arm and grabbed my keys, after locking the door we were on our way.

It was chilly as we walked in the direction of my house. As we walked I was desperately searching my head for something to say and thought I would start with the obvious.

"Have you just moved here? Because I'm sure I would have noticed you around before." Why did I say that? Nice Delilah… ugh!

"Yes." he replied with a smile. "I arrived last night."

Just perfect. Get it together. Start with something simple, let him do the talking. I mentally coached myself.

"What brings you to Detroit?" I asked hoping for a longer explanation this time.

"I've been told there's a lot of opportunity here, so I thought I would come and see what all the fuss was about for myself."

"Whad'ya think so far?" I asked sarcastically.

"It has potential." he announced it as though he was telling himself rather than me.

"Something to read?" He asked nodding towards my journal.

"It's my shush book." I answered.

"A shush book?" he asked raising one eyebrow.

"Yeah, I keep my notes and thoughts in here. Some might call it a journal but I refer to it as a shush book because the things I write inside are secret thoughts that I don't share with other people."

"Is it something like a diary?"

"Not exactly. "I don't really write down everything that happens in my life. I'd never write anything at all if I did that. I write more about my feelings about certain things or little random thoughts that might make a good poem later on."

"So you're a poet." he didn't really say it like a question it was more like and outspoken thought but I answered anyway.

"I wish. It would be nice to be up there with one of the greats like W.B. Yeats or Edger Allan Poe."

"It's interesting that you categorize them together like that."

"Why?"

"Well, a lot of people don't consider Poe as being on the same level as Yeats."

"Well, I appreciate each one for different reasons. You're right that they're different from each other, but if they were the same then what would be the point of liking both? I could just read one."

"So you are intrigued by both love and the grotesque and darker side of humanity?"

"Sure, but I never really thought about it that way before."

"Interesting." Vincent smiled at me and kept walking, he didn't say anything after that but every now and then he would look at me through the corner of his eye and I would catch him smiling.

We continued on, cutting through the now empty park. The sky was bright due to the full moon hovering above us and I was grateful for the light it provided. It was just cold enough to keep people from lingering around outside. I was surprised there was no snow yet but thankful because it made the park the Devil to get through and the longer I didn't have to trudge, the better. It was already October, which meant only a few more weeks left until my twentieth birthday.

I dreaded getting older with nothing to show for my life. With every year that passed that I stayed a single "old maid" I felt more and more like a burden on my parents.

Sometimes I wished I could trade places with Helen; she looked happy enough. I thought about seeing her in the Bakery today. She didn't seem to have any real worries. After all, what was there to worry about? She was only eighteen and yet she already had someone to take care of her and a baby on the way to occupy all her time. But did I want that? Could I still have that? Everyone else thought I was getting too old. By the time I found someone worth marrying, and got married it could take years before I had a family of my own. I'd be in my mid twenties by then. Helen's first child would be five or six already and I'd—

"Delilah?" Vincent asked breaking my concentration and mental breakdown.

"Yes?" I answered trying to block out my thoughts.

"Are you alright? You seem… distracted."

How odd, I thought. The man that has yet to speak a single word in the last ten minutes is worried that *I'm* distracted.

"I'm fine." I reassured him with a smile.

"Are you sure?"

"Yes of course."

He smiled back, then turned his head forward and kept walking.

We were almost to my house. The steps of my porch seemed to be waiting for me and I was happy to see them. Vincent was nice enough but I was glad to be done with this awkward situation of walking in silence.

We walked up the six steps and were now standing on the porch in front of the door. He lifted his hand and started caressing the side of my face with his fingertips, I shivered when his skin touched mine. It was soft but it was also cold. Even colder than my cheeks from battling the chilly wind during our walk.

From the very little experience I had with men I always found them to be warmer than women, it was why they could work long hours in the cold and it not bother them that bad. My father was always warmer than my mother. I can't count how many times they argued over the temperature of the house. Pop would say it was too hot and demand that my mother get a sweater or a blanket if she were that cold.

Just then Vincent tilted my chin up with his finger so I could look at his face and I was instantly lost in the depth of those blue eyes. I was nervous and my heart was racing. Was he going to kiss me?

He leaned close into my face and I closed my eyes and braced myself waiting to feel his full lips press against mine. But I was disappointed when he moved past my lips to stop at my ear instead.

"Goodnight Delilah." he whispered in my ear. He was close enough that his lips brushed against my skin and sent chills over my entire body.

God he smelled good! His cologne was just right, not overbearing, and not a popular scent that I had smelled on other men in passing. It was manly with a hint of something else. Something that made me almost want to take a bite out of him.

As he lifted away, my nose tried to follow him and he was smiling at me when I opened my eyes. I instantly snapped to attention and stood up straight; embarrassed that I had been caught sniffing him.

"Same time tomorrow?" He chuckled, grinning.

I looked at him but what should I say? Sorry for smelling you. Or worse. I'm sorry you *caught* me smelling you. Ugh! I'm an idiot. I didn't know what to say but I'm sure the look on my face must have said it for me.

He grabbed my hand in his and smiled kindly stroking my skin with his cool fingertips. "Same time tomorrow?" he repeated softly, still smiling at me.

I hesitated at first but I finally agreed. "Same time tomorrow." I said with a sigh.

“Good, I shall see you then.” He said, then he kissed the back of my hand sweetly and walked down the stairs.

I stood on the porch for a minute longer and watched him walk down the street, and as he disappeared in to the night I thought to myself, “what a man” and sighed as I walked through the door and shut it behind me.

After clearing my head of the fog Mr. Vanhorne had left. I noticed that Pop was in the living room sitting in his favorite green chair. Personally I thought the chair was hideous but he always refused to get rid of it; arguing that it was “Already broken in.”

He liked to sit there and listen to the radio to help himself relax after a hard day at the Plant. He got home at five o’clock so he had already eaten dinner and was settled in for the night.

I smiled at him sitting contently and hung my coat on the tall wooden rack by the door. He had dark brown hair, he wore slicked back, light green eyes and a warm smile. He wasn’t a large man though, he didn’t make it to six feet tall but he was strong and had a mighty temper when provoked. I guess I got my attitude from him.

I was taking off my shoes when my mother called out from upstairs. “Your dinner is waiting for you on the table.”

“Thank you.” I called back as I headed toward the dining room. I had gotten used to cold food; I had been eating it for almost two years now. I always got home after Pop and he liked a hot meal when he walked through the door so that meant mine sat out for at least an hour before I got home.

I sat down on the wood chair and removed the white cloth napkin covering the white porcelain plate. "Chicken again?" I grumped, but under my breath so my mother wouldn't hear me. I didn't want her to think I was ungrateful but we ate a lot of chicken and I didn't like it much to begin with. So with a frown I ate it anyways because "Waste not, want not." had been drilled into my head from birth.

I washed my dinner dishes and headed up the stairs to my bedroom at the end of the hall. A small space welcomed me when I opened the door. It was modest but clean. My bed sat pushed up next to the left wall, my dresser on the other side of the 2 windows in the right corner and a small bookshelf by the door.

I changed into my long nightgown, shut off the light and crawled in to the bed pulling the log cabin quilt my mother had made me up to my chin. It was much bigger than my single bed with a bunch of different colors incorporated in to the design and I loved it!

Feeling warm and cozy I laid in the moonlight my window let through and thought about the beautiful qualities of this beyond perfect stranger. I was flying high on hope that just maybe he might be the one to take me away from here. Maybe my luck was changing? Maybe he was here to put an end to the harassment and judgement from everyone else that already had what they wanted?

Hope:

A stranger so beautiful, he takes my breath away.
He's a hope, an escape and might be here to stay.
Will tomorrow be better? Is he what I've been
waiting for? I never thought, someone as exquisite
as him, would happen through my door.
Delilah Waters- Oct. 1929

Chapter 2.

I awoke with a searing curiosity about who this dangerously gorgeous man was that now appeared in my dreams? He even appeared in my snowing rose petal dream. Both of us dressed in red, dancing together in a field of snowing white rose petals. Usually I was alone in this dream, spinning and twirling in a blizzard of whirling petals but for once it was nice to have the company.

I got myself together in slow motion at first, lost in the sparkle of his eyes. They were *so* blue. I had never seen anything like them before and the way the light at the bakery danced off them… wow! Was he staring at me? I mean yeah he was obviously looking at me but was he *staring*? I realized that I was just sitting on my bed obsessing instead of dressing so I mentally shook myself out of it so I could get myself going. I stole a quick glance in the mirror. Everything looked the same as usual. Same slightly frizzy red curls covered my head. Same slightly blushed cheeks and rose colored lips. Even the same multicolored green eyes only today they were accompanied by slight bluish circles… Great. I suddenly wished I had done more with myself but there was no time. I took a hair pin and shoved my locks in a quick, make shift bun and headed for the door. I was going to be late… Terrific.

Once at the Bakery, I sat on my little stool behind the counter and allowed myself to get lost in a daydream of how beautiful he looked in red. His pale skin and coal black hair were perfect in contrast to the white shirt and red vest he wore. I wondered what he was doing right now and if he was thinking about me?

Of course he's not thinking about you! I'm sure he has better things to do with is time than think about a girl he barely knows… Right?

Well, then I hope he's thinking about me. How's that!? I smugly asked myself.

Oh no! Am I losing my mind? I wondered. After all I am sitting here alone, arguing with myself… Nah, I reassured myself. You're only crazy if you answer your own quest—

I took a deep breath and tried to compose myself. It's 3:30 now, only two and a half more hours to go.

But suddenly I realized he might not come back. What if he realized there are prettier girls that live around here? Or thought I was boring because I didn't talk enough last night. If so, why would he waste his time coming back?

My heart was racing at the thought of being stood up. "Breathe Delilah," I commanded myself out loud.

I took another deep breath and went back to business as usual, trying to keep myself from going insane.

That was all I needed floating around. "Did you hear? The old maid lost her mind."

"Yeah, I heard she went loony waiting for some boy."

That was *not* acceptable. It was bad enough I was the *old maid.* I wasn't going to be the *old_loony* to go along with it. So I kicked out all my thoughts of Vincent so I could continue my day *sanely.*

I kept myself busy by cleaning around the front counter and straightening up the back room. I swept up the remaining flour off the floor and washed the mixing bowls and bread pans.

I tried to keep moving so I didn't have time to think about him. I hoped picking up and straightening would make the time go by faster.

I was still scrubbing parts of the back room when I heard the bell on the door chime. I threw my rag back into my old metal bucket and ran towards the front of the Bakery. I just knew it had to be… Percival!

"Did you give any thought about dinner?" he said enthusiastically.

I wanted to scream. I balled up my fists digging my nails into my palms and bit my tongue instead. Every day, every day he does this to me! I took a much needed breath to calm myself, and as politely as I could manage without losing it, I gave him the usual excuse.

"Percy," I said calmly. "I'm afraid you think differently of me then I think of you. I don't want to hurt your feelings but I think of you in more of a *friend* kind of way and I don't want to mislead you, so I think dinner would be a bad idea."

"If that's the way you feel Delilah, then okay."

Wow! I thought. Maybe I was getting through? Walking toward the door, he shot me a cocky glance.

"There's always, next week," he said smirking.

"Ahh!" I exploded and I threw my shoe as hard as I could at his head. It missed him by an inch hitting the door frame as he ducked out the door laughing.

"He is persistent, I have to give him that." I said hopping to put my shoe back on.

It was later than I thought, it seemed my neurotic cleaning and annoying conversation with Percy had proven useful. Just what I needed to get my mind off Vincent; he should be arriving soon.

I made a promise to myself. I was going to finish putting away all the left overs, just like any other day, grab my coat, keys and book and start home with or without him. I was not going to sit and obsess over if he would show up or not. So that's exactly what I did.

It was about five minutes to six so I went to the back room to grab my coat as promised. I walked slowly back to the front of the Bakery. My head was down, so at first I didn't realize that he was standing there.

"Oh! You scared me." I said, looking up with my hand to my chest. "I didn't hear the bell ring."

He stood there in front of the door staring at me with that same dazzling smile and blazing blue eyes that had haunted my dream the night before and I had to admit even my dreams didn't compare to the real thing. Tonight he wore a tan suit with a cream colored vest and his long black over coat draped in the same fashion as the night before. In his left hand was a bouquet of white roses complete with some greenery and baby's breath all wrapped together in red paper; they were beautiful.

"How long have you been here?" I asked confused.

"Only a minute," he replied. "Are you ready to go?" he asked reaching to help me with my coat.

"Sure," I answered fastening the buttons.

"These are for you." he said as he offered me the bouquet.

"Thank you. They're beautiful Vincent."

With the flowers in one hand I grabbed my keys and book and then we headed out the door— the bell ringing this time— as I shut and locked it behind us.

We started toward my house just as the night before only this time we walked a little slower. I hoped there would be more conversation on this walk but so far, we were off to a bad start. I took a deep breath ready to start my interrogation but just as I was about to speak, he did.

"Do you mind if we detour a bit?"

"Okay. Where?" I asked curiously.

"There is a bench just off the path," he said pointing to the left. "I thought perhaps we could sit down and talk for awhile?"

He wants to talk, this has to be a good sign, I thought to myself as we walked to the small wooden bench and sat down. I stared at him waiting for him to speak but he just sat there looking at me with frustration on his face like he didn't know where to start. He finally hunched over and put his head in his hands.

I started to ask him if he was okay. I guessed that he had something that he didn't really want to say but had to tell me. Maybe he was going to tell me he didn't want to see me anymore. He seemed gentlemanly enough for that to be a hard thing for him to say. I started to open my mouth to tell him that it was okay but that's when he looked up again.

"I want to apologize for being so dull last night," he said, lifting up to look at me. "I'm not used to talking to people that often."

"Really?"

"Not usually, no. I haven't been very interested in what they have to say now for a long time. You see, people rarely surprise me but I was taken off guard with you."

"What do you mean, taken off guard with me?" I had to ask. I mean, what an odd thing to say to a person.

"What I mean is, I've traveled all over and have never met a human being worth knowing, before meeting you." He sat, staring at me, his big blue eyes lost in my face.

The way he spoke, I felt sorry for him rather than flattered. He spoke as if he had been searching for something with no hope of ever finding it.

I reached out my hand to try to comfort him but he pulled away from me. He was acting so strange. First with his staring at me during our walk last night and then spilling his guts just now and then not wanting me to touch him.

"What's so special about me?" I asked confused.

He smiled. "If I were a betting man. I would put my money on… Everything!"

I wanted to share in his excitement but I just met him! He knows nothing about me.

"I have to admit I have become completely enthralled by you, Delilah and if you allow me, I would like to spend more time with you?"

I sat there trying to comprehend exactly what he was trying to tell me.

Enthralled? Who talks like that? He sounds like a nobleman from a book. Then I wondered if this was possible? A gorgeous man just happens to walk in to my life and confesses that he's "enthralled" after just two meetings?… I don't think so!

"Is this a joke?"

"What?" His smile was gone in an instant.

"Did my father ask you to talk to me?" I demanded. "Because this is not very funny!" I said standing up now.

"What?… No!" He said rushing to his feet. "That's not true at all. I have never even spoke with your father. Why would you think that?" He asked in disbelief, grabbing my arm to pull me back toward him. "I know how I must sound Delilah, but please believe the words I speak are the truth."

"Believe you? I don't know you!" I had to get out of here.

"I have no reason to lie to you." He pleaded.

"Let my arm go!" I said pulling myself away from him. "And. You. Can. Keep. *These*!" I yelled hitting him with each and every word with the roses.

I walked swiftly back down the street leaving him standing there behind me. I could have run home I was so angry. Not as angry at him as I was angry with myself for starting to believe the bull he was telling me. I wanted so much for it to be true and I hated myself for that. For seeming so gullible that he thought he could lay that on me and I wouldn't see through it. What kind of girl do people take me for when they look at me? I thought to myself as one by one tears started to fall from my eyes. It was too cold to be blubbering and the icy wind was doing a good job of turning my cheeks into a salt flavored Popsicle so I did my best to stop my tears as I walked with my head tilted down until I was on the porch. I took a deep breath, wiped under each eye with one of my powdery blue sleeves and hoped that my face only looked swollen from the cold before I walked through the door.

If my father had sent him Vincent could tell him I didn't fall for the gag. I didn't feel like explaining what had happened and the slightest hint of tears on my face would start a conversation I didn't want to have. I took another deep breath before hanging up my coat. Please don't let them talk to me, I silently prayed looking up at the stucco ceiling. I knew if I had to speak, that my voice would surely crack and I would fall apart. I bent down and took off my shoes then put them in their regular place by the wall. Then I started to walk, headed for the stairs.

"Delilah, is that you?" I heard my mother call out from the dining room. Her and my father were sitting in there probably piecing together a puzzle. I froze! Keep it together Delilah. I mentally coached myself. I held my breath hoping it would help.

"Yes Mother, it's me." I chocked out with a slight crack.

"Dinners in the oven," she yelled back. Yes definitely doing a puzzle. Good, she hadn't noticed. I thought relieved. "Okay" I called out still holding my breath, and I ran up the stairs.

There were tears streaming down my face before I could make it to my room. I was crying so hard I was almost hysterical. I shut the door behind me and ran over to my bed and sank my face deep into my pillow where I could let everything go. The fears I had of being an old maid and how far I was willing to go today to escape those thoughts and feel loved. The fact that I almost let a man I didn't know manipulate my thoughts. What a fool I had been for the past two days!

How could you let this happen? I scolded. How could you be so stupid and even worse, so desperate to believe such lies?! What could he possibly see in me that would make him feel that way and in such a short period of time? I'm not especially pretty or talented in any way. I could name off a dozen girls that were prettier than me that I went to school with; most of them still lived here. Of course, most of them were married or engaged too I suddenly realized. Maybe that's why? I'm the only one that's left? I win by default. Congratulations Delilah, you win because there's not another choice. Way to go!

I sobbed even harder at the thought and let my pillow catch every salty tear my body threw at it until I thought there couldn‘t possibly be any more left.

Finally I turned my head to the side feeling that the worst of the sobbing was behind me but continued to lay there as a few silent tears joined the others that had fallen onto my pillow.

Wait! He did say that he traveled, didn't he? So maybe you're not the only choice? It seemed my subconscious was searching for hope. It was all a lie, I argued. I didn't want to hear it right now.

But look at the way he dresses? He must have money to dress that way. So maybe it wasn't a lie after all? Maybe he travels for work? That would certainly explain why he thought I was so interesting. He didn't get out much, because he was always working? And he obviously wouldn't talk to that many people because of the same reason.

What if my father didn't send him? I was so horrible to him! The more I thought about it the more I started to feel bad about just leaving him standing there like that all alone by the bench. I wondered how long he stood there before walking back to, where ever it was he was staying?

Yes, what if he was telling the truth?

I had heard of love at first sight before. I didn't actually know anybody it had ever happened to, but I guess it was possible. Maybe he had a version of that. Definitely not love though, maybe just intrigue? I guess I could at least consider myself intriguing, right?

I do read and write a lot and did at least finish school, that was rare for a girl. I work too, so I'm not lazy. That could be interesting… I hope?

Oh no. I HIT HIM!… I beat him all over with the flowers he brought me to be nice! I wanted to die. I was an awful, AWFUL person. I needed to apologize to him tomorrow after work, that is, if he comes back.

Damn! Tomorrow's Sunday, I don't have work. I realized.

But I could look for where he was staying? With a face like that, I'm sure someone knows where he's staying? I'll start after breakfast tomorrow, I promised myself.

I changed my clothes and crawled back into bed. After my breakdown, I was exhausted and the only thing I longed for was sleep so I closed my eyes and let my unconsciousness take me away.

* * *

The night was black and the street was empty. The concrete was cold and sharp as the jagged pieces bit into my feet but I didn't care. I moved slowly through the thick fog that lingered all around me. With my head tilted back I wiggled my blood soaked fingers through the open air with no concern as to why they were bloody.

I watched as my gore covered body moved through the fog until I came to a halt, almost as if I was waiting for something. I stood there, blood covering my mouth and the front of my nightgown while the fog slowly started to lift and become a light mist. Soon after, a man appeared behind me. I anxiously waited to see his face but my dream self was much more patient and remained standing with my back toward the man, until he wrapped his arms around my waist..

As the fog got lighter my dream self turned to finally see that it was Vincent that was standing behind, holding me. His face looking just as gruesome as mine; blood covering his lips and chin.

I waited for him to be disgusted by the way I looked but he looked… pleased.

He stared down at me with a smile that I returned before we joined together in a passionate kiss; his strong hands entangling in my ruby curls. I could taste the blood that covered his lips and surprisingly it tasted… good! I began to crave its odd mix of salty sweetness and had to stop myself from licking his chin. Instead I let my desire to touch him take over and I pushed my body up against his, yearning for more than the kiss we were sharing. Sliding my blood covered hands into his sleek black hair, I pulled his head back so I could continue to kiss his neck. I started to unbutton his shirt but suddenly, he pulled away.

"What are you doing?" I asked walking toward him with a smile.

"We can't do this. Not now, not like this Delilah."

"Vincent?" I called looking around, but he had vanished.

"Vincent!" I called out, jerking myself upright expecting to see him in my room, but unfortunately I was greeted by darkness instead.

I cringed remembering the dreams gory details as they rolled back into my mind, like the heavy fog..

What would make me dream of something so morbid? I thought to myself laying back down; snuggling into my other (non soggy) pillow.

And why was I that unaffected to be covered in someone elses' blood? More importantly, whose blood was I covered in? Surely someone had to be dead for there to be that much blood? Why were Vincent's lips and chin covered in blood? That was definitely an odd place to be bloody.

After racking my brain, I couldn't come up with any answers so I decided to let my mind rest and instead I focused on the good parts of my dream. Like the softness of his hair as I slid my fingertips through it and how muscular Vincent felt under his shirt. I couldn't help even thinking about how secure and petite I felt by having to stand on my tiptoes to kiss him. Mm… and the softness of his lips…

WHAT IS WRONG WITH YOU?! I chastised. I'm fantasizing about a guy I've only seen twice!… You could do a lot worse? My mind argued. I shuddered as my thoughts immediately went to acne infested Percy. Yikes! Yes, I do believe I'll crawl back into my head where my dark and beautiful man hopefully awaits.

So with a sigh I decided to listen to myself, hoping that when I did go back to sleep my dreams would leave out all the blood but otherwise start back up where they had left off.

Chapter 3.

I woke up the next morning a little disappointed at my dream selection. Unfortunately my sexy dream man had failed to make another steamy appearance after I finally fell back to sleep. Instead I had to settle for what did make another appearance; me twirling and dancing in the same green field of snowing white rose petals. It was a tranquil dream that I had been having for as long as I could remember but still didn't understand why?

It was later then I was used to getting up, no doubt due to the horrible sleep I got the night before. I couldn't extinguish the same burning questions stuck in the back of my mind that had bothered me last night before falling back to sleep. It was just my imagination running wild, I told myself trying to dismiss the memory of my blood soaked hands and face.

Shaking it all off I suddenly remembered what I had planned to do today. Springing out of bed, I got dressed, careful to pay a little more attention to myself than usual. I put on my light blue dress that was just about the same shade as my powder blue coat and accented with black heals. I put my hair in a low bun and covered my head with my black cloche hat. My eyes looked the worse from all the crying but I used a little cream to help fix that and put a little rouge on my cheeks to give them slight color because I didn't like it too bright. I rarely wore lipstick because with the paleness of my complexion my lips always looked brighter but today I even wore a little bit of that just to add to the look. After some mascara to darken my red eyelashes I looked well rested and ready for the day.

I went down stairs to meet my mother and father already sitting at the dinning table about to eat the breakfast my mother had just set out.

My mothers tiny frame was hidden under her pink robe, her face was already done up. Red lips, rogue and dark lashes. Her dark auburn hair was in a scarf to hide her pin curls while they set.

“Good morning,” my father said folding his paper to set it on the table beside his plate. He was fully dressed for the day in a white collared, short sleeved shirt and tan slacks. His hair was slicked back like usual.

“Good morning,” I replied pulling out my usual chair from the table so I could join them.

“You look nice, are you hungry?” My mother asked handing me the bowl of scrambled eggs.

“Starving!” I said smiling at her compliment and grabbing the bowl so I could begin piling the eggs on to my plate.

"I’m not surprised, I noticed you didn’t eat dinner last night. Were you not feeling well?”

“I had a headache and I was just really tired so I went straight to bed.” My mother looked at me and politely smiled, dismissing her worry lines.

“What are your plans for today?”

"I think I'm going to walk around, stop in at some shops and enjoy not working," I replied, reaching for the biscuits. I knew better than to tell my mother what I was really doing. I knew she would not approve of me searching for some strange man that I met two nights ago.

"That's nice. You work so much I think a day of fresh air will do you some good, maybe even help with the aftermath of your headache."

"Me too. It will be nice to see what's new in the shops." I agreed smiling at her.

"And besides, maybe you'll meet someone today. On your walk."

She just had to keep talking.

"Maybe." I said, starting to chew even faster. This time I actually hoped she was right. But I was sure that *my* someone and *her* someone weren't the same someone at all. Plus I knew if I stuck around much longer it was only a matter of time before "how old" I was getting was sure to get worked into the conversation.

"Yes, I think that's a wonderful idea!" Added my father. "You're not getting any younger you know?"

And there it was. I froze, and forcefully pushed a bite of biscuit down my throat to keep from screaming. I needed to get away from here, and fast.

I started to cram food into my mouth as fast as I could. I nodded occasionally and tried to look enthused as they threw out suggestions of the single men that were left. This one's cousin, that one's brother; one was even a coworker of my fathers. Ugh! I tried to stay as quite as possible. I hoped that the quieter I stayed the less chance my age would have to make another appearance. That was all I needed. Like this wasn't bad enough.

Finally! My plate was clean and I was almost free. I stood up grabbing my plate and glass and started towards the kitchen.

"Don't worry about that honey, I've got it." My mother said.

"Are you sure?" I asked sincerely, trying to make it look believable.

"Yes of course. You go ahead." She insisted, waving me away as she picked up the dishes on the table.

"Alright. Thank you."

"Any time sweetie. Enjoy your walk." She shot me a warm smile, then went back to clearing the table.

I knew she would want me to hurry up and get started and I was happy to go. I put on my coat and walked out the door.

And I'm off! I thought as I stepped on to the porch. I knew they meant well but they were both driving me crazy about this age thing and I couldn't handle listening to it right now.

I took a deep breath, ridding myself of their age digs and humiliation and breathed a mental sigh of relief that I had something else to do with my day then sit there with them.

As my foot left the last stair I smiled to myself. Now, I thought, let the manhunt begin!

I walked through town stopping at the little stores along Vernor and Springwells asking if anyone had seen Vincent? I gave his description but there was no luck. No one had seen him. How could this be? As beautiful as he was, how could no one have noticed that face? But nothing! It was as if he never existed at all. Not a single trace of him left. Where was he staying? I looked at all the little apartments that were scattered here and there within walking distance and asked the other men on the street, but still nothing. I had searched all day with nothing to show for my efforts.

It was getting later now as I slowly walked back toward my house. I thought about how he could disappear like that? Maybe he had left? What was there to stay for? He had only been here for two days before being insulted and abandoned by the only girl — in his mind— that was "Worth knowing." Of course he would stick around after that. Wouldn't you? I asked myself, shaking my head in disgust.

I picked up speed now that I was irritated and headed straight for home to grab my journal and then go to the Cemetery. I needed to sit and relax and that was the only place I ever felt free. I thought maybe writing would help with my frustration.

No one said anything to me when I came in to the house and marched up the stairs to my bedroom. It was Sunday so maybe my parents had gone out for the day? My mother insisted Pop take her out on Sundays because she spent all week cooped up in the house while he was at work. I couldn't blame her for that, I wasn't home either so she spent a lot of time alone.

I grabbed my notebook off my book shelf where I always kept it (if it wasn't with me) and headed out of the house to the Cemetery. Once I was there I settled down in my favorite spot in-between a giant tree and a big Celtic cross that sat on top of a tombstone. It was close enough that I could still see my house but far enough away that no one knew I was there.

I pulled out my pencil and in no order what so ever, started to write down the jumble of thoughts running crazy in my brain. Turning the book this way and that to fit as much as I could on one page. By the time I was done with my rantings I had not one but two poems.

Running out of time:

They say I'm far too old now, they say I should find love. But where to look when I'm stuck in this place, enduring every nag and shove. If only they understood me, if only they truly seen. That I have hopes for myself that don't include a man's wealth, they'd let me be free to dream. Maybe I am too picky but why shouldn't I be? It's my life not theirs, so why should they care? The only one living it, is me.

My Shoes:

Old maid, Old maid, that's all that I hear, day after day and now, year after year. I'm glad it's so easy for everyone but me, I get it! I'm pathetic! So just let me be! I'll work at this bakery for the rest of my life, I'll never be a mother cause I'll never be a wife! But I'll never settle for less and that's all

that's left to choose so I'll stay the Old maid walking alone in these shoes!
Delilah Waters- 1929

I inspected my work and I thought they were alright, I guess it never really mattered because I never showed any of them to anyone anyway but I liked reading published poetry and reading my own didn't make me cringe so I thought they were good enough. It wasn't like I was a professional or anything though. I think I did it mainly because I was alone. Who did I really have to talk to? I didn't have a best friend or even family I could confide in so, a simple piece of paper and a pencil were my friends.

I was so consumed I hadn't realized at first that it was dark out. I didn't mind being in the Cemetery at night but it was getting cold on my bare legs and I also hadn't moved since I sat down so my butt hurt like hell.

Stretching and rubbing my sore backside I began the walk back towards my house. I was less aggravated now, but a sadness was starting to creep in as I walked with my head hung, kicking stray pebbles in my path. I couldn't imagine not seeing those beautiful eyes or brilliant smile again all because I was a suspicious idiot that didn't know how to just accept good fortune when it smiled down on me.

I walked up the path to the steps. I started up the first step and looked up to see Vincent standing there, waiting for me on the porch. He was the breath of fresh air I needed, almost as if I hadn't been able to breathe all day until I saw him. I was almost ecstatic and my heart began to race— that is until my memories came barreling back to me from the night before.

“I'm so sorry. I shouldn't have reacted that way when you were just trying to be honest.” I put my head down in shame. I reacted so badly I couldn’t look at him.

He walked down the five steps to meet me and placed one hand on each of my shoulders, to pull me closer. He then tilted my head up with his fingertips and his eyes glistened when they locked with mine. I started to speak, to explain myself but Vincent had his lips already crushing my lips. I was hopelessly lost in the softness of his full lips and the coolness of the inside of his mouth as our tongues slid against each other, in a slow and seductive rhythm. It was the closest thing to perfection I had ever experienced and although the dream kiss was good and steamy, this kiss was *real* and sensational.

He lifted away slowly caressing the side of my face with the side of his hand. Then with his eyes once again gazing into mine, he whispered.

“There is nothing for you to apologize for,” and smiled the kindest most beautiful smile I had ever seen.

I felt better instantly. I laid my head on his chest and wrapped my arms around him for the first time. His chest was hard and muscular but also cool just like his hands had been every time he’d touched me. Why was he so cold? I couldn’t understand. Being that cold all the time surely he would have never stopped shivering? However, he never seemed to notice the temperature difference between us.

We stood there holding each other for a while before I remembered the hopeless search I had conducted earlier.

"Where are you staying?" I asked, leaning my head away from his chest to look up at him. "I looked for you all day and no one knew who you were or where you were staying."

"Why were you looking for me?" He asked looking amused as he gazed down at me.

"I wanted to apologize for reacting so badly last night. I realized how rude I must have sounded and I wanted to catch you before you left to tell you I was sorry."

"Before I left? I wasn't aware I was going anywhere any time soon. Why would I leave?" he asked looking at me confused.

"I don't know… maybe because of me?" I said cringing at the thought.

"Oh Delilah, and what exactly do you think *you* did that was so horrible to make me want to leave? Especially considering I'm the one that made no rational sense last night. You had every reason to react the way you did."

"I did?" I asked in shock.

"Yes." He chuckled. "The last thing I expected to find tonight was *you* out looking for *me*."

"Well that isn't exactly where I was coming from just now." I said softly, not really wanting to explain that I was in the Cemetery. I just got him back, the last thing I wanted was to scare him away with my morbid obsession of sitting with dead people.

"Then where were you coming from? I did notice earlier that you were walking up from the opposite direction."

I hesitated but finally I said. "If I tell you, you have to promise that you won't think I'm deranged and run screaming for the hills… Can you promise that?"

He looked at me humorously and said, "I promise, and to be quite honest I don't think there is anything you could possibly do that would make me think that, of you. But I'm not going anywhere Delilah, I give you my word."

Okay, here it goes I thought and took a deep breath before slowly answering… "The, um, Cemetery." I waited for him to laugh thinking it was a joke or run, thinking I was a loon but he just stood there expressionless. Maybe he was in shock?

"Where you visiting a relative?" He asked, maybe he was trying to give me the benefit of the doubt, secretly hoping I had a legitimate reason to be leaving a Cemetery after dark.

"Not exactly, I just go there sometimes. It's quiet and I can think and that's where I put together some of my poetry."

"Aren't you frightened, to be in a Graveyard alone and at night?" I could tell he was confused so I rushed to explain myself before this conversation got any more bizarre.

"No, I've been going since I was in grade School. It's been the only escape I've ever had because no one knows I go there and if they did, most people would be too afraid to go looking for me."

"Well, I have to say it wasn't what I was expecting. You constantly surprise me Delilah." If I didn't know better I would say he looked… impressed?

"I thought the idea would repulse you?" I admitted, kind of shocked.

He pulled me in his arms once more and whispered. "not at all." He began outlining my nose and lips with his finger, sending a relaxing comfort through my body then he continued in his low tone "I'm intrigued by you in so many ways."

I didn't want this feeling to end. It was a completely different feeling then my everyday life of just being around other people. It was comforting and standing there in his arms I felt like I could relax. Maybe if I did this I wouldn't have to be all alone?

I took a deep breath and tilted my head up at Vincent. My eyelids were heavy but when they lifted, he was looking almost through to my soul as if he knew the epiphany I just had. He smiled at my drowsiness and brushed the side of my face with a single white rose bud.

"I thought I would try bringing just one with me this time; if things didn't go well it had to be less painful then getting hit with twelve." He smiled and held it out towards me.

"You're probably right." I agreed returning his smile as I took the rose from him. Holding it up to my nose, its sweet scent instantly took me back to twirling with my snowing rose petals.

“How do u know I like white roses?” I couldn’t help but ask.

He smiled, “Oh, I have my ways. Get some sleep Delilah. I will see you tomorrow?” he whispered and kissed my cheek.

I smiled back lost in the bliss of the moment. “Tomorrow,” I agreed with a sigh, content in my dreamy world. With my feet dragging me forward and still rubbing the rose against my nose, I walked up the stairs and through the door.

Blue:

Blue, blue... I can't get enough of blue. I can't get enough of his smile or the velvety smooth touch of his hand. There is never enough hours in the day, to get my fill, of this beautiful, beautiful man. I know I sound pathetic but I'm sure this love is true, because he seems to be everywhere I turn, as a breathtaking shade, of blue.

Delilah Waters- 1929

Chapter 4.

I hadn't dreamed of anything disturbing since that night after our fight. I still dreamed of Vincent every night but everything was pleasant, just a collage of us being together in different surroundings. I liked this way of dreaming, almost a little too much, it got harder and harder to drag myself out of bed in the morning. The only thing better than my dreams was the promise that at the end of each day I would see him and *finally* be able to breathe again.

I continued to work at the Bakery every day and Vincent was always there to walk me home after I was done. We had grown close in our short time together and everything was perfect.

I had never met anyone so passionate before. Just one touch from him sent me off, flying into oblivion somewhere. But I couldn't help but compare myself to the other girls in town; ones I thought might catch his attention. I was constantly trying to figure out Vincent's type. Maybe he only liked girls with red hair? That would definitely tip the scales in my favor. On the other hand, maybe it was because my eyes changed colors, going from green to light gray and blue, to honey brown without warning. I always thought my eyes were my best feature.

For whatever reason I was the center of his attention and who could have asked for more than that? He was smart, he dressed nice and always smelled good so who in their right mind would pass that up? Instead I thought about maybe fixing myself to match him? Maybe cut my hair like most of the other girls had into a short bob? Or get myself some dresses that hid my curves to make me look more modern and box-like?

"I'm thinking of cutting my hair." I announced one night as I started to close the Bakery.

"No you're not."

"Why not? It's not the style to keep it this long anymore." I asked, stunned at his remark.

"Because, if you cut off all those long beautiful curls then what will I grab a hold of when I do this?"

He slowly slid his hand behind my head intertwining his fingers in my ruby ringlets and brought me to his lips. My head swirled as his cool lips touched mine, every soft caress felt like heaven and I wanted to devour this man in a way I never thought possible. Every taste as our tongues collided filled me with a craving that only he could sate and it wasn't long before all was forgotten about our conversation.

He lifted me up and sat me on the cool marble counter and I eagerly locked my arms around his neck as we continued to kiss. He moved down kissing me on the earlobe and just underneath sending chills down my body, while his gentle hands discovered each of my curves. Unfastening my dress he started to pull it down baring my shoulders and brassiere straps as he continued kissing my neck all the way down to my left shoulder. His kisses tickled my skin causing a multitude of heat waves through me, melting my body like putty in his hands. He didn't fight fare.

I was lost in every stroke and touch as Vincent started to slide down one of my straps, when suddenly— the door slammed!

"Get away from her!" I heard from the distance.

Vincent stopped and turned his back to me enough for me to see Percy, standing by the door with his fists up.

Oh, for crying out loud! I thought as I pulled my dress up to cover my shoulders.

"I mean it, you get away from her, Mr.!"

Vincent started to walk forward. He had to be at least two times bigger than geeky, little, Percy.

"Are you sure you want to do this boy?!" Vincent asked in a menacing voice, stopping in front of him.

"Percy, get out of here!" I yelled.

"If you hurt her, I'll… I'll kill you!" He stammered.

Vincent laughed. "And if you don't leave now, *I'll* kill you. And I don't mean it figuratively, I assure you." He warned, moving even closer to Percy's face.

In that second Percy's eyes changed. They got so big I was afraid they might pop out, as he stood frozen, locked on to Vincent's gaze.

Percy looked to me then back to Vincent before mumbling "S—sorry for bothering the t—two of you." and tripped and fumbled backward out the door.

Vincent turned to face me and I looked at him questionably?

"What?"

"What'd you do to him?" I asked with a smile. I mean, whenever I looked at Vincent all I could think of was all the things I *wanted* him to do to me.

He shrugged by way of answering and then gave me a devious smile that stretched from ear to ear. "We should go." he said lifting me off the counter to set me back on the floor.

"Yeah," I agreed. "Before they come and try to rescue me from your cruel ravishing." I said laughing at the situation.

"Cruel?" He asked lifting his eyebrow.

"It would seem that way to Percy."

Vincent barked out a laugh, while helping me get my dress put back together. "Ravish, yes. Cruel?… Hardly. He could see full well that you were enjoying every kiss I gave you. And I might add, also giving back." he kissed me sweetly on the lips when he was finished with the last button and held out his hand.

"Shall we?"

"Yes, I suppose so."

We walked down the street in the direction of my house hand in hand and I couldn't help but wonder if Percy had told anybody yet about what he saw? My reputation seemed to be continuously changing in my head. I went from the old maid to the loony and most recently to the town strumpet. Great, I thought shaking my head.

– "About?"

"Hmm…?" I asked confused only hearing a mumble of the question.

"What are you thinking about? You're somewhere else and shaking your head at nothing."

"Honestly?"

"Of course."

"Well, I was thinking that if Percy blabs about what he saw that I'll not only be the old maid that I'll also be the town strumpet." I answered. Honestly.

"That is ridiculous, you're nothing of the sort. Besides, that isn't his opinion of you. He thought I was taking advantage of you. He won't say anything like that."

"Because?…"

"Because I know for a fact he won't."

"It's in his favor to rat me out. He's been asking me out for the past year and I won't go out with him. He might want to get back at me for turning him down."

"And trust me when I tell you Delilah that it is most definitely *not* in his best favor to do that." He laughed.

"And why not?" I asked stubbornly.

"Well, would you want to see me angry and directed at you?"

I thought about it for a second. He was a bigger man and compared to Percy, he was a giant. I hadn't ever seen Vincent mad but the sheer size difference alone would make me not want to mess with him.

"No, I guess I wouldn't." I agreed. "Not angry anyway. That's not to say I wouldn't mind seeing you directed at me though." I finished with a flirty smile.

"Good, because I like to be directed at you, in a non-angry way, of course." He said grabbing me by my waist to pull me up into his arms and another kiss.

The street began to spin and this time I wasn't sure if it was the kiss or if we were actually spinning. I quickly decided that I didn't care as long as I was in his arms.

He set me on the ground again and I breathlessly tried to get my bearings back before I fell over.

"You've got to stop doing that, it's not fair." I complained.

"If you mean stop kissing you then not a chance." He answered grinning.

"No, stop with the earth spinning, left on a cloud, life changing kisses."

"I'm sorry." He leaned down and kissed me softly on the lips. "Is that better?" he whispered his breath right next to my ear.

With my eyes still closed I shivered as butterflies fluttered through my entire body.

"N—no." I stuttered trying to cage my butterflies.

I opened my eyes to see him smiling like a fool as he watched my confusion.

“Not funny!” I grumped as I started to walk away. “You don’t know what that feels like because I don’t leave you in a stupor every time I kiss you.”

“Ah, but don’t you?” he asked pulling me back to him.

“Obviously not,” I fought back. “You don’t look as ridiculous as I must when we pull apart.”

“I’m just older and in better control of my facial expressions, that’s all. I wouldn’t be kissing you all the time if I didn’t get something out of the deal.”

I just looked at him. Okay maybe he did just like kissing me but I think most of it was watching my dumbfounded reaction to kissing *him*.

“Mm… hmm.” I said before starting to walk again.

He chuckled as he caught up to my pace and grabbed my hand in his as we walked the rest of the way to my house.

Spinning:

Head in the clouds, my feet are off the ground. I'm spinning and spinning there's no one else, no sound. Left in a haze when the connections undone, your lips on my lips make me as hot as the sun.

Delilah Waters- 1929

Chapter 5.

"I don't understand why you're so obsessed with your age Delilah? You're not even that old. Believe me?"

"Believe you? For one you're not that much older than me and two, you don't have to hear about how old you are every stinking day. I know I'm not that old I just wish someone would explain that to my parents." I argued sitting across from him on the floor in the back room of the Bakery. I had brought a couple blankets and some pillows from home and together we had set up our own little hideaway in the corner of the room where he was currently reading me Peter and Wendy by J. M. Barrie.

"It would be different if they knew about you or knew I wasn't alone but they have no clue that I have you in my life so according to them *"I'm just wasting away."* I air quoted, frustrated by our most recent conversation.

"You do realize I don't have to be a secret, right? You could tell them."

"No, I don't think that's a good idea. So far things are working out fine. I don't feel the need to jinx it. Besides do you really want to have the father/boyfriend discussion? They're my family and *I* don't even want to talk to them if I don't have to."

Vincent smiled and kissed my nose. "No, I'd rather not. But for you, I would do it."

He was sweet and if the roles were reversed I'd do it for him too. It really was too bad that both his parents were gone. He'd said once that I was lucky to still have mine and from his point of view I guess he was right. But the more they got on my nerves the more I wished someone *else* would take them.

I sighed and fell back on to the pillows. "Wouldn't it be nice to just never age like Peter Pan? Get to see the world with no worries that time is going to run out soon?"

"If you had someone to share it with. Sure." He agreed.

"Ah, but who to take with you? If you choose the wrong person then you're stuck in misery, forever."

Vincent fell back next to me and laced his fingers through mine. "Well I'm hoping to have solved that problem."

"Assuming I'd want to go with *you.* What if I had someone else in mind?" I teased

"Ah yes, our young Percival. If that's not utopia, then what is?" I could hear the smile in his voice as he teased me.

"Funny." I said cringing at the horrid picture that popped in to my mind of me and Percy standing together on our front lawn hand in hand with a slew of children surrounding us that all looked like him. I winced shaking my head, and Vincent laughed.

"You think you're so funny don't you?" I said rolling over on top of him.

"As a matter of fact, yes, I do. And now that I know my humorous ways will get this type of reaction, I'll have to think up more witty remarks."

“Really?” I said pinning his arms above his head. I leaned down muffling whatever clever quip he was about to attempt and pressed my lips to his.

“Do you promise to be nice?” I teased as I lifted my face from his, still pinning down his arms.

“Not a chance.”

I smothered his face with more kisses.

“Now?”

“If I say no, do I get more kisses?”

I laughed realizing that we’d be here forever if that were the case. Not that I would’ve really minded that but it was more fun to torture him at the moment.

“Maybe, or maybe I’ll think of something crueler to do to you.”

“Woman, do your worst.” he said laughing.

“Alright, but don’t say I didn’t warn you.”

I leaned in close and as a smug smile started to spread across his face, I quickly put both wrists in one hand and began tickling under his arms and across his ribs.

“Alright! I promise… I promise!…” He laughed and squirmed, disheveling our pillows and blankets that once laid neatly under us. Of course with his size he could have just thrown me off of him but he didn’t which proved he loved every minute of it.

“You don’t fight fair!” He gasped breathing heavy. He kissed me again and placing his hands on my hips he slid me off him and over to the side so we could continue to look at each other.

"I'm a girl, we never fight fair. Besides it's a little payback for all those life altering kisses you like to throw on me." I answered with a mischievous smile.

"I can't believe you're complaining about how well I kiss you. Don't you think that seems a little unreasonable?"

"Not at all."

"No?"

"No."

"Would you care to elaborate a little for me please?"

"I already told you. I feel like an idiot when I'm standing there disoriented while you're staring at me with that smug grin of yours, thinking you're that cats meow. It's not fair."

"I obviously *am* the cats meow though or you wouldn't be complaining about the stupor you end up in every time my lips touch yours."

"I— " I started to argue but he was right. I didn't have a leg to stand on and he knew it. "Oh hush up!" I snapped, not being able to think of a decent argument.

"That's what I thought."

Appropriately, I stuck my tongue out at him as my response to his overweening ego.

He chuckled and wrapped his arm around me pulling me to him so I could lay my head on his chest. Sighing contently I started drawing imaginary lines and circles with my fingertip over his shirt as he did the same, playing in my hair.

“Where were we?” He asked reopening the book.

“The beginning of chapter 6!” I replied excitedly.

I listened to his voice rise and fall with the words under my head as he continued. I loved listening to him read to me. This was one of the things I looked forward to every day since making our hideout. Sometimes he would bring old poetry I had never heard of too. He already knew I liked some pretty risque writing so he introduced me to a few more Authors like Ambrose G. Bierce, who wrote The Haunted Valley. He also told me about Mary Shelley and said he would try to get a copy of her book. I had to admit, a book about a man made monster brought to life sounded exciting!

It was nice to share something with someone who loved it as much as I did and he never seemed put off by my appreciation for writing of any kind from one extreme to the other. Like today reading about Never Never Land and Lost Boys that never grow up. Tomorrow, who knows, maybe the book about the monster? I liked his unpredictability.

He continued on explaining how the kiss had saved Wendy from her ultimate doom and my first thought was how his kiss that night on the porch had saved me.

“I love you.” I said out loud as I continued to twirl my finger around and around on his chest. I felt Vincent’s body tense underneath me and he stopped reading.

We hadn’t said it out loud yet and now that I had, I couldn’t take it back. I only had to sit there and wonder if he loved me in return? It felt like minutes of silence passed until he said.

"I love you as well."

I popped my head up to look at him. "You do?"

"Yes, I do. I think I have for awhile now. I was just waiting for you." He smiled.

My insides were jumping with joy but instead I sat up and said. "And you didn't say anything?!"

"Well, the last time I tried sharing my feelings I recall getting hit with a dozen thorny roses." He lifted his eyebrow at me.

I laughed, I couldn't help it. "Yeah, I guess it didn't go so well for you did it?"

He laughed too "No, not at all."

"So what was the pause for?"

A very slow smile started to form before yelling "REVENGE!" and pouncing on me faster than I have ever seen anyone move before. He tickled me relentlessly then started to kiss me on the pinwheel floor. The tile was cold on my back and Vincent was his normal cool self on the top. I couldn't hide the shiver that ran up my body and he stopped immediately and he sat up pulling me up with him.

"You're cold."

"I'm sorry."

"For being cold?"

"Yes, I guess so."

"Don't be ridiculous!"

"You're mad?"

"About you being cold? No. The fact that you just apologized over something you have no control over? Yes."

"I'm sorry."

"Christ Delilah, stop apologizing!"

"Then stop being mad!"

He laughed, "It's starting to get late, I'd better get you home before people start to wonder what happened to you."

"I didn't mean to upset you." I whispered.

"You didn't, you just reminded me of something I need to do." He smiled and tapped the tip of my nose with his fingertip. "Don't worry so much, everything's fine. More than fine even, it's perfect."

He led me by the hand towards the front of the Bakery where my things already sat on the counter waiting for me. He helped me with my coat and before I could really refuse, we were out the door.

I couldn't think of anything to say as we walked but my mind was racing over everything that just happened. I shivered, so what? He's cooler than me, big deal? I didn't understand why he was suddenly so upset?

"Vincent, are you alright?"

"Of course."

"You seem upset with me. You nearly pushed me through the Bakery."

"That's only because of the time. I hadn't realized it was getting so late. I don't get to spend as much time with you as I would like, so I got greedy tonight and the time escaped me, that's all."

I knew he wasn't being completely honest with me and I wondered what he was hiding? He seemed a little anxious and I didn't understand why. I was no later than usual. I had already come up with a cover story for my parents, the Bakery needing all the "extra work" and all. I had been rearranging little by little every night after work. Scrubbing ovens, walls, windows, etc.… etc.… usually by the time I got home they'd be ready for bed or sometimes even in bed. They knew I had keys to get in the house and they weren't worried because they figured I was *old* and responsible enough to get home without a problem.

Vincent walked me up to the door like always, even when he was evasive he was still a gentlemen. He kissed me gently and I sighed as we broke apart. I hated not knowing what was going on with him.

"Are you sure you're okay?" I asked as he stood with his forehead rested against mine.

"Perfectly, I promise. I'll see you Monday night. I love you." He kissed me again, this time on my forehead and started down the stairs.

"Yeah, I love you back." I didn't yell it but I knew he heard me because he turned around and winked before continuing down the street.

A secret :

If only they knew you existed and my life isn't what it seems. The discussions would stop and planning would start, of the beginning of our lives for you're the completion of my heart. If only they knew I'm not hopeless, I'm not sitting here just wasting away. They'd relax knowing that there's hope for me yet, a future to behold and brighter days.

Delilah Waters- 1929

Chapter 6.

It was growing closer to my birthday, only a few days left until November 19th and I was starting to get nervous. I was still terrified about getting older. Yes, I had Vincent now but my parents still didn't know anything about him (thank God!) It seemed that Vincent had been right about Percy, (come to think of it, I hadn't even seen Percy since that night) so, as far as they were concerned I was still alone, hopeless and about to be twenty. It was better this way. I wasn't sure what they would think about Vincent if they met him. I hoped they would be thrilled but our relationship was still pretty new and I didn't want them throwing marriage suggestions at him this early so I decided to keep a lid on him for the time being. Nothing like eager parents to ruin a relationship.

But keeping Vincent on the hush, unfortunately meant that I still had to suffer through "age" discussions on a regular basis. My father even recently had a coworker over for Sunday dinner and he was eagerly waiting there for me when I walked in the door.

"Delilah, this is Bradly. He works with your father." My mother introduced. She was dressed to the nines. She wore a light blue dress that flared at the waist and went down to her calves and black heels. Her hair was pinned up with slight finger waves and her makeup was (as usual) done to perfection complete with blush, red lips and long dark lashes.

I was in shock. I didn't know what to say. Bradly was dirty blonde, with brown eyes and dressed in a tan suit. He looked about my age, maybe a few years older and actually wasn't bad looking! Not as delicious as Vincent but not the usual type that they liked to throw my way.

I finally managed "Hello."

I hadn't even removed my coat yet. To say my parents were eager was an understatement.

"Why don't I go set the table and Delilah, honey you go on upstairs to freshen up a bit and when you come down we'll all eat?"

That wasn't a question. In mom language that was make sure you look good before you take that coat off and ruin your chances of marrying a guy that's offered to take you. What a dreadful thought it was to see what they believed my future held for me. A lifetime of loneliness and shame with no hopes of family or happiness.

"Sounds swell, I'll just go get dolled up and be back in a jiffy." I knew she didn't like Flapper talk but I'm sure she knew before hand that I would hate this too so for the moment we were even in our pettiness. I headed up the stairs to change.

I made sure I looked presentable but not go too overboard. I did in fact have a boyfriend but no one knew and I still didn't want to tell them so I was stuck. I had to look like I was trying but not actually try. The whole time upstairs I thought to myself, *This is so stupid.*

I took a glance in the mirror and decided I looked decent enough. I wore a simple black dress, left my red hair down in curls and put on my makeup. It was as good as Bradly was getting.

I made my way to the dining room and the two men were seated.

"Perfect timing!" My mother said coming from the kitchen with the roast in her hands. The table was already set and the men stood to help us both with our chairs.

How polite, I thought to myself and said thank you to Bradly.

"So, Delilah, Your father tells me you work at his Bakery?"

"Yes."

"Is that something you enjoy?"

He was trying but I was irritated that both of them would spring this on me with no warning.

"It gets me out of here. I'm not sure I'm cut out for wife and motherly duties. I like the idea of the modern woman. Why can't we work, vote or do anything a man can do?"

I think my mother choked on a piece of her food. *Another point for me!* (2/1)

"I see. I happen to agree with some of that but I find that most women want to care for their husbands and children. Women naturally have a need to be needed and feel, useful."

He said "useful" in a way that made me feel like he didn't agree at all.

"I agree with Bradly." my mother said and side glanced at me before smiling at him. I knew that look, I'm being warned. *Crap* (2/2)

"Even if you're right, women can be useful in other areas. Just because she isn't married or a mother doesn't mean she's worthless. I'm sure there are plenty of things women could excel at in other areas, if given the chance?" I said politely and smiled my own phony grin for her benefit. Then I took a bite so I couldn't elaborate. *Ha!* (3/2)

I already didn't like Bradly with his smug sexist views; didn't like my parents at the moment either. Yes, this was the dinner from Hell! Part of me wished Vincent would break in and save me. It would figure that the first hot meal I had in a week was with an idiot.

I sat there as they made small talk and finally Pop started talking about work and the newest cars they were working on. Usually I liked to hear about them but I was tired and I had heard plenty for the night.

"I'm afraid I have to turn in now. I have to be up very early, for work." I added in that last part for Bradly.

As I stood he did too. "It was nice to meet you Delilah." he took my hand in his and went to kiss it but I faked a yawn/stretch combination. "I'm so sorry. It really has been such a long day for me."

I turned to both of my parents and smiled "Thank you for dinner, goodnight." I added and turned towards the living room. They both yelled goodnight as I kept walking. I'm sure they both knew I was done with this.

* * *

It was Monday, a slow day. All I had to do was clean and think and I would go back to cleaning to stop thinking. Dinner last night was a nightmare. I hadn't talked to either one of my parents and I wasn't looking forward to the chewing I was going to get from my mother later tonight.

I battled over if I should tell Vincent about it at all. I knew it would upset him and I wasn't going to see Bradly again anyways so it seemed pointless to bring it up. Why hurt him?

I was so sick of all of this! The never ending harassment every day. I already wasn't home six days out of the week and now I did anything else on Sunday to keep from being there seven. I couldn't see Vincent on my one day off because he was busy with business stuff during the days and I couldn't lie about being at the Bakery at night to make it work. I was beginning to hate Sundays. I was actually beginning to hate a lot of things. I needed a break from all of it. This stupid bakery, stupid customers, stupid parents, my stupid birthday! Why do we have to get older? It doesn't seem fair that as soon as we're out of childhood that even more pressure is pushed on us to be married and starting a family of our own, only to repeat the cycle all over again with more children. Who started this?! "It's the way it is." My mother told me that once when I had asked her. Well thanks a million.

My thoughts were interrupted when someone walked in the door. I looked up to see Vincent. Was it six already? How long had I been obsessing?

"Are you ready?" he asked, looking at me a little confused.

"I completely lost track of time," I admitted. "Let me grab my things and we can go." Once again I grabbed my coat and keys and having forgotten my journal at home this time I simply headed out the door beside Vincent.

"I have a surprise for you." He whispered in my ear as I was locking the door. He turned me around and pointed to the running car sitting in the road.

"You bought the Model A?!"

It was beautiful! Red shiny paint, black top and fenders with gold spoke wheels! I couldn't help the excitement I felt; I walked everywhere I went unless I traveled with my father.

"You know about cars?" I clearly had caught him off guard.

I shrugged "My father works for Ford. He tells us about the new models. I doubt my mother pays any attention but I like to hear about them."

"I'm impressed! But to answer your question, I didn't exactly buy it, I borrowed the Model A. I wanted to take you somewhere and I thought it might be a nice change to take a drive instead." He was smiling and I could tell that he was pleased about how happy I was.

"Come." He opened my door and took my hand to assist me as I sat down on the smooth leather bench seat. After he made sure my feet and coat were safely in the car he shut the door. I quickly leaned over and opened his door from the inside so he could get in beside me.

"Thank you." he said and smiled. I winked back. I thought opening his door was the least I could do.

"Are you warm enough? There was an iron unit placed on the exhaust to create heat!"

"Yes." I laughed. "Thank you." He looked so genuinely happy that I couldn't help but giggle.

This baby had a sliding gear shift I noticed but Vincent had no issue with it as we raced down the street. For someone that had just arrived to this city he seemed to know exactly where he was going as he jig jogged through the narrow side streets to Dix. He kept going past my street but it wasn't long before he stopped the car in Dearborn.

I looked out my window to see the bridge that had just been built over the river a couple years earlier.

"Stay right here." He said cutting off the engine. He quickly got out of the car and then opened my door for me.

He offered his hand and assisted me on the slippery pavement and shut my door behind me. He really is a gentleman, always so thoughtful and sweet I thought to myself as he led me to the bridge rail.

"What do you think?" He asked.

We stood there hand in hand looking out at the ebony water. The river wasn't frozen yet and the crescent moon hung over us giving off the perfect amount of light for it to be romantic.

"It's beautiful." I said leaning my head on his shoulder.

"Yes." he sighed. "The crescent moon is my favorite." he said nodding in its direction.

"It is?" I asked curiously.

"Yes. I have noticed that everyone shows more interest in the full moon. She commands more attention because of her size and brightness and I feel the other moons are overlooked. I can sympathize with the crescent moon, her glow is more subtle so it goes unnoticed."

And what exactly does this smart, funny and.. oh yeah, absolutely, breathtakingly gorgeous man, know about being unnoticed? I secretly wondered. He turned to me suddenly vibrant and added "But I have great hope that everything is about to change."

Wait. What?

"I know how upset you are about the birthday you have coming up but I have something for you." He reached in to his left pocket and pulled out a little white box.

Oh no! I thought to myself. This could *not* be happening. I wanted it to happen of course, but no one knew he existed, — except for Percy— he hadn't even met my parents yet. I looked up at him and he was smiling.

"Are you going to open it?"

I took a deep breath and took the box out of his hand. I looked down and slowly began to lift the lid, only to find a teardrop shaped ruby about the size of a nickel that hung on a dainty gold chain. It's a necklace, I thought with a sigh of relief.

"Well… do you like it?" he said eagerly.

"It's beautiful Vince, thank you."

He took the small box from my hands and lifted the necklace up in the air between his fingers.

"Turn around." He said, unclasping the chain.

I turned and lifted my hair so he could put the necklace around my neck. His touch was cold but soft on my skin and it made me tingle all the way down to my toes.

He took a step back and I let down my hair and turned around so I was facing him.

"Perfect." He said looking at the charm that hung just below my collarbone.

"Thank you. It's a very thoughtful birthday present. I love it."

I smiled up at him and kissed him on the cheek in appreciation for the gift.

"And I love you. But the necklace is more than just simply a birthday gift." He said still looking me over.

"Then what else is it?" I asked curiously. Maybe it was an engagement necklace? I mean nothing else in our relationship was normal. Maybe this was just another oddity that was us?

"It will be a reminder that I intend to love you for the rest of your life."

Oh no! It *is* and engagement necklace. I thought with horror. How am I going to explain this?

"Um… Vincent. Is this some sort of… engagement?" I asked in a small voice. I didn't want to assume but I had to know.

"Oh Delilah it is so much more than that…"

"I–

"Just listen. Then you can give me an answer." He interrupted.

"From the first time I saw you through the window at the Bakery I knew there was something special about you. Then the second night I watched you throw your shoe at Percival and knew there was a fire in you as bright as that beautiful hair. Your taste in literature and the day you walked up from the Cemetery just confirmed you were perfect for me in every way."

"You saw that?!" I interrupted.

He laughed and swept one of my curls behind my ear. "Yes, I saw that. But that's not the only reason I love you Delilah. I love how fearless you are, you're smart and strong and stubborn." He laughed. "You never settle for less than you deserve. You're beautiful…" He grabbed both of my hands and put them between his.

"I know we haven't been together for a long time and I hope you don't feel rushed but I know for a fact that I want us to be together forever." He said rubbing both of my hands with his.

"Do you want to be with me?" he asked looking at me with excitement in his eyes.

I didn't know what to say at first? This was crazy! I loved him, I was absolutely sure of it but marriage? When I looked at my future lately he wasn't only a part of it but my future seemed to be completely centered around him. If I wasn't with this man I was dreaming about being with him. He was every waking thought I had and to be honest I felt amazing when he was near me. Did it really matter if we hadn't been together for years? Sure there were things that we didn't know about each other but it could be fun finding out?

I took a deep breath and answered "Yes!" I watched the moon dance off his eyes and he smiled as he took my face in his hands and pressed his soft lips to mine.

I was instantly lifted off my feet as he spun me in the air kissing me all over my face and I giggled with excitement. I was an engaged woman!

He smiled as he set me on the ground again. "This is going to be amazing Delilah, you'll see." He said as he brushed a stray curl off my face and tucked it behind my ear. I smiled brightly up into those deep blue eyes that glimmered like the stars. "I love you Vincent Vanhorne." I sighed wrapping my arms around him. He knelt down and placed his lips to mine. Our kisses seemed to tell the story of our relationship in its entirety, soft at first then heated and passionate bordering scandalous.

He knew just how to make my legs turn to pudding. It's like he held the only map to all my secret places of desire and was determined to conquer them all. My head was whirling in a daze that was fast becoming my favorite place and my body started to sing as his gentle hands started to caress my sides, stopping to massage my breasts as his mouth moved to the little space behind my ear. My breathing was heavy and a soft moan escaped from between my parted lips as somewhere far away something was telling me we were still in public but I could barely hear that part of myself anymore and as long as Vincent kissed me this way and continued to work his magic fingers, I refused to listen to it anyway.

"Delilah?" He whispered then ran his teeth along my earlobe.

"Yes." I managed to push out in a heavy breath.

"Remember you said that."

With my eyes closed he lifted me up and I wrapped my legs around his waist. Supporting my weight with one arm he wrapped his long fingers in my ruby curls and I moaned again as he pulled my head backward to continue his trail of blistering kisses to the side of my neck. I wrapped my fingers in his hair enjoying the… PAIN!

My eyes flew open in shock and I gasped. He was biting me! Not a nibble I mean *biting* me!

"Ah!" I gripped his shoulders with my hands, and dug into him with my fingernails frantically, desperately trying to push him away from me. What was he doing?!

I pushed and pushed with no result until I couldn't even move my arms anymore. The warmth of my body was slowly being drained away inch by precious inch like the mercury leaving the top of the thermometer on a cold day.

Not 10 seconds ago he was the man that I wanted to marry and that I wanted to spend the rest of my life with so how is it possible that everything has come to this? That he's some kind of *thing* and is slowly draining me? I breathed in heavily as my limbs started to weigh me down. I could feel his arms still holding me tight against his body as he quickly pulled and drank and pulled and drank. I was so tired, I just wanted to sleep or I guess, die? That's what this was, right? I was dying? I had spent so much time amazed that he loved me and I should have known better. Stupid Delilah.

Shivers consumed me but it didn't hurt anymore. I couldn't really feel anything any more He laid me on the ground and through my blurry eyed vision I didn't see the sadistic smile I thought I would. He looked at me adoringly.

"Wh—y?" I whispered.

"Shh… I promise it will all make sense soon my darling." He stroked my hair and poured something liquid into my mouth. It was thick and salty; coating my mouth like led based paint as it slid down my throat leaving a dry, coppery trail behind it. Gross.

I coughed and gagged, and was rolled to my side, braced with familiar strong hands as I started to vomit up everything I had eaten earlier that day, and it seemed, everything I had ever eaten at all.

If I make it out of this alive I'm going to kill him! I thought as he rubbed my back while I continued to re-live every food decision I had ever made all over the sidewalk.

My stomach hurt so bad. There's nothing left! I thought as I continued to heave up nothing but sour acid.

The pressure in my head was building, my skull felt like it was going to crack and tears began to fill my eyes turning my vision blurry red. My nose began to drip too and I realized I was bleeding. Blood was pouring out of my face.

My shoulders snapped! I cried out in pain. Snap!… Crack!… Snap!… My fingers and knees started to crack and shift. Dear GOD! Will this never end?

Every time I thought there might be some relief something worse would start. I was so tired I couldn't even move anymore and just before everything went black my conscience whispered.

Happy birthday Delilah...

Chapter 7.

"Delilah?"

Far away I could hear someone calling my name but I didn't want to get up. I was exhausted and literally broken. I probably couldn't move if I wanted to.

"Darling, you must get up… DELILAH!"

My eyes shot open with a jolt of awareness as I gasped in the crisp air.

"Thank goodness. I've been waiting on you for hours now." he said looking down at me.

I tried to make some sense of where I was? He was holding me somewhere… oh yeah, the car. We were in the car he had drove me to the bridge in before..

"You attacked me!" I yelled, sitting up going for the door.

"Delilah, I—"

I opened the door to run but he was right in front of me, somehow? I jumped back, "What are you?!" I asked frantically… "Wait, my heart's stopped beating!" I suddenly realized placing my hand on my chest. Nothing. I took another breath in and still nothing. The world was spinning. "Why isn't my heart beating Vincent?!" I asked outraged.

"Calm down Delilah, your heart is in hibernation. You lost almost all of your human blood so there's not enough in your body to pump. It's perfectly normal, you're going to be fine."

Human blood?... "What... Did you... Do..?!" I yelled, backing up next to the railing of the bridge away from him. Now I wasn't HUMAN! What was I?

"It was the only way we could be together. I asked you if you wanted to be with me forever?" He pleaded walking toward me with his hands out.

"I didn't know I would have to become a freak! I thought we'd get married and have a life together, like everybody else. I didn't know I was agreeing to... whatever this is... What am I?"

I grabbed my head with both hands and ducked back down to the ground as I was suddenly struck with flashes of something, like a dream.

I saw a man, as clear as if I were standing behind him. He was tan and very muscular with long, wavy, black hair that hung down to lay on huge, white feathered wings that rested on his back, touching down to the bends of his knees. He stood strong, in front of a great white light, with something more than confidence, I would guess it was also defiance that gave him such an edge? He didn't shy away from the lights intensity, instead he held like stone to make his point.

I watched with curious eyes as more angels appeared to take sides either with the dazzling light or with the beautiful angel and I too went to stand beside my fellow angels, against the light. We knew there would be consequences for our actions but we simply couldn't stay silent about the unfair treatment we were receiving since he had created *them*.

After all the angels had chosen a side, the angels that stood with the light held a mix of anger and remorseful expressions on their face as they walked toward myself and the other four angels. I screamed out in agony as they ripped the giant white wings from my back. The clouds parted and I was forcefully shoved off the edge to fall towards the ground, far below.

I could feel the immense pressure of the wind on my face as I soared, with the other four through the clouds. I watched as their naked, blood smeared, bodies swirled around and around through the open air, catching glimpse after glimpse of the gaping, bleeding wounds that now marked were their beautiful wings had once been.

We hit the sand hard and it took a long time for us to start to move. The moon shone bright as we stumbled to our feet with confusion. The man with the long black hair looked to the rest of us, he seemed to be piecing things together as he looked at the naked bleeding bodies before him then down to his own body and up again.

Suddenly more people started to gather around us and now there were a dozen strangers with curious eyes circling our group. A woman dressed in animal skins walked to stand in front of the man with the long black hair. She had slightly darker skin and black hair, which hung to her hips. She reached to him and caressed the side of his face and the man tilted his head toward her touch. He nuzzled her wrist and started to smell her skin, then he stopped.

I looked at the pair of them with curiosity. I didn't understand his reaction to the woman's smell. His head was now thrown back and he was breathing heavy. I started to move closer to better see what was happening. He started to shake and when he brought his head down he was something else. His eyes were alight and two teeth on each side reformed themselves, they were longer and came to sharp points at the ends. He lunged at the woman biting her viciously on the neck, sending blood splatter in every direction.

The villagers started to move in a panic, some held spears and ran in the direction of the pair locked in blood and carnage and others ran in the opposite direction to get away from us. I was locked in place and unsure what I should do, until I smelled something sweet that made my mouth water. I sniffed up in the air and could feel the change move throughout my body in a ripple of pleasure. I could hear everything and smell everything and my teeth longed to pierce the flesh of those around me. I lunged at the closest villager and buried my teeth deep until my mouth was overflowing with a sweet heavenly fluid. I swallowed and sucked and swallowed until there was nothing left to suck but I had to have more. I searched but could see nothing but red. I smelled only the sweet odor of what I craved most and I had to find it at all cost.

I didn't know when the screaming stopped but when I could see again, the five of us stood on blood soaked sand, littered with the dead bodies of the villagers. Naked and covered from head to toe in blood, I spun in a circle to fully take in the massacre that had been our doing. We were monsters that craved human blood and had eaten an entire village to get it. I looked to the others and each one was still as confused as I was and just as covered with gore.

The morning light was beginning to peak over the horizon and my body shook uncontrollably. The warning signal was unavoidable. I knew with every inch of my being that I had to hide, right now. I once again looked to the others and got a nod in sequence, telling me that they too shared the same feeling. I ran to one of the huts and shut myself inside, pilling pelts over my body to be sure I was out of harm's way from the light.

* * *

As I began to feel more like Delilah and less like the dark skinned woman that fell, everything started to come into focus. I had a better understanding of what consequences the five fallen angels had faced for their decision to rise against the light. They were cursed to walk the earth in darkness. Never again could the sun warm their skin and they would have to rely on the blood of the very abominations they couldn't stand.

When I could stand up straight again I looked at Vincent. After seeing what they had become, I now understood what I was. I would hunt, I would kill, and I would enjoy every minute of it. Never again would I set eyes on the sun. I was his and he was mine, forever blanketed by darkness.

Under this shell :

Your scent drives me crazy, sending me into a craving I've never known. I look to what's left behind, not to your carnage, but my own.

I revel in this glorious death, each stained kiss delivering life. Because under this beauty, yes, under this shell, I am an angel who stalks the night.

Delilah Waters- 1929

Chapter 8.

Looking down at my hands I noticed my fingernails were longer now, almost resembling the claws of a cat and my skin was as white as porcelain and just as smooth. I touched my face in disbelief to see if it felt the same.

Vincent walked up to me and grabbed my hands away from my face and set them to my sides. He ran his fingertip down the bridge of my nose then reached down to lift my chin.

"You are even more beautiful then I imagined Delilah, immortality looks flawless on you." he said smiling, then he pressed his lips to mine.

I thought his kisses were good before but wow! This was an amazingly different experience. I could taste him like never before, like the finest chocolate desert slowly melting on my tongue. It shot sparks through places of my body that I had never known and made me want to do things to him that I had never done. Things were different now. I needed him in a way I didn't understand, almost like I was starving for his touch and taste and even the smell of him was driving me crazy for more. Which made it that much harder to bare when he finally broke away.

"Come with me," he whispered, grabbing my hand. I laced my cool fingers together with his and we began to walk away from the Bridge back toward the car.

“What was that?” I asked as the car took us back towards my house. I was curious about who the angels were? I had seen their faces but I never got any of their names.

“It was a memory.”

“Was it the same for you?”

“Not exactly. I have a different sire so I shared his memories and experiences. You and I don’t have the same maker so there is a different point of view.”

“If we don’t have the same maker, then who is my maker?” I had so many questions about this whole situation. I couldn’t help but be curious after everything I had just seen.

“Zariah. I obtained a vial of her blood at the last gathering.

“So that was what you made me drink? But why did you use her blood, couldn’t you have um… used your own?”

“No.”

“But why, you’re like them?”

“Yes, I am. They call it Vampirism but I’m not one of the first. As far as I know the Elders are the only ones that can stir. Their blood alone has what is necessary to pass immortality to another before the soul leaves the body, plus it‘s forbidden for a couple to share the same immortal blood.”

“I would think it wouldn’t matter?”

“Normally, it wouldn’t but it is like having the same parents. If you and I had the same bloodline we would be considered siblings.”

"Oh, can we have children?" I thought I should ask. If we couldn't be "siblings" maybe there was a reason beyond it just being disgusting to be romantically involved with my brother.

"No, we'll never have children. I am sorry about that." He looked a little sad at first but he continued. "With the blood comes the gift and it gives a couple a better chance at a long and happy union if we have different gifts and defenses. We're a very competitive species so I think every vampire having the same abilities might cause friction."

"How did you get her blood?"

"Once every decade before Easter, the Elders throw a grand ball so they can meet any new comers and give reassurance to the others."

"Once every decade? Did one just pass?"

"No, in fact, the last gathering was March of 1920."

"So you've had that vial for nine years?!" That was incredible! And also pretty gross. "Are you sure it isn't food poisoning that does this to us?"

Vincent laughed and wrapped one arm around me, "No my Darling, not at all."

"Why did you wait nine years?" I still couldn't believe he had been running around with a vial of blood for that long.

"Don't you know the answer to that one? He asked with a smile. "I was waiting for you."

That was definitely the right answer. I beamed back at him, what else could I say after that?

“Tell me more!” I commanded. It sounded so unreal, like the stories he had been reading to me in our hideout.

“Well, at each gathering one can request a vial as long as you’re old enough and they feel that you are mature enough to handle the responsibility.”

“How old do you have to be?”

“The minimal age is fifty but most under a century get denied.” He answered.

“Why do you have to be so old? That seems like a very long time to wait.”

“In human years it is a long time but being immortal takes some getting used to and they don’t want a bunch of rogue vampires running around killing everybody. It takes a long time to acquire the self-control it takes to stop your urges and even longer to be able to teach another how to stop theirs.”

“Yeah, I guess that makes sense when you put it that way. Wait… How old are you?” I asked smiling at him.

“Let’s just leave it at I’m old enough.” He said smiling back, and then he winked at me

“I saw that they’re angels but who are they exactly? I thought more than five fell with Lucifer when he rebelled. Oh, God! Is the black haired angel Lucifer?” I was shocked, I knew there was no way out now but what if I was some sort of Devils spawn… literally?

"Calm down.” He chuckled. “Different set of angels. Lucifer and the others were the first to fall but more followed as time went on. Carlus, like most wanted Gods love. He didn't challenge him, or give him an ultimatum though. He brought up specific points that the other four agreed with. That's why they were cast down and that's why they were cursed in the way that they were."

"So that's his name? I wondered about that because I never heard his name, or the others either, actually."

"Yes, for the last century or so, anyway. Their original names were stripped along with their position when they fell so each have changed their names numerous times throughout the centuries."

"Why do they do that?"

"To keep up with the time. Names change and they have been here for over a millennium so they have to keep something pronounceable."

"So no one knows who they were originally?"

"No, not that I can recall. There are others, older than myself who might know names closer to their original names but I don't think anyone knows their angel names. I'm sure they have done this deliberately. I doubt they want their true identity known."

"But why would that matter?"

"I'm not entirely sure, but I suppose they have their reasons."

"You said our blood has to be different because of the gifts that are passed down through the blood, so I'm guessing each has special powers?"

"Yes, each have many, in fact. Carlus is very strong, very fast and among his other abilities he's a Charmer."

I'm sure he knew the next question I was about to ask but he didn't get aggravated when I interrupted him to ask what a charmer was.

"They are a very rare talent. Carlus can command blood from someones body by the wave of his hand; willing it to do whatever he wants and ultimately bleeding them dry without ever touching them."

I couldn't help my silence, I was so lost in that mental picture it was hard to focus on what he said next.

"Ian is also incredibly fast and he is known as a Whisperer. Meaning he can whisper and control smaller living creatures, like birds, snakes or even wolves if he's around them.

"Then Zariah, she's a Dancer with the ability to sweet breeze, but do not be fooled by her beauty. Not only can she dance flame; with one blow across her hand in your direction she can smoke you from the inside, leaving nothing but ash behind."

"Julius is a Sleeper, something in his eyes surrenders humans and vampires alike to his will."

"And lastly Nathaniel, he's a Dreamer, with a wink he can make others see anything he wants them to see and let's just leave it as, it's not pleasant."

"Oh." I gasped, thinking of the possibilities.

"Yes, all are great warriors with unimaginable skills and talents that I'm sure most of us are unaware of. The Elders are greatly respected by being the oldest and wisest of the Vampire Nation."

"Can you do something like that?" I asked enthused.

"I am the son of Nathaniel, my gift is and extension from his but each of our human abilities change the gift into something different. I can manifest and manipulate dreams, adding to them what I wish, that's the illusion but I can also Ghost.

"Ghost?"

"Yes."

"What does that mean?"

"I can project myself through the mind to feed on those in their sleep."

"Can I do something too?" I asked hopefully.

"There is one gift we're born with. All vampires can induce somnolence."

"What is that?"

"It's a calming sensation. It makes them more agreeable."

I thought about how much simpler it would be if people blindly agreed with you against their normal instinct.

"Wait, you did that to me didn't you?" I asked thinking about the night we met.

He looked at me and shrugged.

"I knew it! The night we met and I was nervous to leave with you then I suddenly wasn't afraid after you touched my shoulder. That was all you. Did you make me go with you?"

"No. It's not compulsion. The only thing I did was calm you down. You left with me on your own once I removed the worry."

"That's a little better I guess. I was starting to think I was bewitched or something."

He laughed. "Bewitched?"

"Well you know what I mean."

"What about my dreams? Did you ever project my dreams?" I asked, already guessing the answer.

"Yes, but only once. I had to let you know what I was to see if you could handle the truth of it."

"You mean you're the reason for the gory one of us covered in blood, kissing in the fog?"

"Well the kissing part wasn't supposed to happen, I just couldn't help myself, you looked too sexy to resist." he answered lifting an eyebrow.

Yeah sexy, I thought sarcastically. Nothing sexier than a girl covered in blood. I wondered where something like that would come from but I never thought it would have come from him? I actually thought he was responsible for the other ones. The ones that he just showed up in all the time.

"I don't understand, you were *trying* to scare me?"

"Yes, and no. I wanted to brace you for this life and also make sure you could handle the reality of what we are. That's why I was an active part in the dream with you. You didn't mind the gore, in fact, you seemed to be quite aroused by it."

"What an interesting plan." I agreed. "But" I continued in a whisper, running my hands over his broad chest. "I wasn't aroused by the blood; I was aroused by you." I lifted myself up and kissed him on his cheek while he drove.

* * *

We were almost to my street now so I looked at Vincent with pitiful, puppy dog eyes.

"Don't give me that look. You can't go back Delilah, I'm sorry, and we can't stay *here* either. Too many people know you and if we stay we risk being exposed. Besides, it's always easier to eat someone you don't know." He said smiling at me showing off his sharp white teeth.

"I can't just leave and not say goodbye; that would kill them." I said looking at him for compassion.

"If you go in there Delilah *you* might kill them. You have yet to feed and they're human. You might not be able to resist the urge and then you'll really hate yourself."

He was right but I still had to do something.

"I'll write them a note and leave it for them to find in the morning."

Vincent just looked at me and shook his head.

"They're your parents," he said turning the car down the street. He drove slowly all the way to the end and turned the car around before pulling up and stopping in front of the house.

"Are you sure you want to do this?" He asked.

I looked out the window for a moment to give myself a second. "Absolutely."

"Alright." In a flash he was at my door. "After you." He said with his open hand pointed toward the house. I could see the moon light dance on his milky skin and neatly filed fingernails as his hand hung in the open air.

I jumped up and kissed his cheek and ran toward the door first but Vincent shook his head.

"What?" I asked confused. I had a key. It was on the ring with the Bakery keys.

"If you go through the door you might wake them."

"Well how else am I going to get in?" I asked. I didn't have a key for the back door and it was through the ally anyway so I really didn't want to walk all the way around the houses to get there.

"The window." he answered simply.

I looked to the first row of windows, they were about 6 feet away from the ground so I guessed Vincent could boost me up, unless they were locked? It was cold now so I was pretty sure they had already been locked up until spring.

"The front windows are locked." I whispered.

"That wasn't my intention anyway." He whispered back.

"Then what are you talking about?!" I was starting to get frustrated. All he was giving was suggestions with no real solutions.

"Is your window locked?"

"No!" I said as I remembered I had opened it recently to test the weather before I left in the morning.

I ran to the yard and looked up at my window on the second story of the house. It was pretty far away and I wondered how I was going to get up there? I looked at Vincent for a suggestion?

"Jump!" he said looking at me with a smile.

"Are you serious?" I asked. It's easily 18 feet high. There was no way I was going to look like an idiot jumping up and down on the lawn so I whispered "You first."

"Always so suspicious." He joked. "Watch." He knelt down close to the ground, his left hand touching the grass and sprang up into the air landing one foot on the window ledge gracefully and pushed up the window. He looked down and waved me up.

"That's so neat!" I said in awe. I took a deep breath to prepare myself. "Okay Delilah you can do this." I encouraged. I knelt down like Vincent and sprang upward as hard as I could and of course passed the window but Vincent grabbed my waist and pulled me down to him on the cement ledge.

"Thanks."

"You're welcome." He smiled at me and held my hand to help me in the window.

"Okay I know I have paper around here somewhere." I said when we were both inside. I searched my shelves and found my shush book stuffed in between two of my other books. "What should I write?" I asked in a whisper.

“I don’t know, but make it quick.” He replied while he pulled my clothes out of my drawers and set them on the bed.

“Okay, I’ve got it.” I grabbed the pen and started writing. I knew my mother would find the letter so I addressed it to her.

Mom,

I'm sure you are worried about me right now, I just want you to know that I'm okay. I have found someone that loves me and we have decided to elope! I know you were always worried that I would never find anyone so you can finally stop worrying. I'm going to be fine and no matter what please remember that I love you very much. Please give Pop my love and tell him thank you for everything. I don't know where we are going but I will try to write as much as I can. I love you both, Delilah.

I folded the paper and wrote *Mom* on the front then set it on my dresser along with the Bakery keys so she would find them.

"I need something to put your clothes in Delilah." Vincent whispered.

"Okay, I have a bag in the hall closet, I'll go get it, will you also fold the quilt? I'd like to take it with me." It seemed silly but I loved that quilt, I had been using it most of my life.

I seen Vincent shake his head as he grabbed the quilt and I opened the door and stepped through, slowly shutting it behind me.

I started to the closet at the other end of the hallway slowly so I didn't make any noise. I could hear my father snoring loudly and I smiled to myself but kept moving. I tiptoed past their room to the closet and grabbed the big carpetbag and shut the closet door. So far, so good I thought. I turned around and headed back toward my room. Walking past their room again I thought I'd better shut the door this time so I didn't wake them.

I reached in to grab the handle and caught a whiff of something sweet, perfume maybe? It smelled good. I put my nose in the air and breathed in heavily to find out what it was. It was strong, my mother must have sprayed it around the room right before she went to bed.

I closed my eyes so I could further enjoy the smell. Breathing in heavy I sniffed and sniffed until it got stronger and stronger; my mouth watering with each breath. Mm… how delicious, I thought to myself licking my lips and swallowing hard. I leaned down until the smell was right under my nose.

"DELILAH!" I heard someone call out. I opened my eyes to see who was calling me? Vincent was standing in the door way, looking at me. "Get down!" He whispered pointing towards the floor. I followed his finger to the floor and soon realized I was holding on to their headboard, hovering over my mothers head, with my teeth exposed. I fell to the floor and threw my hands over my mouth in disgust when I realized that the perfume, the delicious smell that drew me in… was my parents!

I darted out of their room, past Vince and around the corner back to mine. I didn't bother to grab anything. I didn't even think twice about jumping out of my window. I just had to get out of there, away from them.

I sat in the car trying to control myself and the driver door opened and Vincent got in with the bag.

"I warned you that you could be a danger to them. It's in our nature to find humans appealing Delilah." He said grabbing my hand.

“I almost ate them!” I was panicking now. I rocked back and forth running my hand through my hair because I didn’t know exactly what I should do? I mean, I really almost ate my parents! “I feel like I’m going to be sick…again.” I bent over and put my head between my knees and took some cleansing breaths hoping that would help.

“It’s not your fault.” Vince said pulling me back up and wiping my hair away from my face. “But we can’t take any more risks. We have to get out of the city. The sun is going to rise soon, we need to get you something to eat and get back to my Apartment.” He turned on the car and put it in to gear.

“But what am I going to eat here?” I said nervously.

“Don’t worry, I have an idea” he said, “trust me.”

We drove for a while and I noticed we were headed for Down Town.

“Well this explains why I couldn’t find you.” I said looking out the window at the city. “There was no way I was going to walk this far.”

“I actually wasn’t this far either.” he replied. “I had something else closer to you for the last few weeks but I wanted tonight to be special.”

“Then why didn’t anyone see you around?”

“Because I didn’t want them to. I don’t go out of my way to be noticed Delilah. We blend in and try to be as inconspicuous as possible.”

“You don’t talk to many people.” I said out loud remembering our conversation on the bench.

“Exactly. I told you then that I was speaking the truth.”

“So where are we going?” I asked.

“First, you eat.” He answered cheerfully.

He continued to drive turning this way and that way until he came to a small alley in between two big brown buildings.

“What are we doing here?” I asked, looking around as we got out of the car.

“Shh…” he said, pressing his finger to his lips. His lips looked soft as they molded around his finger and I wanted to lick them right on the spot. Maybe a little nibble or two, just so I could feel the texture between my teeth. I licked my own lips as I stared at his. “You’re getting distracted.” He said with a smile, breaking my fantasy.

“Well you‘re very distracting, or well your mouth is anyway.” I purred smiling up at him through my lashes.

“Delilah, I’m serious. We don’t have the time for this right now. You have to eat and we have to get back before the sun comes up. Can’t you feel the warning your body is giving you?”

Could I? I did a mental check of some kind of new feeling but the problem was that they were all new feelings. Instead I looked for a bad feeling. I guessed that if the sun could hurt me then there should be a warning signal of some sort? Closing my eyes I tried to shut off my lust for Vince and find the warning. I hadn’t realized how bad I wanted him to touch me or for me to touch him. Come on Delilah snap out of it! I mentally slapped myself and bingo! There it was. We only had about forty-five minutes left. How exactly I knew that, I wasn't sure? I guess it was part of my new built in alarm clock and as long as I could keep my public fantasizing down to a minimum then maybe I could not get… well, I wasn't exactly sure what would happen?

I opened my eyes to see Vincent looking at me. "Forty-five minutes?" I said and he nodded and then smiled.

"How did you know I was distracted?"

"Because you were looking at me like you were starving I was the first thing you saw to eat."

"I am. And you are." I answered back giving him a wicked smile.

"There will be time for that later." He said smiling. "Now focus."

"Alright." I promised and gave a little yelp when he slapped my bottom to get me going again.

We walked in silence looking for something. I walked behind Vincent while he searched, occasionally sniffing the air before dragging me further.

I went along until he suddenly stopped. "There, do you see them?" he asked pointing at three overflowing garbage cans that were grouped together.

"The garbage?" I asked confused.

"What's around the garbage Delilah?"

I looked back to all the silver cans. I could smell them from here but I was sure he didn't want me to eat garbage so I inspected a little further.

"The RATS?!" I asked in disbelief.

"It's an old survival trick our kind has used on ships for centuries. They're warm blooded and you have to eat something. Do you really want to attack someone you know? It's late and we're running out of time before the sun comes up, that is unless you'd like to go back to see your parents; it makes no difference to me, and if memory serves you found them to be quite *appealing*." he said with a sadistic smile on his face.

I stared him down furiously at his suggestion. Right now I wished I had something to throw at him.

"FINE!" I agreed angrily.

I flashed over to swoop one of the rats up in my hand. I could hear the chaotic drumming of the little rodent's heartbeat and feel its desperation to escape. The smell was not a sweet smell *at all* and mixed with the garbage odor it was nauseating. I looked at Vince and frowned, crinkling my nose in disgust.

"Bon Appétit," he said leaning casually against one of the buildings. He looked so relaxed I could just kill him for making me do this!

I closed my eyes so I didn't have to focus of what it was that I was about to do. I opened my mouth wide and bit down hard. There was a squeak as soon I sunk my teeth in but I felt the warm thick liquid instantly fill my mouth so that was forgotten almost as soon as it happened. I began to swallow faster and faster. It seemed the more I drank the more not only my stomach yearned for more but also my veins. In their dehydrated condition I felt the heat run through them like liquid fire, jump starting my heart again and instantly moistening my body from the inside. I sucked until there was nothing left. I opened my eyes and lifted away from the hairy carcass that laid in my hands.

I started to feel sorry for the lifeless rodent until I realized what poor condition my body was in and how dehydrated I still felt. I saw there were more of them still in the corner eating old food that covered the ground so I dropped the rat in front of me and quickly grabbed another one, squeaking and squirming, and trying to escape before I drained it also. I repeated this process over and over until there were no more to grab. I dropped the last one and looked down breathlessly as it fell to the ground. To my amazement there were a half a dozen lifeless little hair covered bodies lying at my feet.

I took a step back and looked up at Vincent who was now standing next to me. I felt better, more in control of my body but I was a little unsure of everything else. He simply looked at me and smiled, holding out a white handkerchief between his finger and thumb. I noticed a set of red embroidered double V's stacked one on top of the other and secretly wondered who stitched them before I took the fancy hankie and started to scrub away the blood around my mouth.

"See they're not so bad are they?" he asked, grabbing my hand to walk me around the little pile I had made.

“No, they’re not, and once you’ve eaten enough of them you don’t notice the strange taste as bad.”

Vincent just laughed and put his arm around me as we walked towards the car.

“Wait here.” he said and continued to the car alone and grabbed my bag before shutting the door. “We don’t have far to go. Only about a block.”

He laced his arm back through mine and we were off.

I felt so alive, more than I had felt since I awoke in my new body. My heart was beating quickly now from my dinner and warmth was surging throughout my entire body like an electric current.

My senses were heightened now too, everything was brighter and I could see over a mile away. Even the tiniest details of the trees were visible. Every texture and every grain, the way the different shades of brown intertwined with each other like a lovers embrace. Each naked branch looked like an out stretched hand just waiting to be caressed by the sky.

I was in awe of my new sight and it was hard to not be distracted (yet again) by the simplest things as we walked. It was like I was truly seeing everything for the first time.

We continued to a big gray building at the far end of the street. There were no signs in front and it looked abandoned. The windows were all dark, no lights were on at all and there was no sign of life left anywhere in the building.

We passed through the big black door and there were sets of wooden stairs winding upward to the other floors. I had never been to this apartment building. I hadn't known it existed and by the look of it I'm guessing that no one else knew either.

The inside was dark and smelled of dust and mildew. I gasped as Vincent gathered me in his arms and raced us up to the third floor. In the shape that the stairs were in I was surprised by the silence. They were so old I would have thought it was impossible but he was fast.

Vincent stopped at a faded black door that had a tarnished gold number nine on it. He slowly turned the handle and pushed it open.

I was amazed when he stepped into the room and set me on the floor. I looked around taking in the size of the room and how clean it was. There were no walls. It was completely open with golden wood floors that shinned and looked nothing like the outside of the building or even the stairway had been. The entire room smelt like Vincent, his strong satisfying smell mixed with a sweet hint of something new… Ah, roses. I spotted the crystal vase sitting on a night stand next to the bed, spilling with red and white roses. There had to be at least a dozen of each filling the room with their sweetness.

In the very middle of the room was a big, dark cherry oak, four poster bed covered by a canopy and thick black curtains that hung on all sides, stopping just above the floor. Each curtain was pulled back by a red satin tie, neatly knotted into perfect little bows.

The bed spread matched the curtains and on top sat two red satin pillows and a single white rose nestled in between them.

Out of curiosity I decided to check the vase again and count the white roses, just to see if he stole one from the vase to put on the bed. One, two, three, four… I mentally counted until I got to twenty-four. Wow, not only did he not steel one, but there were two dozen of white alone.

"There's two dozen white and one red." He whispered in my ear, standing behind me.

"How'd you know I was counting them?" I asked curiously.

"Because you count everything." He answered simply.

"I do not!"

"Oh, no? And how many stairs are on your patents porch?" He asked sarcastically.

I stopped. I knew instantly how many were there. I didn't even have to think about it. There were six.

"That's different," I answered. "I grew up in that house. I've been going up those stairs just short twenty years."

"Mmm… hmm… Sure." He accused smiling.

"The reason I was counting the roses to begin with, was to see if you cheated and just pulled one out of the vase to put in-between the pillows." I added in my defense.

"Hey," he said throwing up his hands, with a broad smile stretched across his face. "I believe you."

"Good, you should." I said smiling and starting to laugh along with him.

“Am I really that bad?” I asked sliding my arms around him.

“Not really but I have noticed you count often. I am willing to bet you know how many stairs there are to your old bedroom too.”

I sighed.

“You do know, don’t you?” he asked tilting my head up with his fingertip.

“There’s twelve.” I answered sadly. “And two more before the landing bringing the total to fourteen.”

He knelt down and kissed me, softly at first but that kiss soon erased all my sadness and replaced it with an undeniable longing.

Oh, how I had dreamed of this moment, and now I was finally going to get everything I had fantasized about. But suddenly, I was nervous. I was self-conscience about what I should or shouldn’t do and soon my head was taking over what my body should have found natural.

I pulled out of our entanglement and Vincent looked at me with understanding.

He smiled and kissed my hand sweetly and walked over to the wardrobe.

“I have just one more thing for you,” he said as he opened the door. He reached in and pulled out a baby pink, silk and lace negligée and walked back toward me, holding it out in front of him.

“Something for you to sleep in?” he said as he handed me the garment. My eyes felt like they were going to pop out of my head. I just stood there staring at the nightgown he still held out in front of him, not quite sure what I was supposed to do with it. It looked awful short to be a night-*gown*.

"You can change over there," he said as he pointed to the left side of the room. My eyes followed his finger to see a black dressing screen with dainty red embroidered flowers and delicate green vines that ran up the front of it. The screen was standing in the corner all alone, apparently waiting for me.

I walked nervously to the corner of the room and ducked behind the partition. I stood there for far too long with the nightgown still in my hands, contemplating if it would hurt his feelings if I just came back out in the same clothes? But I decided there was no going back now so I might as well change and get it over with.

I hung the garment over the top of the screen and quickly realized there was matching pink, lacy, panties to go with it. I took off my shoes and stockings first and slid them to the side. Here we go, I thought to myself while taking off the rest of my clothes.

I quickly slipped the nightgown over my head and it slid down quickly, just barley covering my rear. I gasped at the shortness. This wasn't a nightgown at all. This was a night *shirt*! No wonder they gave you a pair of panties. Anyone who saw you in this was definitely going to see them. I ran my hands down my sides and over to my stomach while looking down just to make sure what little bit of fabric was there, was whole.

I peeked out slowly and nervously from behind the screen at first to see if he was looking in my direction —of course he was— just sitting in the chair by the door patiently waiting for me to fully step out. So I ducked back in, shut my eyes, and took a deep breath to steady myself. Opening my eyes I ran my fingers through my hair to straighten it out a little bit. I was sure it probably looked terrible after my ordeal of laying on the ground and jumping and running. But as my fingers made contact I felt velvety smooth waves beneath them and thought that maybe my hair didn't look that bad after all. With nothing left to fix I bit back my nerves about the horribly short night shirt, shut my eyes, and walked out into plain sight.

When I opened my eyes Vincent was standing with a shocked expression on his face.

"Is it that bad?" I asked frailly, looking down.

"No."

"No?"

It was a nice change to see him dumbfounded for once. And I reveled in the moment.

"So, by that face I'm guessing I look pretty good huh?" I said sarcastically looking at the gawking fish he'd become.

He looked me up and down then he smiled like a fool. "Pretty good would be an insult, come with me." He took me by the hand and led me to the full length oval cheval mirror at the other end of the room. Walking toward it I noticed that it was made of the same dark cherry wood as the bed. He moved behind me and with his hands on my hips he pushed me toward the mirror.

"See? You are way more than pretty good," he whispered, his full, soft lips right next to my ear, and his breath giving me goose bumps as it tickled my neck.

I stood at the mirror gazing at the reflection it gave. I couldn't believe it. My skin was snow white and radiant and my limbs seemed stronger and more defined yet still elegant. I was me but I looked more agile.

My eyes were a brighter emerald reflecting the light of the room and almost glowing. I was sure they still changed color like before but I would have to wait and see.

My hair was a flawless cascade of rich, ruby red curls that stopped just above my hips with not a single frizzy in sight.

I couldn't help but touch my face and hair, just to make sure they were real. I had changed so much, but yet I hadn't. I got really close to the mirror to take a closer look at my face.

"Wow," I whispered to myself in disbelief, touching my milky soft skin.

"Pretty good does not quite cover it, does it?" Vincent asked turning me away from the mirror and back toward him.

Oh! Had he been shirtless before? Had I been so self-absorbed that I hadn't realized that this beautiful hunk of man was shirtless? I froze in that instant, mesmerized by how breathtaking he really was with his flawless skin, and broad shoulders. Not to mention how muscular he was. His body was chiseled all the way down to bellow his belly button.

I couldn't help but run my hands down his chest; it was like touching sculpted marble draped in the finest silk. I had never seen a naked man before to compare, but I was positive that Vincent had them all beat when it came to his overall beauty. I was in awe as I tickled my fingertips down his smooth chest and lower to his stomach and the little muscles that sat stacked up there, stopping to curl my finger around the little trail of ebony hair that ran downward from the bottom of his bellybutton. I wasn't sure how far down I was allowed to go and stopped when his breath hitched. I hadn't even realized that we were both breathing hard until then but there was a smoldering look in those deep blue eyes that told me to keep going.

I slid my hand down between the band of his pants and the muscle of his stomach and rubbed him until I could feel him growing in my hand. My eyes widened and Vincent looked down at me and smiled. Staring up at him I slid my hand down a little further and watched as he closed his eyes and parted his lips. Then slowly I pulled my hand back, tracing my delicate fingers up too, making him moan with pleasure.

I had to admit I liked being able to do this to him. My way of a little payback for his earth shattering kisses, I thought smugly.

After another up and down he stopped my hand and pulled it free from himself. He lifted me up and I wrapped my legs around him just like I had done on the Bridge. He began to kiss me harder and more ravenous then he ever had before, intertwining my tongue with his in a way that made me melt with desire as he walked me to the bed.

Laying me back on the bed he slowly slid his strong but gentle hands up my nightshirt caressing my breasts and setting my skin on fire. “You’re so soft.” He breathed in my ear. The vibration on my ear caused a spark that ran down through my belly, moistening between my thighs.

“Oh!” I gasped and arched to push myself further against his touch, as he pulled and massaged my nipples. I needed him to fill that ache he was causing with every touch.

Softly he pulled the negligée over my head and continued to cover me with sensual, soft kisses starting at my lips and slowly working to my neck, running his full lips affectionately over my collar bones.

His mouth was warm on my skin and hot to my sensitive nipples as he teased them with tip of his tongue. He let his teeth brush against me and I moaned in response as he sent shock waves throughout my body. This was torture, a sweet, all-consuming torture that I couldn’t get enough of.

He slid his hand down into my panties and began to mimic my up and down motion from earlier. Sliding his fingers in the wetness that awaited him there, I now understood why it had looked so pleasurable and struggled to catch my breath with every motion he made. “Vincent.” I pleaded. My body was tightening like chains being twisted around and around creating a tense knot. Every tongue flick on my left nipple sent more electric shocks down to meet the fingers that were working their magic inside me. I cried out, not knowing how much more pleasure I could possibly consume before Vincent started to trail sensual kisses down my belly stopping to kiss each hip bone while he removed my panties and tossed them to the side.

"I do recall you wanting to make a meal out of me? But I believe the pleasure shall be mine first." He grinned a most devious grin and before I could say anything he buried his face in-between my thighs.

"Oh!" I gasped as he softly licked and stroked me with the tip of his tongue and soon my gasps were replaced by moans as he circled and teased my most sensitive spot over and over again.

The emotion flowing through me was unimaginable and I gripped the sheets with both hands as my breathing grew even heavier. With my knees trembling, I slid my hands up, winding my fingers in his thick, black hair as my body continued to build. With each and every magnificent flick of his tongue a small piece of me tried to escape until I could no longer keep myself together, and I erupted.

I was so sensitive, shock waves continued making my body quiver each time the tip of his tongue touched me until he stopped and began his upward trail of kisses, first on my inner thighs, then each of my hip bones, my bellybutton and breasts stopping briefly to tease and nibble each of my nipples again. Each kiss felt like silk as he continued the short distance to start kissing my neck. "Ah!" I yelped as his teeth pierced my skin, catching me completely off guard, yet again.

Sinking his teeth further into my skin he then plunged his hardness inside me. I moaned as he filled me up completely and with every slow thrust I craved more of him but he stayed at an even rhythm driving me crazy.

He nipped and kissed my jawline before he moved his lips to mine and I could taste the sweetness of my blood on him making my heart race in response.

With my blood singing, I became that starving woman again that was eating for the first time. I let my desperate hunger direct my movements to find the friction I so desperately needed.

That night we became one entanglement of passion with no conception of time and completely cut off from the light and the waking world around us. Our bodies intertwined like mating snakes, coiled together. We were two separate beings, but created for one another, and perfectly pieced together to create one.

Exposed:

Touch, Taste, Pleasure and Pain; I surrender to you completely. Every fear, and every flaw erased leaving none, for the first time revealing me.
Delilah Waters- 1929

Chapter 9.

We boarded the train headed for Chicago. It was close enough that we could get there within a few hours so I could grab someone to eat without making a scene.

Vincent chose seats at the end of the train so I wasn't tempted by the all "possibilities" in the other cars.

"By cutting out the temptation, we cut out the risk," he told me as I followed him to the back of the train.

As we passed down the hallway, I looked in at the little yellow canary fluttering around in its iron dome cage; squawking nervously in my presence. I thought seriously about putting us both out of our misery. Until I saw the little blonde girl trying desperately to calm the bird. She couldn't have been more than seven but her big blue eyes were filled with worry for the little creature so I knew it must be her pet. Instead of stopping I just smiled and nodded at her as I continued to walk past to get to my seat at the end of the train.

Vincent and I sat close to each other and talked of what was to come in the many years ahead of us. Things we wanted to do and see.

He told me of his days in Paris and how beautiful it was. He promised we would go back once the people that knew him there died.

"It has been many years," he said "and many of them are old now in their late seventies, but better to be safe than sorry. I wouldn't want anyone to notice that I remain unchanged by time."

I smiled at him, just those three little words alone made me happy "unchanged by time." I too would remain unchanged. No more worries of being and old maid, doomed to repeat the cycle of marriage, children, old age and death.

The thought of remaining young and with Vincent forever was more than I could have ever hoped for and I could hardly sit still. I was so excited! It hadn't even been a whole day since I became an immortal and I was already doing so many things I had never done. Last night, or well, this morning, had been amazing. I never knew that being touched by someone else could make me feel that way. Or that *I* would enjoy touching someone *else*, but Vincent made it so easy to love him. He was smart, so much smarter than me, and passionate with a hint of sarcastic, yet gentlemanly humor that I adored. He had patience and was understanding and whenever I needed him, he was there.

I leaned forward and pressed my lips to his passionately. I could tell I had caught him off guard, but it only took a second for him to reciprocate.

"Not that I'm complaining, but what was that for?" he asked winded, when we broke apart.

"For coming into my life and saving me from being a lonely old maid. And for last night." I couldn't help but smile at the thought of how perfect we had been together.

"You are quite welcome," he said smugly and I knew of course he was just referring to the sex.

I rolled my eyes at him and smiled. He returned my smile with a big cheesy grin of his own then put his arm around me to pull me in close to him, and kissed the top of my head. “Just you wait Delilah, You haven‘t seen anything yet.” He whispered as he twirled one of my ringlets in-between his fingers. He sounded so excited to show me everything he could and I smiled again and snuggled a little closer and wrapped my arm around his waist. We stayed cuddled up together for the remainder of the train ride and I was as content and happy as I had ever been in my entire life!

* * *

It was a short trip to Chicago and before we knew it, it was already time to get off the train.

Vincent carried my bag and his as we started to walk down the street towards where we were staying. We had plans to travel more but I wasn’t sure if Vincent owned a house or how long it would take us to get settled somewhere.

“Where are we going?” I looked around but I had never been to Chicago before so I wasn’t sure where we were.

“There is a Motel just a little further that I have already made arrangements for us to stay in until you get settled in your new skin; so to speak.”

“How long is that?” I asked, confused by his statement.

"However long it takes Delilah. You haven't even been a vampire for a full twenty-four hours and you have yet to eat anything that's really worth eating. Why?"

"I thought we were going to somewhere more permanent, sooner than that, or traveling to somewhere far away."

"Are you in a hurry?" he asked in a chuckle. "You do realize we have until forever? You still have a human conception of time, my Darling. We are in no hurry anymore to do anything. The only constriction of time we have is the time between sun set, and sun rise."

I was actually glad that he brought up the subject of sunrise because the vision hadn't explained in further detail what would happen if we were in the sun. So curiously I had to ask.

"What will happen to us if we *are* exposed to the sun?"

He stopped suddenly and I had to freeze to keep from running him over. I expected it was something dangerous or I wouldn't have felt the warning like I had before but I wondered why he would have that reaction to my question.

"Well, due to the curse, the sun would burn right through us; causing the most excruciating pain that you could not even imagine."

"How do you know this?"

"Because I've seen it first hand, and believe me, it's not something you ever want to endure."

He started to walk again but I was frozen in the thought of slowly burning to death in the sun. Seeing my flesh smoke and cinder as I screamed out in agony unable to save myself from my own doom. I had to mentally shake myself to rid my thoughts of the horrible images.

"Are you coming?"

I looked up from my spot to see Vincent stopped a few feet ahead of me, waiting.

I unstuck my feet and pushed the sun away from my mind. It was another problem for another night. Instead I decided to lose myself in the scenery as we passed by, enjoying all the little details I would have never have been able to see if I were still human.

The colors that I could define in the dark were breathtaking. The night-time sky and its swirls of navy blue mixed with light and dark gray and outlined finally in black. The stars that I always thought were just white I could now see that they were white with speckles of yellow, light blue, red and bright green running through them.

I kept myself busy gawking at the scenery until we reached the room. It wasn't as nice as the first room but it had a little charm about it. The bed was smaller and not surround by thick curtains which made me nervous after the sun explanation I had just got from Vincent. There was two small, light, wooden chairs over in the corner and nestled in-between was a petite round wooden table. There wasn't really a place to put our things just a small dark, wooden hope chest at the foot of the bed, but I guess it would do for now.

I looked at Vincent, worried about the small window in the room.

"Any suggestions?" he asked looking back at me.

I took a look around the room and noticed the cover on the bed was burgundy. "Will this do?" I asked pointing.

"Looks like it might." He answered with a grin.

We stripped the comforter off the bed and we both secured it around the window.

"We can use my quilt on the bed until we leave?" I offered.

"Sounds good to me."

Vincent hung the curtains over the quilt we put up just to be safe while I finished unpacking our things. It didn't take much time because I only had one bag and Vincent didn't have very much either so it wasn't difficult to fit our things into the chest.

When I was finished Vincent was still standing near the window. "Would you like to go for a stroll?" he asked reaching out his hand.

I felt a little nervous to take it. I knew exactly why we would be *strolling*, but the dehydrated ache in my veins was begging me to, and my heart was almost at a standstill again, so I reached out hesitantly but put my hand in his.

We walked out of our room and out of the building. I wasn't sure where to go or what I was supposed to do.

"What if I can't do this?" I asked, looking into Vincent's loving eyes.

"Of course you can, this is your nature now; what you were designed for. Remember the way you felt at your Parents?"

"Actually I've been trying to forget." I answered, eyeing him.

"I'm going to ignore that look and instead tell you that now is the time to remember it."

"Remember the overwhelming pull towards what you wanted most. The smell, the way that smell made your mouth water. If you focus on those two things they will make the connection between you and your prey. You have to let go of everything else and follow your instincts."

It sounded easy enough and I guess I *had* already done it before, with my parents (I was really trying to forget that) so why couldn't I do it again? The answer was, I could and more importantly I was going to.

Maybe Vince could see my internal battle because he stepped behind me and put his strong hands on my hips and whispered. "I'll stay right behind you. You won't be able to see me but remember I can see you so don't be frightened, I would never let any harm come to you."

He kissed my cheek goodbye and vanished. I just stood there at first not knowing how to start. I decided to walk a bit, turning down different streets looking for something to catch my eye.

Suddenly, I found what I was looking for; a Speakeasy just down a little ways from me with drunken people stumbling out of the front door. This should be easy enough I thought. They're already zozzled so to see me wouldn't be alarming right away.

First I strutted past the three men. They were stumbling and leaning on each other for support. I was counting on them to find me attractive and of course it worked like a charm.

I heard one whistle as I passed by and I shot the group a flirty glance over my shoulder to lure them in. I started to walk again, but slowly, so they had a chance to catch up.

"Hey Doll," one called out, and I could hear him stumbling towards me, trying to find his footing. I continued to walk further away knowing the others would follow.

I shot another glance back and let out a soft giggle to entice them and bring them further into my little game as I turned around the corner into the alleyway.

Walking halfway down, I stopped, keeping my back toward the three men so they couldn't see my face as they stumbled around the corner.

"Don't be that way, we just want to talk to you." One of them slurred.

I decided to close my eyes and let my other senses guide me. I tried to remember the delicious smell from my house and focus on finding it.

I inhaled deeply through my nose and caught a bunch of different scents. First was the scent of the wet snow covering the ground underneath my feet, a wet dirt and sulfur kind of smell. Then the wood smoke mixed with a sour garbage odor being carried through the air, but none of those were what

I was searching for so I tried again and sucked in through my nose a little harder… and there it was. That sweet, lovely, mouthwatering scent of… life. Only this time it was mixed with harsh overtones of whiskey, and a lot of it.

I opened my eyes and smiled as one of the men touched my shoulder. I didn't know if the others were as close and at that moment, I didn't care.

Slowly I turned, smiling in the most bloodthirsty way, to glimpse the horror his expression held at seeing what this little lady had in store for him. His eyes bulged and his heart drummed a melody that sung only to me, awakening the monster I didn't know was lying inside. My mouth began to water and my teeth were sharp and at the ready. I knelt in close and sniffed his scent once more before grabbing his head and lunging my face forward, sinking my long, pointed, teeth into the pulsing vein that had been calling my name.

He struggled fiercely, but compared to the strength his blood was feeding me, he was as productive as the rats had been struggling in my grasp the night before.

I sucked hard, this time enjoying the taste. It was sweet with no sour aftertaste, suddenly reminding me of the blood I had tasted in the dream Vincent had given me. The only difference now was the hint of whiskey which made me light headed.

I drained him completely and let him fall to my feet. I looked up with the same smile on my lips and saw the other two men standing, frozen, in fear not too far away.

I lunged at the bigger one with dark hair hoping he would be more of a challenge because he started to run.

I grabbed him from behind, ripping his head to the side with one hand causing his neck to break under the pressure.

Biting him with even more force than the first. I felt his vein burst as I tore through his flesh losing myself in the hot, sweet liquid that overflowed my mouth, spilling down my chin; warming my icy, porcelain skin before it dripped to the awaiting snow at my feet.

I felt his adrenaline flow through me as I drank and licked at the spraying vein in his neck. The more I drank the more excited I got and holding his sagging, lifeless body was no inconvenience, even for my smaller frame.

As I sucked out the big man's last drop I looked over to the corner and saw Vincent swoop down from the rooftop of a nearby building to finish off man number three.

I dropped the remains of my dinner and wobbled over towards Vincent. I was so high off of whiskey and adrenaline that I was still smiling.

Stepping over his kill that just collapsed to the ground I slid my hands up the sides of Vincent's head. Kissing him hard, forcing him backward into the brick building behind him.

This was another totally different experience. I had never been drunk before. But I couldn't say I didn't enjoy it. To feel out of control of my body and just let my desires take over was nice, especially when my desires led me to Vincent.

We stood there for a long moment kissing. I was covered in blood, rubbing it all over Vincent's face.

"So, how was that?" I asked winded and a little smug when I pulled away from his face.

"Mm... I have to admit it was more forceful than usual but that made it that much more erotic."

"Not the kiss Vince," I said rolling my eyes.

He smiled at my appearance, quickly reminding me of how he had acted in my dream.

"You did excellent! Just as I knew you would. I have to admit I've never seen any other (new or old) take on more than one at a time, but your lure was genius."

Touching my face with his hands he continued to smile as he wiped off the blood covering my mouth and chin with his handkerchief.

"Well technically I only killed two. I said smiling. "You finished off the third." I reminded him, while he continued to scrub at parts of my face.

"Yes, I came down to catch him while your attention was… otherwise engaged." He said as he nodded over at the dark haired corpse laying on the ground.

I followed his eyes to the gruesome scene of the two men laying opposite each other on the ground. Yikes!, I thought at first glance. Victim one wasn't as bad of course, blood just on his neck and coat collar. The second was a total blood bath; soaked from the neck down it seemed and even his hair was matted with red stickiness. Both men still had their eyes open, mirroring the same shocked expression like they couldn't believe this "Doll" had killed them.

I really wasn't the guilty type but I thought about my human self, and what I had thought about my horrific dream that night. I had been appalled and confused as to why I would ever dream of anything so gruesome. But look at you now, my conscious replied. You just created something far worse in reality and enjoyed every minute of it!

Vincent took my hand and led me towards the bodies and one by one we took out their wallets and whatever money they had.

"Why are we doing this?" I asked in confusion as I tossed the wallet back down onto the corpse.

"It's better for us if humans believe that this was some type of robbery. Humans are greedy by nature so it won't be hard for them to believe that other humans are responsible for the murders if money was involved."

"Oh, what will happen to them now?" I asked as we walked out of the alley.

"What do you mean?"

"I mean there are three dead men in an alley now that weren't there before. What will happen to the bodies?"

"Oh, well, someone will find them and bury them somewhere after some type of religious ceremony I suppose. Why do you ask?"

“I was just curious of who cleaned up after us? You know, a kind of who’s stuck with the dishes after dinner kind of thing.”

Vincent looked at me with a confused expression on his face for a brief moment before shaking his head and saying, “You shouldn’t burden yourself with such thoughts. It’s better to think of them as inconsequential and go about your night. Who they were and what happens next is irrelevant to us.”

I wanted to ask him why but after thinking about the situation, he really was right, so I changed the subject.

“So is it my turn to watch now?” I asked playfully, squinting my eyes at him.

“Do you wish to watch?” he asked curiously.

“I would like to; if you don’t mind?”

His eyes glistened with excitement in the moonlight as answer to my question.

“Follow me to the rooftops and I shall show you how it’s done.” He gave me one of his cocky smirks before he scaled the brick of one of the nearby buildings and disappeared.

Leaping on to the brick I used my claw-like nails to scale each brick with ease. I wasn’t bothered at all by the rough texture of the faded red blocks under my palms, and within seconds I was on the top of the building.

The city looked so different from this angle. Rooftops stretched out in front of me like the black squares scattered on a checker board and the streets looked like nothing but little gray lines that formed the maze of the city below.

The sky was bigger and the stars and moon were brighter than before; almost hurting my sensitive eyes. The moon however bright, was somehow still unnoticed by everyone else on the streets.

I remembered what Vince had said before about the moon and I understood now what he meant. The large, white half circle was undoubtedly there and undoubtedly beautiful, but completely unnoticed by the public that roamed the streets underneath its glow, as were we.

To my surprise Vincent stayed on the rooftops leaping from one to the other in silence. I followed behind a few feet apart to give him some space.

I watched carefully to learn any kind of technique that might be helpful in the future as he crouched down, lurking on the rooftop. I got closer to the edge of the building to spy on who he was shadowing.

It was a woman, she was young, with short blonde hair and wearing a long, knee length, light brown coat and tan heels.

She was rushing, maybe to get out of the night air or maybe she was running late? It really didn't matter, I could tell by Vincent's posture that she was never going to make it anywhere ever again.

He slid down the wall with ease not making a sound when he touched the ground. He confidently and gracefully walked forward behind the unsuspecting woman.

I watched as he flashed in front of her, startling the woman, leaving her frozen on the side walk in front of him.

She gasped. "Oh! I wasn't expecting you there," she said, looking up at Vincent's eyes.

He extended his hand out toward her face as he spoke. Softly he whispered to her while running his long white finger down the side of her face.

"Shh…" he said, putting his finger from the other hand to his outstretched lips.

She didn't speak, instead she stood there in front of him like a breathing statue. She remained completely calm and relaxed as he bent her head to the side and bit down.

I watched as he drained her. As her hands and arms began to weigh her down and as he braced her arching body with his strong arms as more of her started to fall backward.

It was beautiful, so delicate and graceful, there was no struggling or screaming, she simply went to sleep and would never wake up.

He lifted his face from her neck and looked up at me. Though there was much space between us I knew he could see me with great clarity. The admiration left on my face as I stared down at him would be very obvious to his inhuman eyes.

He laid the woman down on the ground in front of him and after going through her purse, leapt onto the roof to stand beside me.

"That was beautiful, so poetic, she just stood there and she didn't struggle or even try to move. And you thought what I did was genius. No *that* was genius!" I gushed, completely captivated by his finesse.

"How did you do it?"

"I told you, all of us have the gift of somnolence."

"So I can do it too?"

"Yes."

"How?"

"Concentration. You have to concentrate very hard on your prey to soothe them, think about being calm and reflect that on to them."

I thought I would try it just to see if it would work. I closed my eyes and concentrated very hard on Vincent to see if he would get the least bit drowsy; but I was suddenly interrupted by his thunderous laughter instead.

"What's so funny?" I demanded when I opened my eyes.

He was standing there in stitches unable to speak at first while I stood there waiting for some kind of explanation as to why he was still laughing.

"You should have seen your face," he cried, bent over chuckling at me. "I told you to concentrate and there you stood with your eyes clenched together frowning and faced towards *me*. Did you think I would fall over and begin to snore?" he asked *still* laughing.

"I'm glad you find this amusing," I answered coldly. "No, I didn't think you would fall over snoring. I thought that if you began to feel it then I would know I was doing it right; but forget it!" I stormed away and jumped off the roof to head back to our room.

Before I could stand up right he was by my side.

"I'm sorry I laughed at you, but if you would have seen that face you would have laughed too." He chuckled, grabbing my arm to keep me from walking away from him.

"And this is you apologizing?" I asked annoyed because he still held his stupid grin.

"Yes." He agreed serious now. "It's my fault to begin with. I forgot to tell you that it doesn't work on vampires, so even if it was working I wouldn't be able to tell you because I wouldn't know myself, and for that I apologize also."

"So, do you forgive my inconsideration?"

I glared at him for a moment for making me feel stupid, and also because I didn't want him to know right away that I'd forgiven him.

"Yes, I forgive you, but I will have my revenge, Mr. Vanhorne, you just wait." I threatened with a smile as we weaved in and out of the streets on the way back to our room.

"Is that a threat, flowing from those lips?" He asked smirking back at me.

"Why, yes it is."

"I'm shaking in my shoes." he said gesturing to his feet.

"Good, you should be. Be afraid, be very afraid." I warned, squinting at him.

"And when should I expect this reprisal?" he asked smugly.

"Oh, it could come at any time. Maybe tonight, maybe tomorrow, or maybe even a month from now. Either way you'll never see it coming."

"Ah, I see… like this?" he scooped up a big pile of snow and lunged it forward hitting me on the side of the head before I could duck out of the way.

"Oh, well two can play it that way!" I yelled, grabbing a pile of my own to throw at him. I let it go streaming through the air at his head. Of course he moved just in enough time so my snow ball hit the side of a building.

"Missed me!" he teased.

"I'll get you eventually!" I yelled throwing snow ball after snow ball that all seemed to miss him. He was fast when he wanted to be. He was moving towards me and I still couldn't hit him!

He grabbed my arms to stop me before I could grab another mound of snow "You have terrible aim." He whispered before kissing me sweetly.

"No I don't, You move too fast." I mumbled in between kisses and he laughed.

"Life with you my darling is never boring." he said brushing my hair away from my face. With me still in his arms. We kissed on the street while the snow swirled all around us, it was like being on the inside of a shaken up snow globe with the city as our backdrop. The moonlight shined brightly reflecting off the new fallen snow, lighting up the night until it mimicked the day. Life was perfect.

Chapter 10.

It had bee a whole month since we arrived in Chicago and I was enjoying everything about the nightlife here. I had gotten the hang of feeding (things weren't quit as gory as they started out) although sometimes I still got carried away. I couldn't help it. I would get so excited and it was fun to toy with them. To chase them just for the love of the hunt and feel their fear and adrenaline run throughout my body as I sucked away their life, drop by precious drop. I lived for that game and night after night Vincent watched with amazement as I slaughtered the living with enjoyment.

I have to admit I didn't understand when Vincent would speak of vampires he knew that felt sorry for their victims after the kill. I never looked at it that way. As far as I was concerned, I had no more remorse for my dinner now that I was an immortal than I had when I was human; eating a chicken or a cow.

Sitting in our little room contemplating where we should go for dinner, I was surprised when I heard a knock at the door. No one knew we were here. Did they? And if so, who knew? Vincent never mentioned we were having visitors. When I opened the door, a couple stood there silently, I guess waiting for me to address them. Instead I stared, not knowing either the man or woman that stood in front of me but knowing instantly that they were both immortal.

The woman was pretty. She had very pale skin and dark brown hair that she wore short, tucked under a black cloche that had a big silver flower on the left side of it. Her eyes were the color of dark chocolate and they shined as the light bounced off of them. She was dressed in a black dress coat and was smoking a cigarette, connected to a long black holder.

The man was just as modern looking. He had olive colored skin with slicked back, dark hair and big brown eyes. He wore a gray and black pinstriped suit under a long black unbuttoned coat.

By the end of my brief assessment, Vincent was at my side.

“Ramiel, Fidelia!” He greeted as he gestured them into the small room.

“Heya Vin-nay, the woman gushed dragging out his name.

Vinny? I thought with disgust, looking the woman up and down again.

“It is good to see you old friend,” the man said with a slight accent.

“And you; both of you.” Vincent answered, nodding to the woman.

“What’s it been, seventy years?”

“About that,” said the woman smiling.

I stood there not knowing if I should just introduce myself and get it over with because it was obvious that Vincent or “Vin-nay” had forgotten that I was even in the room. Instead I nudged Vincent in his side with my elbow *hard* and smiled up at the couple standing in front of me.

"I apologize, how rude of me" he chuckled rubbing his side. "Delilah this is Ramiel and Fidelia; old friends of mine from my days in New Orleans.

"Guys, *this,* is Delilah." He said hugging me around my waist.

"You forgot to mention just how lovely she is in your last letter Vincent." Ramiel gushed, smiling over at me.

"Did I?" Vincent beamed with a hint of his usual smugness.

"It's nice to meet you both," I interrupted, putting out my open hand towards Fidelia first.

"You too," she replied, gently grabbing my hand in hers.

As soon as my hand was free Ramiel was there taking it with his. "Pleasure," he said softly, then he lifted my hand to his lips and gently kissed the top of my skin. I would have blushed if there were any blood in my system but they had just interrupted our dinner plans.

After a little conversation it seems they had stopped in to visit us after the news spread of my "arrival" into the world of immortality.

They were very curious about my skills and amazed when Vincent told them how well I had adapted to the change.

After getting acquainted a little more I could see that Fidelia was much bolder then I had originally thought. She was just slightly taller than me and I could see after she removed her coat that she was very fit under her long, black, slinking dress. She was direct and she spoke with an accent that I actually recognized.

One of my customers that came into the Bakery sounded a lot like her. Everyone called her B, short for Beatrice. She had come from New Jersey and had that same way of pronouncing her words.

Fidelia's wasn't all New Jersey though, I guessed some of the other was acquired from all her traveling; a little bit picked up here and there that I didn't recognize.

Ramiel was much smoother than his mate. He was a tall man, a couple inches or so taller then Vincent, with a thickness about him, but not over weight, and as hard as it was to miss him, he wasn't nearly as bold or as loud as Fidelia. It was easy to see that she did all of the decision making in their relationship.

Both looked like they belonged in a high class Club, dancing and drinking with the rest of the city on a busy night and that made me feel out of place standing next to the two of them. It was worse when they spoke of their travels together. The only places I had ever been was Detroit Michigan and now Chicago Illinois. I had absolutely nothing to add to the conversation. I knew nothing of expensive things or the night life in exotic places.

For my sake Ramiel shared the story of how he and Fidelia met each other long ago.

They met in Ramiel's homeland of Spain in the late 1600's both already vampires making sure to hide what they were from the world.

“Fidelia, was the most beautiful woman I had ever laid my eyes upon, well, I guess it was a little more than my eyes.” He said with a knowing smile.

I started to tell them that I didn’t need *that* much information when Fidelia interrupted and said “Yep, he ran smack dab into me, knocking me to the ground.”

The confusion must have been very plain on my face because they both gave an amused smile and then Ramiel continued to explain.

“The Salem witch trials began in 1692 but accusations of witchcraft started long before that. Back then everything was considered witchery, unfortunately many of the accused were simply ill and unstable women. In those times you could be burned alive or hanged just for knowing how to stop a fever or simply because they wanted your land.”

“Could you imagine what would have happened to us that night if they had caught you feeding on the living?” Fidelia laughed in her high pitched voice as she laid horizontally at the foot of the bed, propped up by her elbow.

“It was a very close call. The sun had just set and I had been feeding close to the woods. Sure I knew it was dangerous, but back then if you didn’t catch something just after dusk then you would have to go into the home while everyone slept, and that was even more dangerous to attempt.”

“I heard footsteps approach and I let my victim fall to my feet. Moving cautiously I climbed one of the big oaks and waited for my stalker to show themselves. Only smelling the blood that covered the ground and my face I lunged from the tree, and landed…"

"Smack into me." Fidelia interrupted...

"Of course when I realized I had just tackled a woman in the woods I immediately rushed to my feet apologizing…"

"For how "clumsy" he was. Fidelia said giving air quotations with her fingers.

"At least I apologized, my love."

"But when he stopped blubbering over me and finally realized that I was immortal…"

"That was it. I knew right then that she was the one for me."

"I… on the other hand wasn't so sure."

"Are you trying to get yourself hanged? I asked looking at the corpse lying next to the tree. Of course he had no answer and just stood there like the village idiot, staring."

"I couldn't speak at first, you should have seen her in that white bonnet. She was really stunning.'

"Oh, I'm sure. Vincent agreed smiling a cheesy grin at Fidelia.

"Aaanyyyway," she continued. "He finally found his tongue and spit out the reason he was in the tree in the first place."

"It was not usual for me to kill so out in the open like that but I was so desperate for blood that night and couldn't wait for something less conspicuous." Ramiel finished.

“I had to admit I was a little turned on by the time he finished explaining his bloodlust and lack of control. Who doesn’t love a bad boy, right?” Fidelia chuckled.

“So I asked her to accompany me for the rest of the evening and show me some of her… techniques.” Ramiel smiled as the word *techniques* rolled off his tongue, seductively wrapped in his Spanish accent.

“And of course I agreed because he obviously needed the help and let’s face it, he aint hard to look at either.” Fidelia smiled then winked at me.

“After that night we became inseparable but we had to move constantly to avoid being detected,” Ramiel continued. “Sure there was no way of knowing what was leaving the bodies of men and women lifeless on the street, but back then people were a lot more superstitious and everyone had their beliefs about what we were. Some thought us to be Demons; others thought us to be the Devil himself.”

“My favorite, by far,” Fidelia paused to hit her cigarette “was all the ways they thought up to get rid of us,” she continued as smoke slowly poured out from in between her lips. “Garlic, wooden stakes, crosses, ha! crosses made of wood.” She snickered rolling her eyes. Hitting her cigarette again, she held it out towards me, having switched positions crossing her legs under her.

“You want a drag? “I looked at the smoke pouring out of the top and wrinkled my nose at the stench of it before shaking my head. “No. But thank you.”

"Suit yourself." She said seemingly unconcerned that I didn't want it. "You would not believe the rumors I have ran across over the years?" she continued. "Right down to we can't see our own reflection. Humans, soo eager to believe whatever they're told. I wonder sometimes how they've lived this long?"

"So… who's hungry?" She asked suddenly, popping up off the bed. "I just love a new city, such a bigger variety to choose from!" she gleamed.

In a weird way I think the story actually triggered her bloodlust. But I wasn't opposed to the idea. It had been too long since my last meal. There wasn't the slightest flutter in my chest anymore and being closed in with Fidelia's nonstop cigarette smoke made me want to get out of that room even more.

I didn't usually let myself get this drained but it seemed my last dinner hadn't stuck around very long this time and it was a lot later than I had anticipated from all the catching up and reminiscing.

The four of us left the room together and I was a little uneasy about having two people I didn't know well watch me hunt for dinner. I had performance jitters just thinking about it. I hoped they would go off on their own but it looked like I wouldn't get so lucky.

"Are they really going to watch us?" I whispered to Vincent as we walked.

"I'm assuming so. It doesn't look like they're going to leave. It will be fine, just be your usual charming self. He winked at me.

I didn't share his optimism but stayed quiet.

"Alright newbie, you're up!" Fidelia snarked.

I was beginning to like her less and less as the night continued. I looked to Vincent and he smiled and gave a slight nod.

I rolled my eyes and left them standing there together as I prepared myself.

I was starving so it wasn't that hard to find what I was looking for. I zeroed in on a heavy set older man was walking down the street, he had a slight limp that slowed him and it was obvious that he supported most of his weight on the long black cane tucked under his left hand. I watched as he struggled in the snow to get across the street and couldn't help thinking that I'd be doing him a favor to put him out of his misery.

I didn't usually go for something this easy but I was desperate tonight. It had been too long and my body was paying the price. My skin was dry and my veins were empty leaving just shells to support the weight of my skin. As a result I was slower, weaker, and easily distracted. I felt like I was suffering from sleep deprivation.

I decided to let him go the easy way so I simply walked up to him and smiled. He lifted the black hat off of his white hair with his right hand and nodded, "Ma'am?" he said in a friendly but low voice before lifting his head and replacing his hat. I nodded back still holding on to my smile (after all there was no reason to be rude) then I lifted my hand to the side of his face.

"Shh… I whispered softly. Stroking the side of his cheek with delicate fingertips I watched as his eyes got heavy and drifted close for the last time.

Afterwards I met with the others on the roof top they had gathered on to observe.

Vincent greeted me first with a soft kiss then we turned to Ramiel and Fidelia.

"I have to ask," said Ramiel with a slight confused expression. "Why did you choose to be so kind to him? When Vincent explained your… *appetite* in his letters it sounded… let us say, more ravenous."

"Usually it is," I explained calmly. "But I didn't feel up to it tonight. Besides, what kind of challenge could he really have been? He was what, seventy?"

They both looked over at Vincent.

"Got one with a conscience do we Vinny?" Fidelia said snidely past Vincent before jumping off the roof.

I looked at Vincent and he could see instantly that I was annoyed by her sarcasm. He grabbed my wrist and pulled me back before I could jump off the roof behind her.

"Don't worry about Fidelia," he whispered trying to nibble at my ear.

"Exactly how long are they staying for?" I barked pushing his head away from mine. "Because if she spills one more snotty remark towards either of us, Ramiel will be going alone." I replied with a malevolent smile.

"Calm down Delilah," he chuckled darkly. "They're not the enemy here. They're both just curious about you. No need for any bloodshed."

I shot him a furious glare before we stepped off the roof, hand in hand.

When we hit the ground Ramiel and Fidelia were waiting for us.

"Are we ready?" Ramiel asked.

I was sure he heard me by the way he smiled and tilted his head.

I didn't say anything because I honestly didn't care whether they both heard me or not. I just nodded and started to walk forward with my hand still in Vincent's.

We followed them this time, letting whatever they were shadowing lead the way. It was a couple, about in their thirties walking with their dress coats buttoned up to the top to help protect them from the bitterness outside.

Vincent and I stayed back out of view when we saw them split up. One went to the left and one to the right but it seemed that Ramiel was taking down the woman so that left Fidelia the man. They disappeared with one quick movement and Vincent and I decided to do the same leaping on to a different roof top to better observe their plan of attack.

We didn't have to wait long, both sprang at the same time; ripping the couple apart from each other in opposite directions.

I wondered if this is what I looked like when Vincent watched me? They were ruthless, not caring in the least bit to muffle the screams of their victims. Instead they drank viciously, letting the blood soak their faces and their clothing until the screams were replaced with gurgles as they let their prey fall to their feet.

They stepped over the lifeless corpses hand in hand and stopped to smile at one another; both smiles covered in blood.

I grabbed Vincent's hand and we started to the ledge of the roof when I heard a very loud bang. Before I could look over at Vincent to see if maybe he knew what it was. I watched Ramiel fall to his knees, his hand still clenched to Fidelia's.

Chapter 11.

I was in shock, "What happened?" I whispered unable to really speak. Then Fidelia let out a pained filled shriek.

"Shh…" Vincent said pulling me quickly down to the snow covered shingles of the roof. He put his finger to his lips but didn't make a sound as he pulled me closer to the edge of the building.

There were six men underneath us standing in front of Fidelia while she held on to Ramiel's heartless, blood soaked body, screaming.

She quickly lunged at the closest man tearing out his throat and sending him grabbing and gurgling to his knees before he fell over. She was so quick that anyone else watching would have thought the man had simply fallen over.

I looked at Vincent for some kind of advice on what we should do but he just looked at me and shook his head. Of course we were outnumbered but they were *human*.

I watched as four big men grabbed her, two on each side holding tight as she snarled and strained against them.

The last man took out a long, silver sword and with one swift movement he sent her head to the other side of the street, splattering more of the white dusted ground with red.

I gasped and ducked back down putting my face on my arm and the cold roof. I didn't want to see any more. Then I heard another slice, followed by a thud and I knew Ramiel's head had just been sent to be with Fidelia's.

That's when they spoke.

"Grab the heads, and put them in the bag with the heart, we'll fill them with garlic and bury them on holy ground. Burn the bodies." A scruffier voice told the rest.

"What about the other two?" A different man asked with a lighter and (I'm guessing younger) tone.

Take their heads too. Just to be safe. Burn them with the other two." The scruffy voice answered.

I heard two more finalizing chops before the splashing started with a overwhelming smell of gas. The striking of the match made me jump and Vincent pulled me a little closer. I could smell the blood and smoke as the fire burned the remains of the two couples.

I laid on the roof top inhaling the remains of Vincent's longtime friends as they burned in silence, not wanting it to be real. I thought all this time that we had the upper hand when it came to us and them.

I just had to find out what was going on. I needed answers. We had to get off this roof but as I went to move I heard the scruffy man speak again.

"Keep an eye out, there are more of them around. Luke found another body about two blocks away with the same punctures and make sure you put Mark in the truck, he died harshly enough, the least we can do is offer him a decent burial."

"Sure." A different voice agreed.

I wasn't sure what to do now. Do we wait for them to leave before we move? Should we try to escape now and hope that there aren't more of them? How many more could there be? I grabbed Vincent's hand and looked over at his face, looking for some hint of hope or direction.

It was wary and I could tell he wasn't sure what to do either so I looked away and tried to concentrate on a plan.

Okay, we had about an hour until sunrise, if we could get off this roof undetected then that would give us more than enough time to make it back.

Worst case scenario was if we couldn't get off the roof in enough time to make it to our room? There had to be a place that we could hide out, right?

My heart started to race at the thought of not making it somewhere in time. That was *not* an option! There was no way I was willing to accept that. So if we had to, we would fight our way out. Of course there were only the two of us but at least we had the element of surprise on our side and even if we didn't kill them all, we still had our speed so we could make it somewhere in time to escape the sun.

That was it, we were getting off this roof! I refuse to lay here and do nothing until we burn to death, I told myself. I would rather they chop my head off first, at least that would be quicker.

I grabbed Vincent's hand again and this time I whispered to him "We are getting off this roof. I know if we can just get down then we have a shot at making it to our room."

He nodded in approval and we both peeked up slowly to see if the five men were still lingering around beneath us. I didn't see anything or hear anything and from the looks of it neither did Vincent because he started moving to the other side so we could climb down.

"Stick to the shadows," he whispered as our feet touched the ground.

Sliding my hand in his I nodded and we started out, at first slowly peeking around the corner of the building to see if there was any one around then blurring from one shadow to the next as fast as our feet would take us.

It was a short trip back to our room and I was more than happy to see it.

"What the hell happened back there and who were those men?" I asked slamming the door.

"The Rising Sons, as in s.*O*.n.s" he answered in a low tone.

"And what does that mean?"

"They are a group of stalkers, they track immortal beings and kill them." He answered in the same defeated tone as before, sitting down on the edge of the bed.

"And you're just telling me about them *now*?" I accused, raising my eyebrows.

His face looked like it had aged ten years in the last hour. He simply sat there on the bed looking at me with horror stuck to his features.

I reached out my hand to rest it on his shoulder before speaking.

"I'm sorry for what happened tonight but I have to know what's going on; from the beginning."

"The reason I never said anything about them before is because I thought they were extinct. No one's seen or heard anything about them in over two and a half decades."

"How many are there?" I asked, still in disbelief.

"There could be hundreds, stretched out, maybe more." He breathed staring at my face.

"How much do they know about us?" I whispered unable to be upset anymore.

"If they are the same, then they know enough." he said looking back. "They study us and pass down the information from father to son and have done so for centuries that's the reason behind the spelling."

"If so, then why the big lapse in time? Why take over twenty-five years off?"

"I don't know, maybe to increase their numbers?" he suggested.

"Or, because they're not the same? These men could just be one group of hunters. I only seen six, if there were more out there don't you think we would have seen them by now?" I asked hopefully.

"No, not for two vampires. They wouldn't want to give their numbers away. If we thought that they were alone then they would seem like an easy target and after an attack the rest could come from behind to finish us off."

"How do you know all this?"

"Because I've seen it. Remember what I told you about the sun?"

I looked up at Vincent after remembering his words and I knew now what had happened.

"When?" I asked with compassion.

"March of 1620 in London. A small group of us had gathered early for the Nations Ball and had decided to see the sites of the new city. I had only been a vampire for six months and I was still under the care of my Sire, Noah."

"They came from all sides as dawn approached. I still don't know how they were able to detect us but they attacked out in the open. Most made it back to safety but a handful of us were forced to seek shelter in a Barn to escape the sun. Of course they tracked us there but Noah knew I was no match for them because of my age and lack of a defensive gift, so he hid me in one of the stables under the hay and stood with the rest to fight."

"I began to argue with him; telling him I could fight with him and the others when he first started pushing me towards the back of the barn.

"This is madness!" I was saying. "You know I can stand with you and the others, Noah. You're treating me like a juvenile."

"Silence!" He said pulling me by my arm towards the shadows. "You are a juvenile, you have no defense and if you stand with us you will fall. Now stay put and no matter what do not come out until it's safe for you to do so."

"Quickly he through the hay over me and rushed to stand with the others."

"They burst through the doors, showing no mercy, slicing and stabbing their way through to cover all the exits. Including Noah there were only five vampires so they didn't stand a chance against the 30 large men and homemade weapons."

"Noah was the last one standing and to my amazement the small group had taken out most of them; there were only five men left. But I knew he would never make it. Soon, my teacher, my friend, and most importantly, my father, was going to die and I would be left to face eternity alone."

"They started to close the gap around Noah, pushing him towards the light that was beaming in over half the Barn floor. He walked backward, cautiously looking for another exit. But where to go? The sun was everywhere. There was no escape and any movement he made towards the shadows would lead them to me, and I knew he wouldn't do that. He would rather die then put me in harm's way."

"So he did the only thing he could. He lunged forward at the closest man, tearing his head clean off with one swipe, and it was over, they had him. They carried him, biting and screaming into the light and tossed him further out."

I watched as he burned, screaming out in agony unable to get back to the shadow of the Barn. I sat silently, my body trembling as he was charred alive, unable to do anything to save him."

I could see the pain in Vincent's eyes as he spoke about Noah and what had happened in the Barn that day and unfortunately there wasn't much I could offer him at that moment to ease his pain.

I had been miserable and sad in my previous life but nothing could compare to the sorrow of losing someone you loved and I was fortunate enough to have never experienced that firsthand. I felt so sorry for him and almost worthless to not be able to offer him more comfort so I did the only thing I could and pulled him in tight, looping my arm around him as I held him close to my body.

We laid on the bed tucked safely in each others arms and I played with his hair and watched him sleep as the hours before sunset and our getaway, slowly ticked by.

Lost forever:

Holding on to a body, clutching in screeching pain, I watched silently, unable to move, as two lovers were slain. All that time is lost forever, never again to be found. Yes out of fear I watched from above as their blood sprayed across the ground.

Delilah Waters- 1929

Chapter 12.

We traveled by train headed for Louisiana. The night sky led us closer to our retreat and raised our hopes that just maybe we would get away from them alive, well, sort of alive anyway.

Eating would have been complicated but with Vincent's ghosting abilities, he said it was easier for people to wake up weak and not know what happened then not wake up at all and us be suspects.

"By keeping as many dead off the train as possible we lessen our risk of being discovered." He told me.

Vincent always bit the back of their neck or the inner part of a woman's thigh (which I'm sure he just hated) so it wasn't noticeable.

I didn't like that he was feeding off women in such an intimate place on their bodies. I would rather he just kill them and get it over with but Vincent was always thinking of the bigger picture; instead of getting caught up in the moment. Ultimately saving us from exposure.

I, on the other hand, did not think ahead. I loved the kill, it's what I lived for and I argued that they were nothing but food and we should be able to eat at will *and* in public, being as we were the superior race.

Of course Vincent didn't agree saying "Living our lives in secrecy saves us from having to hide."

"What the hell do you call this?" I asked gesturing around with my hands as I paced back and forth in the baggage car. Being on the train for so long we had to use it so the sun wouldn't creep in. "We lurk in shadows and on rooftops, hiding in the dark so we remain "unseen." If that's not hiding, then what is?"

I couldn't help but get irritated when I believed that we should have the upper hand over our food.

"You're young Delilah and so eager for blood at any cost, but I have lived through the worst and I have seen what they can do with just 30 men, who knows how many they truly have? We're not hiding. We're being cautious. There's a big difference in what we're doing now and what we would have to do if they found us out." He said lounging on the pallet we set up.

Vincent didn't share my annoyance over the matter. It was simply a way of life for him that he accepted a long time ago.

"Well that doesn't mean I have to like it." I said still aggravated about our situation and over how calm Vincent was being about it all.

He stood suddenly before saying "Do you know how unbelievably sexy you are when you're mad?" And smiled his high beam smile he knew could melt my heart.

He never fought fair. He knew if he playfully changed the subject that I would go along with it and let go of the other topic without a fit.

Of course, it worked. So with a sigh and a slight smile I asked "And how sexy it that?"

"Very!" He said grabbing me around my waist to stop my pacing and pull me closer.

I went along easily as he pulled me with him to the blankets. He caressed the side of my face with his finger before kissing me sweetly on the lips.

"I know how you feel Delilah," he whispered after pulling away from our kiss, "but this really is the easiest way."

He leaned his head to the side to reveal his neck to me.

"Go on my darling, I know how hungry you must be."

He was right, I was hungry, so I didn't refuse his offer. I leaned in closer and let my teeth break the skin on his neck.

I sucked and licked delicately, after all, this wasn't just another victim, this was the love of my life and I didn't want to cause him unnecessary pain.

I felt his heat run through me like fire bringing me back to life. My heart began to hammer away and I felt the intense love that we shared as it engulfed my body.

After I was done we both laid, cuddled together. I rested my head against his chest to listen to the soothing sound of his slowing heartbeat that was getting to be so familiar. Neither of us moved from our state of haze, him from blood loss and me from the calming sensation his blood always gave me.

"Why is drinking from you different then drinking from humans?" I asked after I could think clearly again.

“Because you’re drinking immortal blood. Our body changes it making it a personal connection to us, sometimes even transferring emotion along with it. Because I love you, you tap into that love and it flows through you as strongly as it does me, giving you a stronger feeling and more of a connection.”

“Is it wrong for me to feed from you?” I asked curiously.

“It is frowned upon, yes, in times other than passion, but the risk of being exposed is much higher if we both feed so this is safer right now given the new developments about The Rising Sons. Besides it is only for a couple of days, then we will be able to go back to our original diet.”

I wasn’t sure I wanted my old diet back. Yes, I loved the hunt, the adrenaline was like a drug to me but I was enjoying the smoothness of his blood far too much to want to go back to strangers blood. Drinking from him left me heavy, like gravity was sucking me down and I was beginning to love that feeling more and more. No other blood had ever given me that feeling, not even spiked blood.

I thought I would try his weakness for concealment to better win my case.

“Wouldn’t it be easier to keep feeding this way? I mean, this way no one’s dying so it would keep The Rising Sons off our trail. People would think that they got bit by some kind of, I don’t know… bug or something?” I asked nonchalantly trying to hide how eager I was to prolong my pleasurable experience.

"Yes, it would," he began and my eyes started to dance with excitement "but, it would not be enough to sustain us for long. If we continued this way it would eventually take its toll on both of us." He finished.

Yes, he saw through me and put his big *but* in the way of all my hope.

"What do you mean, take its toll on both of us?" I asked confused by his statement.

"What I mean, is that both of us would suffer side effects. I would remain weak and unhealthy and you would become dependent and very possessive over me, to the point you could lose your mind altogether."

"I didn't know that vampires could lose their minds. Aren't we above the regular laws of crazy and sane?"

"Not at all," he answered. "In fact we may be more susceptible because we're in between both the living and the dead so our minds don't belong to either one."

"Where *do* we fit into things; if we aren't alive and we're not dead?" I couldn't help but ask, it was something I had secretly wondered about since I had changed.

"I'm not sure," he answered honestly. "We're cursed Delilah, that's the only way I can explain it. So I guess it doesn't matter anymore then knowing that. Our abilities to levitate, our speed and strength, they all exist because of human blood, the more life we take the more we thrive. We live on death."

I laid there for a while stuck inside my own thoughts not able to speak. I kept going over everything I had been taught at Church when I was a child. How much God loved us all and the afterlife that awaited us when we died.

I guessed all of that was gone for me now. For one, I was never going to die. For two, if for whatever reason I did die there was no longer a place for me in Gods' kingdom. I was an evil being that lived on death, so what did that mean for me now? Hell? I had heard of Hell and from the description the Preacher gave I definitely didn't want to end up there, and even worse I didn't want Vincent to end up there.

What would I do if I didn't have Vince? He was all I had. I traded in my family, my life and even my soul for him. How would I get over losing him if he were to be taken from me?

I couldn't bare the thought of that happening to us. We had already talked about our long and happy future together and to sit and think about losing him was morbid and a little stupid considering we couldn't die.

But after seeing The Rising Sons slaughter Ramiel and Fidelia I wasn't sure about anything anymore. Sure it had seemed simple enough. We were immortal so as long as we stayed out of the sunlight we were fine but now we also had the human hunting parties to dodge and that changed things drastically.

"Promise me that no matter what happens that you will save yourself?" I asked Vincent while lying on his chest.

"What?" he asked a little confused.

"I know that in theory we shouldn't die, but I want you to promise me that if anything ever goes wrong that you won't worry about me, that you won't wait for me. That you will run if you have to and *save yourself*!" I stressed out the last part so he would know I was serious.

It must have worked because Vincent leaned up and took me with him so he could look at my face. He took my head in-between his hands and said "I promise, that if anything ever happens that *both* of us will make it out, I cannot live without you."

He kissed me tenderly and hugged me, then he leaned in close to my ear and whispered "I love you and I won't let any harm come to you."

Staring into the distance I whispered, "I know, I love you too," and internally finished but it's not me I'm worried about.

Chapter 13.

We got off the train right on schedule. The sun had already set so we were completely in the clear. Well, as in the clear as two vampires being hunted down could be.

There was something very mysterious about this place with its new sounds and smells and I wondered how long we were going to stay here and where we were going to be staying?

I looked around but of course nothing was familiar. It seemed that the only thing that never changed was the night time sky. No matter where I was it was the same; welcoming me home no matter my surroundings.

I took a deep breath and stepped off the train. I smiled and gave the moon that awaited me a little nod of appreciation.

"How long are we staying here?" I asked trying to make conversation as we walked.

"As long as we'd like, I have a plantation just on the other side of the river."

"You mean we're not staying at an Inn?" I couldn't hide the shock in my voice.

"Not this time." Vincent answered as he helped me into the boat that would take us to the other side of town.

* * *

We reached the Plantation and it was beautiful. It was the type of lavish white home that I never imagined myself ever living in. Two stories tall, many windows decorated the front and it had large white pillars that sat in front. The yard that it sat on was the biggest piece of land I had ever seen. In the yard held huge Oak trees that twisted and curved upward reminding me of spider legs, easily reaching over a few hundred feet tall.

When we walked up the path we were greeted by a dark skinned, slender man. He had a short graying beard and salt and pepper colored hair and looked like he was in his forties.

"Mr. Vanhorne, Mrs. Vanhorne," he said kindly, with a southern accent as he nodded to us both with a warm smile across his face.

"Good evening Red," Vincent replied warmly.

"Red, this is Delilah. She's now the lady of the house. If she desires anything would you see that it's done?"

"Yes sir, of course," he looked over at me and gave a slight bow "Ma'am."

I nodded back still awestruck over Mrs. Vanhorne. I knew that our life was now joined forever but I hadn't given us being married that much thought. Of course that's not what I told my parents in the letter I had left them, but that was because I didn't think (I'm an immortal being that thrives on death and leaving to go live in sin with a 300 year old vampire) would go over well.

"Can I take your bags for you sir?" he asked holding out both his hands to take our things from Vincent.

“Yes, thank you Red.” Vincent answered handing him the bags.

We followed Red the rest of the way up the porch and through the big, white double doors into the house.

As he disappeared up the stair case with our things I turned to Vincent. “Mrs. Vanhorne?” I said with a raised eyebrow.

“Well, I thought it sounded better than eternal partner or consort. Besides, I didn’t hear you refuse the title?” he answered smugly giving me back some of my own eyebrows.

I couldn’t help but smile when he said it like that and honestly, I did want to be Mrs. Vanhorne. Delilah Vanhorne I thought to myself. It sounded good, better than good, it sounded important, like a famous actress.

“Would you like to see the rest of the house?” Vincent asked breaking my concentration and useless mind chatter.

“That would be great.” I agreed with a smile.

He led me through the foyer and into the parlor. It was enormous, bigger than the entire down stairs of my parents house back in Detroit.

The room had cream colored walls, with strategically placed gold sconces that held frosted globes to give a soft glow to the room. The light wood flooring shined and the room smelled of wood polish. There were two caramel colored sofas and two cream colored chairs with a caramel floral print that made a circle in the middle of the room. Centered in between, was a dainty wooden coffee table with intricate detailing all along the tables edge and wooden legs that curled upward at the ends that matched both the couches and chairs wood legs.

The room had three large windows and of course they were covered by very long, thick, hunter green curtains that fell to the floor and to top off the look was a lit fireplace that added more glow and warmth to the room.

I walked over to the curtains to get a peek at the view and all three windows overlooked the front yard and the enormous trees.

Next we were off to the dining room and why there was such a big table for just three people was beyond me. Especially considering two of those people didn't even eat.

There were ten chairs. One at each end and four on each side of the huge rectangle shaped table. The whole set was done in that dark cherry that Vince seemed to love so much and was set with white porcelain plates trimmed in gold, crystal wine glasses and polished silverware as if dinner was being served any minute.

I didn't really need to see the kitchen, after all I was never going to use it anyway so Vince led me up the stairs to the bedrooms; all *eight* of them.

Each one was decorated in a different —yet same— way. All were clean with elegant bedding and thick curtains to match. Each had one larger bed or two smaller beds along with a wooden wardrobe. Some had a vanity included but all in all they were simple. The only thing that changed from room to room were the colors of the bedding and the way the furniture was arranged.

After the fourth bedroom I got the point so Vince showed me to our room. He stopped in front of two great big white doors at the end of the hall and pulled them open to reveal the largest bedroom I had ever seen.

To my surprise the bed set from our first night together was there. The same four poster bed, draped in curtains; the lavish bedding, all of it.

"How did you get the bed here?" I asked in disbelief, forgetting about the rest of the room.

"I had it shipped of course." Vincent answered nonchalantly.

"Do you normally carry around your furniture with you when you travel?" I asked sarcastically.

"Not always, but sometimes I have it shipped here or there depending on how long I intend on staying. I like to sleep comfortably."

"Oh yes, of course you do," I teased.

"You planned on staying in Detroit for a long time?"

"I had, but I found you much quicker than I had anticipated."

I thought back to our conversation the first night he walked me home from the Bakery.

"Potential." I said smiling.

He didn't respond with words instead he just smiled at me and left me alone to unpack and get settled in.

I hung up our things in the big wardrobe and noticed that there was a vanity that matched the rest of the set over on the other side of the room. I walked over and sat on the little stool and put my hairbrush and other things on the table in front of the oval mirror.

I stared at my reflection still unable to really grasp what the change had done to my appearance. I was used to the white skin. I saw it every night on Vincent and on my arms and hands.

What I wasn't used to was my face. I hadn't really looked at it much so the intensity of my kaleidoscope eyes and the long dark eyelashes that encased them were still a surprise at first glance.

My ruby red curls made my eyes that much more extreme in contrast and the paleness to my face made my full lips look almost red.

I had just fed from Vincent so there was a blush to my cheeks and overall it looked like I was wearing makeup.

Girls back home would kill for this look, I thought, then I laughed out loud at myself.

"What's so amusing?"

I looked up to see Vincent's reflection looking at me with an amused smile of his own lighting up his face.

"I didn't hear you come in." I said a little embarrassed.

"Yes, I guessed that when you starting laughing at your reflection. But I still don't see the joke, you couldn't be more stunning."

“That *is* the joke.” I answered smiling. “I was staring at my face and the first thing I thought was, girls back home would kill for this look.”

“And that’s funny because…?” He prompted, still as confused as ever.

“Don’t you see? It’s funny because I do kill for this look.”

Instantly understanding lit up his deep blue eyes and he let out a dark chuckle. “I guess it is a little funny when you put it that way.”

I smiled back still looking at him through the mirror and he walked to me and kissed the top of my head.

“You need to get over your beauty, it will always be there, you know? You will forever be young and you will forever be beautiful. No amount of staring or laughing is going to change that.”

“I’m just trying to get used to my features, that’s all. I haven’t had a lot of time to get used to this part yet; it’s still new to me.”

“What did you used to look like?” I asked curiously staring at his reflection.

“We all look the same Delilah. The only thing the change does is take what we already have and make it better, bolder. My eyes were always blue but now they’re richer and more noticeable. My hair was black but now it shines more. I was always taller but the change made me thicker, expanding the muscles I already had and making me more fit“.

“Except for the bone shifting to make us more agile most of what happens to us is our eye sight.

We see things that others can't, so it seems that our appearance has changed more than it actually has; we are finally seeing things as they truly are."

It made sense, I remembered seeing the stars for the first time, *really* seeing them and how much more color they had then I had originally thought.

"I guess you're right. I noticed that a while ago but I didn't think about it when looking at myself." I took another glance at myself in the mirror and shrugged off the shock before standing up and turning to face Vincent.

"You always know the right thing to say." I said laying my hand on his chest then kissing him sweetly on the cheek.

"Centuries of practice. He said smirking.

"Yeah, I keep forgetting how *old* you really are." I said grinning.

"Mmm…," he mumbled as he nodded his head.

"One day I'll catch up to you." I teased. "Then maybe I'll be able to comfort you when you get upset."

Confusion replaced his amusement "What are you talking about?"

"I know Ramiel and Fidelia's deaths are still bothering you Vince and I don't know what to do and that makes me feel horrible because I can't help you."

"Oh, darling. I couldn't have asked for a more compassionate person to be by my side right now. You've been comforting and understanding through this whole situation. Losing them has been difficult, yes, but it's not just the loss of friends that is upsetting me, Delilah."

"It's not?"

"No."

"Did I do something? Or *not* do something?" I asked nervously.

"Of course not!" he shouted extending his arms to look at my face.

"The reason I can't rest easy is because you're still in danger. Every night, the Rising Sons are slaughtering us and I don't know what to do about them." He sounded so desperate and frustrated that I was shocked he let me see him that vulnerable.

Vincent pulled me back in, hugging me close to his chest and as he spoke he stroked my hair.

"It's my job to protect you, Delilah. I brought you into this life and I will be damned if worthless *humans* are going to harm you!" He tilted my face up and kissed me sweetly before heading for the door.

The son:

It's impossible to outrun the Son. Day after day it will rise and with them our demise. Stand and fight in safety of night or burn in the in the day of our enemies light?

Delilah Vanhorne - 1929

Chapter 14.

It was New Years Eve. It had been a couple weeks since we arrived in Louisiana and I have to admit there was a certain spice to the blood here.

Vincent seemed to be more brutal then before too. He said it was the variety that had triggered his bloodlust but I knew a lot of it was frustration because of our current situation.

Don't get me wrong, I enjoyed watching him gouge out throats as much as the next vampire but it was just so unlike him. I had gotten used to the tamer version of Vincent so it still came as a bit of a shock to watch him hunt down his prey in such a ravenous way.

Tonight would be slightly different though. There were parties all over in celebration of the New Year, which made it all too easy to get food.

Vincent made sure we looked the part. He wore a nice three piece black suit. While I wore a red dress and red heels. I swept up my hair for the event leaving just a few loose curls to hang down, here and there. To all the bystanders we were just two people out on the town ready for 1930. If they only knew the truth.

It was nearing midnight and we had made drunken friends on the river. They seemed nice enough and I kind of wished they were already immortal. I think Vincent and I would have gotten along with them well, if we hadn't been about to eat them.

I gave Vincent the, it's time glance, and we lead them to a secluded area away from the busy and packed part of the river.

"Where are we goin? It's almost time." the woman who's name, I think, was Jody asked, as she laughed and stumbled, holding on to her drunken escort.

I laughed as well pretending to be just as drunk and confused while I held on to Vince.

Ten… Nine… I looked at Vince and smiled. On eight we both turned and lunged, each of us sinking our teeth into the neck of our victim at the same time.

The poor couple never seen it coming. To drunk and stupid to understand what was happening or even attempt a getaway.

Seven… Six… Five… Four… Three…Two…One. Happy New Year!!!!!! We let the dead couple fall to our feet and turned to face each other. I smiled at Vincent watching the devil dance in his eyes and nothing else mattered at that moment except when my lips found his.

Soon a blood stained kiss was all that remained of what had happened. We sent the couple floating down the river as an after party snack for the alligators (I'm sure they didn't mind) before we set off, stumbling back to the party.

No one questioned our whereabouts when we arrived back to the other drunken party-goers and me and Vincent danced and partied with the rest of them until it was almost dawn. We said our goodbyes, before plucking off another couple on our way out. Yes, I believe I'm going to like 1930, I thought as Vince and I stumbled drunkenly arm in arm.

* * *

As we entered the house, Red was there to greet us.

"Sir… Ma'am." he nodded.

"Good morning Red," Vincent said happily.

"Good morning. Eventful night sir?" He asked smiling at Vincent.

"Yes, the Misses and I had a very eventful night between the two of us we took down four." He replied.

I was shocked at how casual he spoke in front of Red. I hadn't known that he knew what we were, let alone that Vincent talked about it *with* him.

"Ah, well, I'm sure after a night like this you and the Misses will be needin your rest."

"Yes, thank you Red, and as always, inform me of any disturbances."

"Yes sir. Good night." He looked at me with a smile on his face and nodded again. Good night Ma'am," he said and walked away.

When we got upstairs I was still in shock. He knew, and not only did he know, but he was okay with it? He knew we killed living, breathing people and didn't care?

I sat on the bench in front of the bed to remove my shoes. After I couldn't stand it anymore I spoke.

"He knows?" Was all I could manage.

"Yes, he does."

"And he doesn't care?"

"No, he doesn't."

"Why?" I couldn't help but ask.

"Why, what? Why does he know or why does he not care?"

"Either one or both for that matter. If I were human I would care."

"Would you?" He asked skeptically taking off his shoes. "I showed you what I was, yet here you sit."

"Yes but I wasn't certain at the time of *what* you were. I thought it was only a dream." I fought back.

"Did you? If I were to have a dream as vivid as the one I gave you I certainly wouldn't have been out looking for *me* the next day." he smirked still undoing his tie.

"You still haven't answered my question." He was right. He did warn me, but I didn't see it as a warning at the time because I didn't know what it meant.

"He knows because it's his business to know. He accepts what I am, what we are. It is all he has ever known. As did his father and his father before him."

"But why?"

"His Grandfather worked for me. He knew what I was and accepted it. Then he raised his son to do the same, and so on."

"But they weren't *slaves* right? And Red, he's here of his own free will. Right?"

“Of course he his! We’re more like family and I never owned slaves Delilah. It was common practice but it was something I never agreed with. I’ve always made more than enough to pay my workers. His grandfather caught me feeding once so I made him a deal. I would give him a considerable bonus in exchange for his discretion. He agreed, and our families have been under each others care ever since.”

“Red, helps me with anything I need done, no questions asked and he also runs the business and household when I am away. I trust him with everything I have. I’ve known him since he was born. He’ll also help you with anything you ask for.” He kissed my head and walked towards the bed.

I sat there for a minute still nervous about Red knowing so much about us. Vincent so sure that he was no danger to us and they had lived this long together with no problem so I guessed until he proved otherwise I wasn’t going to (as Vince would put it) “burden my thoughts.” Maybe it would be nice to have someone else to talk to?

I stood and slipped into one of the many night gowns Vincent had bought me since my transformation.

It was my white one that had lace ruffles at the bottom and white ribbon ties in front. It was short though, stopping at my thigh about two inches above my knee.

Vincent said that if I had to spend all day in bed I might as well sleep comfortably.

I think he just liked seeing me in skimpy lingerie but who was I to argue? I couldn't help it. I liked it when he spoiled me. When he had nice things delivered in big boxes. I had never gotten really nice things growing up.

Mostly everything I had gotten was handed down by older women in the family so when it got to me it was outdated and shabby. This was definitely a change for the better.

I sat down on the bed and pulled the cool satin sheets over me. I leaned over and kissed Vincent good night before laying down. I was full after our night on the town so that added to my drowsiness.

"Will you do that thing you do?" I asked as I yawned.

"What thing I do, my darling?" he asked while curling me into him to put his arm around me.

"You know, the dream thing, while I'm sleeping?"

"What would you like to dream about?" He asked while playing with one of my curls.

"Surprise me." I said sleepily. "Make it something nice that we can both enjoy."

"Alright, but you have to go to sleep first."

"I love you." I said starting to drift off.

"And I love you back, sweet dreams," he whispered still playing with my hair.

I took a deep breath and let the sweet image of moving water pull me down into unconsciousness.

The scenery he chose was beautiful. We were on a beach somewhere and it was daylight. Instead of regular ocean water he chose to make the water just as deep blue as his eyes and it swished and moved poetically, before crashing onto the white sand.

The green mountains surrounding us peeked into the light blue sky and big fluffy white clouds strolled by letting the sun shine through amazingly bright, but miraculously it didn't hurt my skin or even burn my eyes.

I hadn't realized how long it had been since I had seen it and the warm rays caressing my body in my baby pink cotton, mesh dress felt amazing.

Of course Vincent was there with me,in a white shirt and rolled up light colored pants, his hand in mine letting the warm water run up on our bare feet as we walked on the water lines edge.

The beach was secluded except for us and the big rocks that sat at the other end, so we laid down on the warm sand, side by side so we could stare at the clouds together.

This was the one thing that Vincent and I would never share in real life so I was thankful for the dream he chose to give me.

"Have you ever played the cloud game?" I asked him staring straight up.

"No. What do you mean?"

"I mean, look at the clouds and see if they resemble something."

"Like something I've seen before?"

"Yes, like that one," I said pointing up in the air. "It looks like a heart. Do you see it?"

"Yes. It does."

“You find one now.”

“Hmm…” he said, searching the sky as the clouds continued to roll past.

“There!” He suddenly blurted pointing up, like it might escape. “That one is the same shape as the ruby droplet I gave you.”

I couldn’t help but smile at his enthusiasm. I had seen him dangerous and that usually lead to sexy and fantasies of me doing scandalous things to him but I rarely got to see him *cute*, and at this moment he was so… cute.

“Oh hush,” he said when he noticed I was staring at him with a plastered on smile.

“What?” I asked in a chuckle.

“You know very well what.”

I couldn’t even help myself. “You look so cute right now.” teasing him through my smile.

He smiled back and nudged me on the shoulder with his hand.

I laughed as I lightly rocked back towards him and when I looked at him he started to laugh too.

As our laughter died down I stared back up into the clouds enjoying how real they seemed. Wow he was good, and I wished I could do something this neat.

“When did you find out you could do this?” I asked still staring upward.

“Do what?”

“This!” I said widening my arms for emphasis.

"It took a while at first. I didn't think that I was going to receive a gift but after a few months I noticed little things and then on my first birthday I received the rest all at once."

"Well it's already been a couple months and I don't feel any different yet. I would love to be able to do something like this."

"Don't worry, some of us have to wait a little longer than others but in the end all of us are gifted in some way. As for this, (now he waved his arms) this is not a possibility for you. You and I have different blood which means different gifts."

"I know that, I was just hoping that whatever I got, I would be as good with my gift as you are with yours."

"I don't have any doubts about that. You've already learned so much in your short time as an immortal that I'm quite positive your gift will surpass anything I can do."

"You really think so?"

"Absolutely my darling, just be patient, you'll see."

He was always so understanding in any situation. He said it was due to his long life but I liked to think it was out of love and compassion for me too.

I laid wrapped in his arms as he stroked my head with his fingertips. I didn't know it was possible to be this relaxed in your dreams but between the warmth of the sun, how the grainy white sand had felt in-between my toes, and the salty smell of the ocean as the waves crashed to the shore, it was easy to wish that we could stay here forever.

Red:

One knows our secrets, he knows we stalk the night. He knows we kill the living but with that he's alright? I now have my suspicions but I'll wait and trust in Red. If he breaks my trust, I'll use my teeth to rip off his head.

Delilah Vanhorne- 1930

Chapter 15.

A few months had passed and I was surprised at how fast time went by when you didn't worry about it anymore.

It was already March and it was time for the Elders Mardi Gras Ball. Vincent had told me about the Ball the night I changed but I hadn't really thought about it then but now I was nervous about meeting the Elders.

When we had awoke earlier that night I asked him why they gathered here and he told me that Louisiana threw this party every year but that they didn't always gather here.

"There are gatherings and parties thrown all over at this time of year. Some are in France others are in Venice, Spain and even Germany; the Nation moves from location to location."

"The masquerade concept started in Italy. A Carnevale is what they call it there and the Elders have been throwing these kinds of parties for years now."

"Why is this time of year so important?" I asked.

"Well, the day before Lent is the day that humans gathers to feast. The streets are crowded with people and no one is the wiser to large parties held at night."

"I have something for you, stay right here," he said motioning to the bed. Before I could say anything he was already right back in the room carrying a very large, rectangular box.

He sat the box on the bed in front of me and he sat beside me to watch me open it.

I sat up and crossed my legs so I could pull the box closer to me. When I lifted the lid I saw a half faced mask laying on a bed of fabric. I lifted it out to see that the mask was black with gold outlined teardrop shaped eye holes that curved upward at the outer corners.

A swirling purple pattern covered it, curling around in different patterns along both cheeks of the mask and continuing up the bridge of the masks nose, leading to an oval shaped emerald that held in place three long black feathers that sat in the middle between each eye hole.

Each feather was detailed with green vine-like lines that snaked upward turning gold midway and finishing the feather in solid gold at the very tip.

I sat the mask down on the bed beside Vince, and stood up so I could lift the bulge of fabric out of the box.

As I pulled upward I realized it was a dress, but not just any dress, it was a ball gown. A lavish, big and beautiful ball gown that went all the way down to the floor.

I took it over to the beveled mirror to see what I might look like in it.

Holding it up next to my body, I could truly see how beautiful it was.

The dress was black and didn't have full sleeves, instead it had ruffle straps that would leave the rest of my arms bare and intricate gold and green designs done with tiny beading that ran down the bodice.

The skirt portion of the dress was a delicate black material that was done in a draping fashion so that it split down the middle to reveal the green chiffon in-between.

I was in awe and I couldn't help twirling with it still in my arms to watch the skirt flow out in the air.

"So… you do like it then?" Vince asked standing by the bed watching me dance with the dress.

"I'm sorry, it's beautiful. I love it!" I gushed, when I realized I hadn't said anything since he handed me the box.

I rushed over and lovingly kissed him in appreciation. "Thank you." I said when my lips left his.

"You are quite welcome," he said smiling with satisfaction and I watched as his eyes danced with joy.

He loved to see me happy and seeing him happy made me that much happier.

"You have to get dressed now or we'll be late." He announced before kissing me again softly and heading for the door.

"I'll be quick." I reassured him. "Meet you down stairs in twenty minutes?"

"Alright." He agreed and shut the door.

I dressed as quickly as I had promised and went to the mirror once again to check myself and put on my face mask.

With all my curls securely pinned on top of my head I was free to tie the ribbon of the mask so it wouldn't fall off.

There! I thought a little smug; I was done.

As I walked down the stairs I caught the first glimpse of Vincent. He was standing at the bottom waiting for me in a black tux.

His hair was slicked to the side like usual but he too was wearing a mask. The base was black like mine but there were no feathers. His mask was much simpler, it had white smoky swirls that were a lot thinner than the purple ones on my mask and the ends of every point were tipped in gold, making his eyes sparkle even more and the nose on his mask was less subtle then mine; his coming to a sharp point.

I stared in wonder still walking down the stairs. He was so gorgeous to begin with, and seeing him like this was breathtaking. With the mask covering the top half of his face it made his full lips look that much softer and welcoming and I couldn't wait to get to them.

With his white gloved hand extended I put my hand in his and stepped off the last stair.

Before he could do anything else I kissed him; my mask to his. His lips were every bit as soft and wonderful as I knew they would be and greedily I devoured their softness with the passion that was overflowing my body.

Finally satisfied I pulled back away from our kiss.

“Sorry.” I said a little light headed.

“For what?” he asked winded.

“Attacking you when I stepped off the stair.”

He laughed. “Well I had the same idea, you just beat me to it.”

I laughed along with him “It seems we both weren’t expecting the other to look so tempting.”

He smiled and grabbed my hand again and twirled me around slowly so he could look at me in the dress.

“You look sensational,” he gushed while still spinning me.

“Really?” I asked excited when I stopped. I couldn’t help but smile at his enthusiasm; it was contagious.

“Yes, really.”

“You too.” I said still a bit awestruck by how delicious he looked. “And I love the mask.”

He bowed gallantly and kissed the top of my hand.

“Shall we then, Mrs. Vanhorne?” He asked staring up into my eyes.

“We shall, Mr. Vanhorne.” I replied smirking, and with my hand in his we walked out the door.

Chapter 16.

I had no idea what to expect when we arrived to the Ball. Vincent wouldn't give me any clues about it. He said I would have to see it for myself. So I wasn't expecting it to be so gorgeous and so… *huge*!

When we walked through the door I looked up to the ceiling first. It was domed and held many golden chandeliers with white candles burning to light the event. As my eyes traveled down the walls, they were interrupted by crimson, pleated material draped down, hugging the walls to give their creamy color some contrast.

The floor was a sea of cream and gold swirled marble that shined like ice and on each side of the room was a large fountain in the shape of a naked woman. Their eyes were closed and their lips were set into a soft smile. They each had crossed legs at their feet and stood with blood pouring from cupped hands down their fingertips and into a small pool below.

I hadn't known that there were so many vampires period, not to mention so many in one place at one time but they were everywhere. Some were standing in smaller groups talking, others were dancing with a partner and those who didn't want to stand were sitting at the elegant round tables conversing through the warm glow of candlelight that encircled each table.

There was food here other than the fountains, I could smell them and I wondered if they were off limits to the rest of us. Maybe they were only here for the Elders amusement?

Vincent seemed right at home, I on the other hand was nervous. I was nervous that I might say something stupid or do something that I wasn't allowed to do. I didn't know how I was supposed to act around the creators of all our kind?

After all, what could I say? Thank you for being cursed, or thank you for allowing Vincent to curse me? Yeah I'm sure that would make for great conversation. In a situation like this it was definitely a better idea if I kept my mouth shut.

I let Vincent lead me around and introduce me to the immortals he knew. They all wore masks of course so the best I could do was remember their names.

After my introduction to most of the room we stopped at a little group standing by one of the red columns. There were three couples talking among themselves.

"Hello Brother," a blonde woman said nodding to Vincent.

"This is Angeline and her mate Ezra." He said as he gestured to them.

Angeline; what a beautiful name I thought.

"Thank you." she said smiling.

"For what?" I asked confused. I hadn't said anything.

"For thinking my name is beautiful."

"But I—

"You didn't have to." she cut me off and winked.

I was even more confused now. I had never said anything I only thought that her name was beautiful.

"Exactly! You thought it."

"Angeline is a reader. She can hear your thoughts." Vincent informed.

"Oh, I guess I have be careful around you then huh?" I said laughing.

Angeline laughed along with the rest of the group and that made me feel a little better, but not much.

"Don't worry. I don't listen in on that much. I just like to play around with people that don't know yet. Vincent and I are siblings and we have a similar sense of humor so he let me know that he hadn't told you when the two of you walked up."

"Oh he did, did he?" I gave Vincent a hard look which made everybody laugh again.

"That one's got spunk Vince, you better watch it." Ezra warned.

"I think she's fabulous! Now if you'll excuse us we're going to get something to drink."

She looped her arm through Ezra's and shot me a smile and another wink before heading off towards one of the waiters holding red Champagne flutes.

I like you too I thought, hoping she wasn't already too far away to hear me.

"Delilah, this is Sawyer and his mate Amari." Vincent continued.

I nodded to them both. “Hello.” I said with a smile.

Sawyer had the same milky complexion as me, with dirty blonde hair and was wearing a black tux and a mask similar to Vincent’s.

Amari’s skin was a caramel brown color and through the holes in her white and gold mask I could see she had honey colored eyes that seemed to reflect the light as it bounced off the masks gold rays. Her dark brown hair fell in light waves down to the middle of her back, gracefully laying on her white strapless gown.

They both nodded back in acknowledgement and smiled.

“And last but not least, Delilah this is Nariyoll and I don’t believe I know your lovely young lady?” Vincent said as he gestured with his hand to the last couple.

“Hello, my name is Hazel.” She introduced herself giving Vincent her hand.

“Nice to meet you.” he said with a nod.

I heard a flutter and the realization hit me.

“You’re human?” I mused.

I should have noticed right away. I had smelled food as soon as I came in but she wasn’t standing that close at first. Plus she was pale and half of her face was hidden.

“Yes, I am, but as I’m sure you’ve noticed not the only one.” She answered.

I now understood why I could smell them so strongly. They were a part of the party and not just the afterward snack.

“Remember what I told you about the age restrictions?” Vincent broke in.

“Yes but I didn’t know anyone was allowed to bring humans?”

“Usually it is forbidden, it all depends on what you plan to do with them, and in this case Nariyoll wishes to change Hazel.”

I looked to Nariyoll, after all, he was standing right there.

“But why bring her?”

“Because I’m underage. I was hoping that if the Elders met her then they would be willing to make an exception.”

This time I looked to Vincent. “Do they do that?” I asked in wonder.

“They have, but it is rare.”

“And what if they don’t?” I asked curiously.

“I die.”

We all looked over at Hazel, in the debate I had forgotten she was there. She was just standing there, no fear, completely nonchalant looking.

“You say that now but are you really prepared for that?” I was dumbfounded as to why someone would come knowing that they may not live through the night.

“We’ve discussed that possibility, but I don’t see it turning out that way. The problem is that if I wait another fifty years I'll be sixty-nine and who wants to live forever being that old? I love Nariyoll and if I can't have him, then that will mean the end of my life anyways."

"I understand that love," Vincent broke in. "But you are very young to have possibly just thrown your life away?"

"That's a risk I'm willing to take," she said as she took Nariyoll's hand in hers.

"You are a brave girl, and for both of your sake I hope it works out for you." Sawyer broke in.

"Thanks, but I think we'll be fine."

She was way more optimistic about her life being spared then I was at that moment, but hey, if she wants to get herself killed then why should I care?

"You shouldn't."

I looked over to see Angeline coming through the crowd with her glass, Ezra in tow.

"And you shouldn't waste your time *here* either. Vincent I'm taking her with me, I want to show her something."

She grabbed a hold of my hand before I could protest and I watched a smile spread across Vincent's face as she drug me away.

What are you doing? I thought. After all I really didn't need to say anything out loud.

Giving you someone more interesting to talk to.

Wait, that was in my head. You didn't say anything out loud.

I know, it's part of the gift. It works both ways; I can hear your thoughts and I can push you my thoughts. We can have an entire conversation in your head.

This is strange.

I know, isn't it nifty?

That's not the word I used Angeline.

Hey! Not everyone knows about this part of the gift but like I said before, I like you so I'm sharing this with you.

Does Vincent know?

Yeah, I've known him a long time, he was around when I was just figuring out how to use it.

How long have you known him?

Almost two centuries now.

Wow! I don't care how long I've been a vampire it still amazes me how old some of you are.

Hey! Vince is older than I am.

I know that, but you seem so young to look at you. I would think you're in your early twenties and you talk differently than he does too. You're more.....

Modern?

I nodded.

Yes, well, I try to keep up with the times. Changing when needed. Vincent on the other hand feels that he shouldn't have to change certain things, and for him that works.

Plus I'm a woman, we have to stay one step ahead.

I couldn't help but smile when she put it that way. She was right.

Do you really think the Elders will let Hazel live? I thought.

Who fucking cares? I can't believe he brought her here. Personally I hope she's dinner; she's a snob.

Wow! I thought in shock. I had never heard a woman use such aggressive langue like that.

Oh, yeah. I say what I like when I like. I'm not much for sugar coating. Sorry to catch you off guard.

No need to apologize, I just had a mother that preached "ladylike behavior" my whole life.

Yeah, so did mine. But she's dead and there's nothing holding me back anymore from living whatever way I damn well please. I suggest you do the same. We are forever Delilah. Why waste your time with meaningless restrictions?

I paused for a second. There was a lot changing for me and so fast I wasn't sure I could keep up.

I took the conversation back to Hazel.

I just can't help but wonder. I still have never met the Elders. How do they normally react with humans knowing their business?

Usually, not so well, and with her attitude it's a good possibility she's toast.

Her light blue eyes danced with excitement through the holes in her green and gold mask as she spoke.

She wore a emerald green, velvet gown that had a V neckline in both the front and even more dramatic in the back that hugged her tiny frame on top and flared out more after her hips. Her short blonde curls stayed frozen in place on her head as she gracefully ducked and moved through the crowd.

I had never met a woman like her, she cursed and seemed to do whatever she wanted, even around men.

My observation was cut short when a beautiful woman began to walk toward us.

Her skin was the color of milk chocolate and her irises were moving clouds of gray smoke blowing in the wind.

Her mask was the most extravagant I had seen yet. Wispy bands of gold made the whole mask, letting her chocolaty complexion show through the weaving of the gold. It lay on her cheek bones, crossing over, going up the bridge of her nose to leave a fountain looking design in the middle of her forehead. Then thinner bands lead from the bridge to encase her eyes before reaching outward at the corners like raging flames that soared upward to the mountain of shiny black curls that rested on the top of her head.

Her gown was just as regal. The same wispy gold strands stretched down in golden rays capping her shoulders before breaking into one thin band of gold that merged with the corners of the white silk and continued down to make the gowns plunging neckline.

The skirt of the gown met just under her breasts, the two pieces of silk joined together with a delicate gold roping. The gown was long and flowing and seemed to trail along behind her as the sea of vampires parted and bowed their heads while she walked toward us.

I didn't need to be told who she was; I knew instantly. I knew from the moment I saw her that she was an Elder, and not just any Elder, she and I were bound by the same blood.

"Daughter," she said stopping in front of me.

I too bowed my head. Technically she wasn't royal. In our world she was even more important. She was the reason we existed at all, and that definitely deserved respect.

I lifted my head and smiled. I was nervous but not as much as when I had arrived, there was something familiar about her that soothed me.

I opened my mouth to speak when I heard Vincent.

"Zariah," he said bowing.

"Vincent," she said with a nod. "And this must be your consort?" she said as she looked at me.

"Yes, this is Delilah," he said hand gesturing towards me.

"It's nice to finally meet you." I said with another small bow.

"And you. I heard you have taken quite a calling to the change?"

"That's what Vincent says." I answered.

"But you disagree?" She chuckled, spreading her very full lips into a smile.

"Not exactly. But I feel that I'm falling behind. I haven't received a gift yet to set me apart from anyone else."

"Never fear my Daughter, you are still young. Your specialty comes with time as does the knowledge to wield it. You underestimate yourself but I see great strength in you. I understand why Vincent has chosen you for this life. Be patient, things will happen when you least expect them."

She looked at Vincent and nodded still smiling before slowly making her way back through the crowd.

Chapter 17.

"You know she doesn't usually do that right?" Angeline asked breaking the silence Zariah had left over the room.

"Do what?"

"Talk to the Kiddies."

"What are you talking about? Vincent said that was the reason they held the Ball. To meet the new ones and reassure the old ones that they're still around."

"Angeline is right. They never talk to them one on one without cause. Zariah must see something in you."

"Like what?" I asked confused.

"I don't know." Angeline answered. But I'll bet it has something to do with the gift you're getting. Maybe she can sense it? It is her blood, maybe she can sense something that we can't?"

"Maybe, but now I feel uncomfortable being singled out."

"You're not the only one being singled out. Look." Angeline nodded for me to turn around.

I looked around and saw that the entire room had turned their attention to me and the ones surrounding me during our conversation, and they were still staring and whispering about it.

I don't know what to do, everyone's staring. I thought, so Vincent wouldn't hear me.

I do, Angeline thought back.

She smiled politely at the crowd of gawking spectators before calmly saying. "I would turn around if I were you."

I don't know what they saw in her eyes (or in their head for that matter) but after a second of blank staring the entire crowd turned around and sparked up different conversations.

Wow! What did you do?

Nothing, I just showed them the possibilities of your gift. The very graphic possibilities of your gift.

I just smiled, I could imagine. It was probably something like me in a rage hurling fire balls at them.

You're close, but my imagination may have gotten the best of me. I gave you red fire beams that shot out from your eyes incinerating groups at a time.

I looked at Angeline questionably raising an eyebrow. She just shrugged. With that we both burst out laughing.

"You're crazy!" I choked out still laughing.

"Yes, I am." She answered proudly with a sigh.

Poor Vincent just looked at us with an amused expression having missed the entire conversation.

"Is she at it again?" I heard a new voice ask.

We all turned to see Ezra standing there with a smirk.

I had got so caught up with Angeline earlier that I had completely overlooked Ezra.

He was tall and slender with wavy black hair that was combed back and slightly tan skin. He wore a white tux with green velvet bow tie and a gold, white and green mask. He had hazel eyes that shinned through the mask holes, a broad smile and matching dimples on each side of his cheeks.

"I believe so." Answered Vincent. "I seem to have missed the joke."

We both looked from Vincent to Ezra. The expressions of pure confusion they both held were exactly the same, then we looked from them to each other and lost it again.

Angeline's laugh made me laugh, it was bold like her with a slight high pitched ring to it that made it that much more genuine.

When we had finally stopped laughing we noticed the boys had started their own conversation; losing all interest in what we were talking, or in our case, not talking about.

I still had a smile on my face when I realized that the room had been called to attention.

Everybody turned to see what was happening in the front of the room.

The five Elders stood in the front of the room in between the two fountains perfectly still while five men in matching white tuxes with matching black masks each carried a very large wooden chair, with green velvet padding, and set it behind each Elder.

With perfect synchronization they removed their masks and sat down.

The entire room (myself included) followed suit by removing our masks and bowing.

Carlus sat in the middle chair. He looked like he hadn't aged a day. The only thing that was different was his hair; it was short now and slicked to the side revealing his flawless bronze skin, chiseled jaw line and high cheek bones. His lips had a slight pout to them and his big brown eyes seemed to burn through me, calling out in a soft whisper, saying "Come to me."

I immediately had to drop my gaze before I lost control of my actions. I steadied my breathing as the urge to walk to him slowly left my body.

Intense isn't it?

I looked over to Angeline and gave her a quick nod.

Wow, I thought it was bad from my angle but seeing it through your eyes was even worse.

Is it like that all the time? I thought. I really hoped it wasn't.

Not always, he just likes to really turn it on sometimes. With how strongly you felt it I think he was purposely singling you out.

Why me?

Maybe he was trying to see how strong minded you are? Zariah must have told him she thinks you're special.

But I'm not! I argued.

They seem to think you are.

I didn't think anything after that I just looked up at them trying to avoid eye contact with Carlus.

After a minute I realized I didn't know which Elder was who out of the three left.

"Who are the men on each side of Carlus?" I whispered to Vincent.

"On the right is Ian and Julius and on the left is Zariah, as you already know, and Nathanial."

I looked over to Ian first, he had short, black hair that was slicked back revealing a younger, thinner face then Carlus but it was just as beautifully sculpted. He was of Asian decent and had glossy black eyes. It was like staring into a well. They were dark but the light of the room danced off them making them stunning.

Julius had slightly longer, dirty blonde hair that had a slight wave but was combed to the side neatly. His lips were perfectly matched in size and his eyes were green like the grass on a summer's day and he wore a cocky half smirk on his face that made me think he was the trouble maker.

Now seeing the entirety of Zariah's face I understand why Vincent had called her the lure.

Her chocolaty smooth complexion made her that much more noticeable in comparison. She carried an undeniable confidence as she sat the only woman in the group.

Her eyes were still a silent storm of gray smoke swirling around. But seeing her entire face now was breathtaking. I was glad she had worn the mask earlier. If I had seen her face in its entirety I wouldn't have been able to talk to her so easily.

She too had high cheek bones but her face was a little fuller then the others so the distinction was more subtle. She had a wider nose and very full lips. They looked like soft pillows arranged into a welcoming smile.

By her side sat Nathaniel. Just glancing at him in his fitted tux you could tell he was much more muscular then the others. His shoulders were broader, his chest looked fuller and I was willing to bet if he stood next to the three other men, that he was much taller too.

His slightly messy, brown hair added to the uniqueness of his features, and the cocky smile spread across his face proved that he truly didn't care what others thought of him. He obviously liked to stand out and with eyes like his, he did just that. His eyes were limpid leaving just the black pupil and a very faint rim that looked light blue around his iris.

I continued to gaze off in their direction until Carlus spoke snapping me back to attention.

"My Children. I welcome you. We gather here tonight to celebrate the births of the passing decade and to bring forth those who wish to create new life in the coming decade. So I ask those of you who wish to create new life to please step forward now?"

There were three vampires that entered the circle, two male and one female. I didn't know the other two but I did recognize Nariyoll, he was standing at the end.

I looked around for Hazel, I figured she wouldn't be too far away and I found her standing on the left side where the crowd curved to make the half circle around the Elders.

The first one to be called on was the other man. He was muscular in his black tuxedo with white vest and white bow tie. He had very neat, slicked to the side, black hair that reminded me of Vincent's.

"Ah yes, Sevilen. It has been a long time."

"Carlus." he said with a bow.

"We received the news about Ira, it was a great tragedy to lose him. He was beloved by the Nation."

"Yes, that is why I have come to request a vial. My Sire is gone and so, now I am alone. With The Rising Sons resurfaced I wish to make a mate to travel with."

"I understand your situation Sevilen but with the resurfacing of The Rising Sons do you think it wise to create a defenseless mate with unpredictable urges?" Zariah asked.

"I do see your concern, yes, but I have been on this earth for many centuries now. The last year I have spent alone in my grieving and now I wish to move on. As for defenseless, I would never leave anyone defenseless. As you well know, I have acquired many talents over the years, and I plan to travel quite a bit of distance in the coming years."

"Yes, I know of your abilities but are you sure they will be enough? After all, Ira has fallen and he was older and even more gifted than you."

"I'll admit that we were caught unprepared. We had no news of their resurfacing and perhaps Ira and I both got too comfortable in our lifestyle, a mistake that has cost me dearly." Sevilen wiped under his eyes with his handkerchief to collect the blood stained tears before they could run down his face. "I just want to move on with my life and I do not wish to wait another decade to start. Please, won't you give me the opportunity to redeem myself?"

Carlus seemed to pause for a moment before speaking again. "We all share in your suffering, and I will tell you that you have made quite a compelling case here tonight. After we speak with the other seekers, we shall deliberate and then give you our decision, you may take your place with the others now."

"Thank you, Carlus," he said before he bowed again and walked back into the crowd.

"Sarila, I did not expect to see you among the seekers." Zariah mused.

Sarila looked confident as she stood, in her dark, purple gown. It was strapless and had different colored gems covering the bodice that shimmered green, blue, pink and yellow in the light. She had short blonde hair that was done in finger waves with purple and green gem pins on the left side. Her crystal blue eyes shined brightly against the paleness of her skin and a small band of freckles that spanned across her nose was the only color on her face. She wore no makeup but she didn't need it anyway. She was simply pretty.

Sarila bowed. "Honestly I never expected to be here either."

"What can we do for you, Daughter?" Carlus asked with a grin.

"I have met someone and would like to bestow them our gift."

"Does this person know of the awakening?" Nathaniel broke in.

"No, he does not, but I have spent time with him and I believe he can handle the truth of our secret."

"Do you have strong feelings for this man?" Zariah asked.

"Yes. I do."

"And what are your plans to elude The Rising Sons?" Carlus asked.

"I already live discretely. My plan is to continue in the same manner, only sharing my eternal love with someone deserving."

"I do know how responsible you have been over the centuries. I really hope your love is as deserving as you believe. We will take your request under consideration." Zariah said lifting her lips into a smile for Sarila.

"Thank you all." Sarila said before bowing and walking into the crowd.

"Nariyoll, I believe you have special circumstances, do you not?" asked Carlus.

Of course Nariyoll bowed before speaking. "I do." he answered.

"And?"

Nariyoll's face remained boyishly smooth as he spoke, only his fidgeting gave away his nervousness.

He looked about nineteen or twenty and had short dirty, blonde hair and innocent baby blue eyes.

"I ask for the vial in the name of love. I too have met someone I believe to be worthy and I wish to share eternity with her."

"But you are underage, are you not?"

"I am. But I fear if we wait another fifty years that it would be unfair to Hazel, she will be an old woman by then."

"And it's been brought to my attention our young Hazel is with us this evening. But yet you stand before us alone?"

"Yes. She stands in the crowd awaiting your answer."

"Well bring her forth. Let us see if she is truly worthy."

Nariyoll waved his hand and Hazel walked to the inner part of the circle to stand by his side.

"My dear, do you know the consequences of your actions here tonight?" asked Carlus.

"I do."

"And yet you came anyway?" asked Nathaniel.

"I did."

"That was either very brave or very foolish on your part." said Ian.

I didn't expect Hazel to answer that one and she didn't. She simply stood there ready to take whatever they decided to give her.

“Are you prepared for a life of secrecy?” Ian asked.

“Away from everyone you have ever known including your family?” added in Zariah.

“I have no family, my parents died when I was very young and I love Nariyoll so I am prepared to do whatever it takes to be with him.”

“So we see.” said Ian.

Carlus narrowed his eyes for an instant as he stared at Hazels young face and just as quickly he snapped back and I wondered if I was the only one that noticed that look. And what it was exactly he was thinking for him to look at her in such a way?

“Very well.” He yelled breaking my concentration and bringing me back to the party.

“I have heard plenty tonight. We will take you in to consideration also. You may leave the circle Nariyoll.”

Nariyoll bowed, and he and Hazel walked away.

“Let us move on to more interesting news. We have a new arrival to celebrate tonight. Carlus spoke.

“Delilah, would you please step forward?”

At first my feet were glued to the floor waiting for him to call another name. He didn’t.

I walked slowly towards the center of the room while couples parted to let me by. I stopped in the middle and bowed to show my respect.

"Hello again. It is nice to see your face in its entirety, my Daughter." Zariah said nodding her head slightly at me.

"And what a beautiful face it is!" Carlus gushed.

"Thank you." I said slightly confused. I really couldn't see what all the fuss was about?

"I have known Vincent for many years now and I have to say he has excellent taste. I can see greatness in you and with the red hair I think Zariah was a wise choice for you. I can see that you will be a great force to be reckoned with my dear."

"How are you adjusting so far?"

"Everything is going well. Vincent has been more than patient with me; he's an excellent teacher."

I thought I would talk about him, maybe it would take some of the attention off me.

"Yes I can see that. You act much older than your age. He has done a fine job with you." Zariah agreed.

"He has also shared with us how level headed you remained during The Rising Sons attack on Ramiel and Fidelia." Carlus broke in.

Was there anything they didn't know? I thought in amazement.

Carlus didn't speak but he shook his head from side to side subtly; answering my silent question.

"I just knew we had to get out of there." I answered honestly. "But unfortunately by the time I understood what had happened to Ramiel, it was too late for Fidelia."

"You did the right thing. If you had gone up against them I have no doubt that you and Vincent would be dead. You have yet to receive any of your gifts and Vincent was in no condition to defend the both of you." Said Zariah.

"Something must be done about them. They have been shown leniency for far too long!" Broke in Julius. I think it was the first time he had spoken the whole night.

"What do you think Delilah?" asked Carlus.

"Me? Why are you asking me?" I asked in shock.

"Because you are the newest to arrive in our world. Your opinion of them remains untainted by grief." Carlus answered, like I should have known that from the beginning.

I thought for a second and he was right, I had never been affected by them the way Vincent or any of the others had.

"What I seen and heard that night on the roof and from the story Vincent shared with me about Noah and the others, I believe Julius is right and it is time to stop sitting by while our people are slaughtered for the sake of blending in." I answered calmly.

In the corner of my eye I saw Julius smile at my words. I think he had been trying to sway the others for a long time and I was sure he thought I might be the one to do it.

"We have "blended in" for many centuries. That is what keeps us alive." Zariah mocked. And honestly I was surprised at how snotty she sounded. Throughout all the different conversations tonight she had been calm and comforting. But suddenly that was no longer the case. And that bothered me.

"No." I answered coldly. That's what keeps *some* of us alive."

"You were astonished that I called on you for your opinion but you seem to have given this much thought, young one." Carlus said, with an amused smile spread across his face.

"It's something Vincent and I have argued about. He agrees that we should lay low in order to blend in." I answered.

"Where is Vincent tonight? I would really love to hear his thoughts on this matter.

"Vincent would you please come forward?" Carlus called.

Vincent wasn't far away. He stepped forward from the group of spectators and walked up stopping by my side.

He bowed respectfully then stood silently waiting for them to call on him.

"Is it true you are content with concealment?" Ian asked.

"If it saves others? Yes. But I'm starting to believe it makes no difference anymore. There are only so many places we can go. I believe the reason they have regrouped is to exterminate us completely." Vincent replied.

"I am afraid you are correct my friend, so what would you have us do then?" Carlus was talking to Vincent but I spoke up first.

“The opposite of what we’ve been doing. Let’s let them know what we can really do when provoked!”

A few people gasped at the thought but it was broken by cheers here and there by others that thought it was a good idea.

“I must admit I love your spirit child but do you understand the risk we would be taking if we did that?”

“I understand that it doesn’t seem to matter. Our kind is still dying rather we’re careful or not. What I suggest is that we show them who’s boss. Are the humans afraid of their cattle? Of course not! I think it’s time to be what we were meant to be. We are the dominate species and I think it’s time we acted like it, instead of cowering in the dark while our kind continues to be massacred.”

“Your suggestion sounds good in theory but how would we put those plans in to action? We cannot simply walk up to their doors and reveal ourselves,” asked Zariah.

I shook my head before answering.

“We won’t have to. If we just carry out our normal lives we won’t have to find them; they’ll come right to us.”

“And if they come?” Zariah asked. “What then? We have no idea how vast their numbers are or how much they know about us. This is suicide!” She was clearly against this idea.

I opened my mouth and Vincent placed his hand in mine to stop me from arguing. It was clear this wasn’t going to end well for me if I kept going.

Zariah also looked annoyed as she closed her mouth and then she glared at me from her seat.

Carlus looked at her and back to me and grinned before he spoke.

“Well, I think this has gone far enough for now. Shall we will deliberate?”

The rest of the group nodded once and so it began.

Chapter 18.

We all waited, softly carrying on different conversations as the Elders deliberated.

They didn't have to speak aloud, they carried the entire conversation in their heads. Must be an Elder thing? I thought watching them as their eyes clouded over and they blankly stared ahead in a daze.

One would give an occasional nod of understanding and then continue to stare in that trans -like state.

Creepy looking aint it? I heard Angeline's voice in my head say.

Definitely. Do we look like that right now? I thought back.

No, not like them. We may have a blankness to our face but nothing like that. They don't just talk in their heads they also see each others thoughts.

Can you hear what they're talking about?

No. She giggled. *They block us all out from hearing them unless they want us to hear them.*

Oh.

I'm surprised you to want to go up against The Rising Sons. She thought.

Why are you surprised?

Because, it's not what someone as young and defenseless as you would normally suggest.

Do you think it's a bad idea?

Shit no! I think it's what we should have done ages ago. I just can't believe you are so eager.

Well, like I said, we should have the upper hand. Pretending all the time to be something we're not is ridiculous.

I agree. You know, I really think they're considering your idea.

What do you think is going to happen if they agree?

We'll start a war I suppose, but not without cost to our side.

Yes, but we'll lose them anyway so why not go down fighting!

Ezra was right, Vincent better watch you.

You know, they say that birds of a feather flock together? I thought, giving her a lifted eyebrow and cocky grin.

Yes, I have heard that, so I guess we're just two crazy ass peas in a pod about to go up against a bunch of angry cows.

I smiled and tried not to laugh at that. *Well at least we'll stand up for ourselves. I really don't understand how you all have lived this way for all these centuries. I have only been doing it for a few months now and I've had enough. How do you do it?*

It's all we've ever known, all we were taught. Of course none of us like it but it's how we have been able to coexist without the whole world finding out about us. If the Elders agree with this it could mean the beginning of a new world for us; you may have just made history.

I guess we'll find out. Look. I thought and nodded over Angeline's shoulder to where the Elders had suddenly come back to reality; losing their glazed over look.

"First things first, we had decided to grant all three of our seekers a vial of eternal life, so would the three of you please step forward?" Carlus announced.

The three seekers walked into the circle in the same sequence as before.

"As you all know you cannot share the same bloodline with your mate so as I call on you will you please make your request to the Elder of your choice?"

"Sevilen, make your request."

"I would like to request your life's blood Carlus? You are the strongest of us all and I believe you would pass on the best chances at a gifted life."

Carlus only took a second to think about Sevilen's request before saying. "I accept your offer with gratitude and again I offer my condolences for Ira. I hope you find great happiness with your new partner."

"As do I, thank you Carlus." he said before a little nod.

"Sarila, make you request."

"Zariah," she spoke. "We have known each other for a very long time now and I admire you. I ask you to bestow your gift upon my beloved?"

“Yes Sarila, we have known each other for a very long time. I am flattered and delighted to accept your request. I wish you luck in love and as always in life.”

“Nariyoll would you please have Hazel come forth?” Carlus asked. Hazel came into sight again to stand by Nariyoll’s side.

“Are you truly ready for this? After this, there is no going back for you.”

“I understand,” she answered calmly. “Yes, I’m ready.”

“This is a special situation we have here. Hazel, taking into consideration that you are here tonight I am going to give you the choice. Make your request.”

Nariyoll started to protest and Carlus simply put his hand up to stop him.

Still looking at Hazel he urged her. “Go on.” he said

At first she just stood there not saying anything, then she spoke up.

“I’m afraid I don’t know that much about any of you, so I ask this instead, based on what you have seen of me tonight would you please make a suggestion on who would be better suited for me?”

“I suppose that is a reasonable request but Nariyoll I am disappointed that you have brought her here with no knowledge of who we are.”

“I apologize Carlus but I was not aware that she would have to make the choice herself.”

"Then tell me, who have you chosen to bring her into this life?"

"I was going to request a vial from Zariah as well."

"Why her?"

"They are both women so I thought it was befitting."

"Is that the only reason?"

"Zariah is very talented and I thought it would make for a gifted companion."

"Yes well, I believe Zariah to be a match for many, just not for Hazel. I believe Julius would be better suited so I will suggest him."

"Julius, will you bestow your gift to Hazel?"

"I will accept her request on one condition; it is to be done here, tonight."

"Do you accept his condition Hazel?" Carlus asked looking to her.

She locked her gaze at Nariyoll.

"Yes. I accept," she answered, her eyes never leaving his."

"Very well then, it is settled."

"Let the festivities begin!" Carlus snapped his fingers, then the same five men that had brought the chairs reappeared with a big rectangular piece of black marble that was the length and width of a person and almost five feet high and set it in front of the five Elders.

They set a large blue and gold urn on the floor beside the white marble and walked away in the same direction they had come.

"Nariyoll, would you please bring Hazel over to stand by the marble altar.

The two of them walked to the altar hand in hand and turned to face the Elders.

"Are you ready my dear?" Carlus asked Hazel.

"Yes, I'm ready." She answered, still as confident as before.

"So be it then. Nariyoll you know what you must do."

Nariyoll and Hazel turned to face each other.

"I love you," Hazel whispered.

"Forever," Nariyoll whispered back running his finger down the side of her face. He brought her in close to him then sunk his teeth into her neck.

I wasn't surprised that Hazel didn't scream the only sound she made was a gulp when Nariyoll bit down. He held on to her, supporting her weight as she slowly fell backward, her head dangling to reveal her tear streaked face to the on looking crowd.

He lifted her lifeless body and gently set her on top of the marble. He opened her mouth then stood by her side silently awaiting Julius.

Julius arose from his seat and walked to where Hazel lay. He then bit his own wrist before holding it above Hazels lips letting his blood flow into her mouth.

After her mouth was full he removed his wrist from her face and the slash he had made healed instantly. He nodded to Nariyoll before returning to his seat beside Ian.

We all watched as Hazel rolled into a ball and I remembered doing that too because of the cramping.

Blood was trickling out of her eyes and nose and her heart was beating so loud I'm sure everyone in the room could hear it.

I realized what the urn had been for when she started to throw up in it, over and over. When she had finally stopped is when the cracking sound of her bones readjusting rippled through the room; this time she did cry out. I couldn't really blame her. I knew from experience that it hurt like hell.

She lay there, her eyes and nose still bleeding while her cracking continued. I could see the exhaustion settling in.

After awhile her hands fell dead at her sides seeming to give up the struggle. Her heart started to slow its chaotic drumming until it stopped all together, giving her a moment of silence to let her features catch up.

Her skin lost all its color going bone white and her long, straight brown hair, curled up into soft waves around her face. Her lips once stained red were now a light pink and at the end of her delicate fingers were longer, slightly pointed fingernails.

Nariyoll leaned down and kissed her softly on the forehead before moving beside her ear and whispering "Wake up my love."

With that she opened her eyes. Nariyoll stared down at her face, smiling at her. He took the handkerchief from his pocket and rubbed off the left over blood from her eyes and nose.

She sat upright and swung her legs over the side of the marble, her wide, dark eyes lost in the room in front of her with wonder.

"How do you feel?" Nariyoll asked her.

"I feel–

She cut off and dropped her head into her hands, curling up her knees near the edge of the marble.

She was completely consumed in the vision. I knew we didn't have the same Sire so our experiences weren't the exact same but I'm sure the goriness of his past was just as shocking. When she finally raised her head, her eyes were even wider than before; she looked… scared.

"I'm evil?" She whispered in a horrified tone, sliding off the altar.

I had never seen a terrified vampire and after how sure she was before, I wasn't expecting this reaction from her.

"No, we're not evil my love; we are life, eternal life." Nariyoll answered calmly with a smile.

He walked to the waiter standing on the side and grabbed two glasses from his tray before walking back to Hazel.

"Drink this and you'll feel better." He said trying to hand her one of the glasses.

She didn't take the glass, instead she was backing away from him.

“Drink Hazel, trust me. You have already been through the transition; the rest is easy. This is what we wanted, a life together, remember?” he urged, walking towards her with the glass.

“I can’t.” She pleaded with red tears welling up in her eyes.

“Yes, you can, it is who you are now. Nariyoll argued.

“No! Not Me!” She yelled shaking her head violently. “You’re all the spawn of Satan! You’re murderers! You told me I wouldn’t have to kill people. You never said you kill without mercy and for your own pleasure, it’s evil and I won’t be a part of that.” She cried.

“Nariyoll! Get a hold of her or I will!” Barked Carlus.

“Please do not do this Hazel, please drink; stay with me,” he begged moving toward her with his hands outstretched as red tears slowly ran down his cheeks.

“Stay away from me!” She yelled at Nariyoll as she started to run for the door.

She didn’t get far. My eyes followed her as she suddenly stopped in mid stride, completely frozen.

I looked around and found that Carlus was now standing with his left hand stretched out in front of him, palm out.

I looked back and forth between Carlus and Hazel. When he lifted his arm higher, her feet left the floor leaving a two foot gap between her and the marble tile.

I watched in amazement as her body mirrored each move he made with his hand. He slowly turned his hand so his palm faced towards himself and her body slowly turned in the same direction so she too was facing him now. Then with a bend of his fingers she went soaring through the air towards him.

He pushed out his palm again and she halted in front of the marble platform, his voice menacing as he spoke. "I will give you… one… last… chance girl. Will you join us, or no?"

With her eyes wide she sobbed. "I… can't."

"So be it."

"NO!" Nariyoll cried but it was too late, as soon as Carlus closed his hand Hazel started to bleed out of every hole she had.

She gurgled and choked as what blood she had left, poured out of her eyes, nose, ears and mouth. It ran down her face and the front of her dress, even her legs had streaks as blood ran down to her feet. Her sad eyes looked over to where Nariyoll stood crying, her bloody lips parted and she smiled at him before her face went blank leaving her lifeless body to hang in the air dripping.

Carlus opened his hand and Hazel fell, half into the small puddle she had made and half into Nariyoll's arms.

"Why Hazel, why?" he cried, stroking her hair over and over and rocking on his knees with her bloody body in his arms.

“Nariyoll, step away.” Zariah commanded, standing up. “She made her choice now let us be done with this.”

“No, I will not just leave her here like this.”

“Neither will I, now step away!”

Nariyoll looked at Zariah with anger in his eyes and he didn’t budge.

“I know what it is you mean to do with her; so do it.” He said coldly.

Zariah didn’t say anything she just gave him a slow nod. She closed her eyes for a moment and took a deep breath and when she opened them her pupils were gone and there was red flames dancing within the gray smoke.

I followed her gaze to where Hazel still lay partly on the floor and partly on Nariyoll’s arm.

She raised her hand to her soft lips and blew gently across her palm in Hazels direction. A sweet scent filled the room. It reminded me of honeysuckle and I remembered Vincent calling this sweet breeze.

Black smoke poured out of Hazels body as her skin and hair turned gray. The veins in her face turned black first then her face began to cinder, falling away under the gentle touch of Nariyoll’s fingertips until all at once her body turned to ash and fell to the floor.

Smoke and blood covered Nariyoll’s once handsome features as he sat staring off into nothingness; caressing the fabric of the gold gown she had worn that night with his free hand.

I felt sorry for him. I couldn't imagine having to watch as the person I loved was killed, let alone in such a brutal way.

Finally the vampires in the white tuxes came and slowly helped Nariyoll up, the dress dumping even more ash on the floor before they walked him through a door leading him someplace unknown.

Chapter 19.

No one spoke. After all, what was there to say? Had that ever happened before?

Once. I heard in my head. *A long time ago.*

I looked over to my right and saw Angeline coming to stand next to me holding on to Ezra's hand.

I don't understand why she acted that way? She wanted this. When I awoke I didn't really know what was going on either at first but I didn't do that!

Sometimes people can't handle the change. It becomes too much for them to process at one time and a lot of times religion gets in the way of their acceptance of killing. She answered.

Wait,why did bleeding her out kill her? Our bodies run low or without blood all the time.

Well, I would guess if we truly did get bled dry we might die too but she wasn't fully awake yet. She hadn't killed or fed on the living to cement her in to immortality. She was still partly human. With nothing to keep her going, she was just a frail as them.

What a shame. I thought.

Fuck her! Do not pity her. Pity Nariyoll for having fallen for such a lunatic.

Where did they take him? I wondered

Somewhere he can mourn in privacy. She answered.

Just then three of the white tuxes came back out. Two carried off the marble altar and the third cleaned up what was left of Hazel and took away the blue and gold urn.

What are they going to do with the ashes?

Who knows maybe they'll throw her in a trash can out back, but I'm sure if Nariyoll has anything to say about it she'll be given to him.'

"On to the other topic of this evening." I turned my attention to Carlus as he spoke. "Delilah has made a valid point tonight. The Rising Sons have resurfaced. If the past does in fact repeat itself then I'm not sure concealment will work. I don't know if being bolder will have the threatening effect she thinks. So we'll leave this decision to you. If you feel that you need to be more discrete, then so be it; if not, then be prepared to handle the consequences. But remember this, to bring them down on one; you bring them down on us all."

He had a good point but I wasn't afraid. After what I just saw we could handle The Rising Sons. What was the difference from what could happen and what *was* happening already?

"This concludes tonight's festivities, please feel free to dance and enjoy the rest of your night. We thank you all for coming and to Sevilen and Sarila you can obtain your vials before you leave. I sincerely hope your efforts are not wasted like Nariyoll's were here tonight." And with that Carlus gave a small nod and he and the rest of the Elders walked together through the same door they took Nariyoll through earlier.

When the music finally started again, Vincent held out his hand to me.

"May I?" he asked.

"You may." I said putting my hand in his.

He led me to the sea of swirling couples and we merged on to the floor effortlessly, swirling and swaying with the melody.

"I noticed she woke up pretty fast, you said you waited on my for hours?" I asked as we danced.

"Everyone's different my love, as you just seen. You had no insight and didn't react like her."

"I'm glad things didn't go that way for us."

"So am I but I knew you would adapt well."

"How?"

"Your dreams."

"What dreams, I thought you only gave me one dream?"

"I did only give you one, but I started peeking in on your dreams from the very first night we met and you were always dreaming of me, even your familiar dream, the one of you twirling in the falling white rose petals included me; so I knew."

"So, that's why you brought me white roses? I always secretly wondered about that."

"What better way to find out what people like, then to look inside their head?"

"You have no shame do you?" I teased right before he twirled me out.

"Well, I had to make sure you did not end up like Hazel." He said after he pulled me back in. "Then, after I gave you the truthful dream and found you while you were looking for me, I knew you were hooked completely." He said giving me his big cheesy grin.

"I still don't know why?" I said dryly.

"Why, my good looks of course."

"Yeah, it's a good thing you've still got those because it's not your personality."

He laughed. "No, definitely not the personality."

I couldn't help but laugh too as he continued to spin me around and around on the floor.

I laid my head on his chest and closed my eyes wrapping my arms around him and he effortlessly changed to small circles with me tucked away in his arms. After seeing what Nariyoll had just gone through I was grateful for the life and love I had with Vincent; he made me complete.

Um... Delilah, you should look around before you hit your head on the ceiling. I heard Angeline's voice say.

What are you talking about? I thought back, annoyed that she was interrupting my blissful moment dancing with Vincent.

Just open your eyes.

I mentally sighed. *Fine!* I thought annoyed.

I opened my eyes and looked up to see Vincent's loving face looking right back at me.

Happy? My eyes are open. What the hell are you talking about? I thought.

You won't be that arrogant once you've stopped staring at Vince and actually looked around, or rather looked down. She giggled.

I reluctantly looked down so maybe it would shut her up.

"Oh, boy!" I gasped.

"Calm down, and keep your hands where they are."

"How did we get up here?" I asked in a panic.

"You. It is your first gift," he said smiling.

"Great, how do we get down?"

"Well, what were you thinking about to rise us up here?"

"Nothing; I wasn't thinking about anything!"

"Then what were you feeling?"

"I don't know… I guess… grateful."

"Then try to feel the same way you were feeling, and think about going down instead."

"I don't know how to do that!" I cried.

"Relax, we are immortal even if we fall we can't die. Just calm down," he whispered in my ear before he kissed me gently on my cheek.

"Okay." I took a deep breath and then closed my eyes. I tried to remember what I was thinking about.

Angeline do you remember what I was thinking about when you broke though?

Yeah and I also heard the last thought you were thinking about. You still want to shut me up?

Focus Angeline, I need your help here and I didn't think I was floating around the room. I just thought you were trying to bother me. Sorry.

Yeah, well next time you'll listen huh...? You were thinking about Vincent; you're always thinking about Vincent. I actually think you might be a little obsessed.

Ugh, what about Vincent?

You were just happy with him. Unfortunately there was nothing dirty what so ever going on in there.

You've been a big help Angeline. I thought sarcastically.

Hey, I wasn't in there the whole time, I have a life too you know. It's not often I get this many subjects at once to spy on. she laughed.

Great, okay just think about Vincent and get down. I focused on his breathing and remembered the dream we shared on the beach together, the sound of the heavy waves crashing up onto the sand, the warmth of the sun on my face and playing the cloud game.

When I was relaxed I thought about feeling the floor beneath my feet so we could twirl around again. Over and over I thought about twirling on the marble swirled floor with Vincent still in my arms.

I opened my eyes and seen that the ceiling was getting further and further away as we got closer and closer to the floor.

“See, I knew you could do it!” Vincent said enthusiastically as our feet touched the floor.

“Yeah I wish I could have been that sure; I thought we were going to be stuck up there.” I said looking back up at the high ceiling.

“So how’s it feel?” Angeline asked.

“What?”

“Your gift.”

“Yeah, you’re one of us now.” Ezra added.

“I– It feels great!”

After the panic left I was filled with the excitement of finally belonging.

“But… what does floating have to do with what Zariah can do?” I asked confused.

“Well, it’s not considered floating. They call it Rising and I’m sure she can do it also. I told you that they have abilities that most of us are unaware of.”

“Will it get better?” I really hoped I didn’t start rising for no reason all the time and actually get stuck somewhere.

“What do you mean?” Vincent asked.

“Will it be easier to use and control?”

“Of course, and once you’ve practiced you’ll be able to do more then go up and down. I noticed it forming in you your first night as an immortal." Vincent said in his matter of fact way, with a smile.

"How?" I asked bewildered.

"When you shot past the window. It's not usually that easy to spring up quite that far your first time and if I had just let you go I am sure you would have passed the house altogether."

"Why didn't you say anything?"

"Because you wouldn't have believed me. I've been telling you all along that you would receive a gift to just be patient."

Vincent raised his hand and a tall waiter carrying a silver tray full of red champagne flutes came over. Each of us took one and the waiter carelessly walked away.

Angeline raised her glass. "To Delilah's transformation, may she always keep her stubborn ways!"

Then Ezra went next. "To the beginning of a long and gifted life spent defying all the rules put before her, which I look forward to seeing, immensely." Ezra gave me a wink and I smiled and nodded, tilting my glass a bit in agreement.

Finally Vincent raised his glass. "To my beautiful and talented Delilah, you make eternity the joyous gift it is meant to be, and I don't know how I survived without you for all those years. Congratulations my darling."

"Congratulations!" They all said raising their glasses to clank them together.

I smiled and raised the flute to my lips. Of course it was blood but I was surprised how warm it still was and it was human.

I got lost in its taste and warmth as the blood ran down into my body; the sweetness was overwhelming and there was a hint of alcoholic bliss that drove me to paradise.

I stayed lost in my head until my glass ran empty and I was —once again— forced back to the party.

"It's fresh?" I announced bringing the glass away from my lips.

"Of course, did you expect otherwise?" Vincent asked.

"No, I guess not but I didn't expect it to still be warm. How is that possible?"

"There are vessels here that supply the party." He answered.

"Vessels, you mean humans?"

"Yes humans, they give blood in exchange for money."

"Is there anything you can't buy?"

"I don't think so… For the right price, that is." He added smirking.

"I've noticed there are human dates here too though and no one seems to care."

"That's because they're Taps." Angeline answered.

"Taps?"

"Yeah, Taps. They're humans that are kept around for convenience; most of the time the hosts are sleepers." Ezra broke in.

"Why?" I asked confused.

"Because they can hypnotize their prey making them believe being bit it something pleasurable and afterwards they can erase their memories altogether."

"So, they won't remember being at the Ball tonight?"

"They might, they might not, it depends on if their host wants them to or not. I'm sure none of them remember what happened here tonight with Hazel though; more than likely that's already gone."

"Oh, that's good that they won't remember that part at least. We don't need the humans knowing the possibilities of what goes on here." I said glancing around for another waiter.

"No.That's why the humans that come here are to be changed, slumbered or killed. Otherwise it would cause panic." Vincent added.

"Oh good," I lifted my hand to signal for another glass. After he stopped I put my empty glass on the tray and grabbed another full one. "Anybody else?" I asked looking at my little group.

"Don't mind if I do." Angeline tilted her glass and downed the rest of the blood inside then placed her empty flute beside mine and grabbed another.

Both of the men just sat their glasses on the tray refusing anymore and I thanked the waiter as he left.

"So… what do you think about the Rising Sons, Ezra?" I thought I would ask, he was the only one in our group that I hadn't talked about it with.

"You mean exposure?"

"Yes exposure, do you think we should hide to keep us safe?" I asked slowly tilting my flute for another sip.

"I'm not sure." he said hesitantly. "It doesn't seem to be working anyway, so maybe it would be a good idea to just take them out and get it over with."

I could tell he was still battling with the idea of going against everything he had been taught about concealment.

"If we do that, it's not going to be easy." Vincent said.

"Yes brother, but nothing worth doing ever is." Angeline answered.

Chapter 20.

We said our goodbyes to Angeline and Ezra as well as a couple of the others and left the party in plenty of enough time to get something to eat. Vincent had eyed me and Angeline suspiciously when we both reached for a third glass at the ball. He promised there were would still be plenty of party-goers left on the streets to make grabbing dinner easy afterwards.

After the long debate with Ezra and Angeline over exposure of our kind, I wasn't sure what I wanted to do. Should I just grab someone out in the open or continue to drag people into empty allies and behind buildings, hidden in the shadows?

Did I want to be exposed? What if they got the best of Vincent because I didn't have a defensive gift yet? Could I live with losing him because I was determined to have things my way?

The answer? No, I couldn't. There was no way I could live knowing I was the reason Vincent was dead. So I wait, I told myself. When I get better control over the gift I have and get something defensive, then I will go after them.

Surrounded by all the tasty varieties made my mouth water with anticipation. I couldn't wait to sink my teeth into them.

The glasses at the party hadn't been that big and was just the "Appetizer" (according to Vincent) so I was ready for the main course.

Walking in the street I caught wind of the most intoxicating scent. It was unlike anything I had ever smelled or tasted before. And as I turned to follow it, I spotted its source. It was a young woman, she too wore a mask covering the top half of her face. She was laughing at some unheard joke but there was something about her big brown eyes that made me want her.

She had tan skin, long, brown curly hair and a beautiful smile. As she swayed offbeat to the jazz band that played she tilted her head back and began twirling around with her arms open. At that moment I knew I had to have her.

Her veins called to me like no others ever had, leaving me feverish and hungry to taste her, like some unseen force was pulling me in her direction.

Lifting the side of my dress I danced, slowly, making my way through the crowd towards her and reached out my hands to take hers. I could feel her heart beating through her warm palms while we danced together on the street.

Twirling and laughing, with her heat radiating around me, it wrapped me up, cocooning me, making me warm with desire. Her skin seemed to glow, and her touch made me feel alive in a whole new way. I knew I had to have more of her. I bent down and closing my eyes I breathed in deeply through my nose taking in every bit of anticipated flavor I could get. Pressing my lips to hers I kissed her sweetly wanting to taste her before I tasted her. She was sweet and warm and ALIVE and I needed that life. I needed her blood to awaken my heart and soar throughout my body. I needed that fire I was sure was there, hidden within her. I moved to her neck and breathed in the intoxicating smell that had pulled me in the beginning, her smell. I smiled knowing that in a very short matter of time I would have it all. With my head bent to the side of her neck her lips pressed against my ear and she whispered something in a different language that I couldn't understand. I hugged her in close to me and with the same anticipating smile I sunk my teeth into her neck.

I continued to dance and twirl her away from the crowd as I sucked. Lost in the reality of her tasting every bit as good as I had fantasized about just moments ago and I blissfully sucked every deliciously precious drop out of her body until there was nothing left.

When I laid her on the ground she still looked just as serene as she had dancing on the street and I marveled at her beautiful features in awe as to why this one human had such an effect on me?

She was beautiful yes, but so were dozens of others I had tasted so far. So why was she able to put me in such a haze?

"I see you found yourself a Gypsy?" Vincent asked turning the corner interrupting my bewilderment.

"A what?" I asked wiping the trickles of blood off my mouth.

"A Gypsy, they originated from Northern India a very long time ago but spread out over time. If you believe the stories, they're rumored to have special powers."

“I couldn’t help myself it was like her blood was calling to me, something pulling me towards her.” I explained.

“I’ve heard of this before, long ago. It’s a spell that the Romanies use to call out to vampires, a sort of suicide calling.”

“Suicide calling?” I asked in amazement.

“Yes. I have never seen it done personally until now, but it has been told for centuries that when a Gypsy knows her end is coming she will call out to a near vampire to end her suffering.”

“But why? Wouldn’t they be afraid of the way one of us might do it?”

“No,” He said shaking his head. “That’s part of the spell, something that tells you to remain peaceful and reminds you to be gentle while it is carried out.”

“She said something to me right before but I couldn’t understand her.”

“Yes, she said thank you.”

“You understand Gypsy?” I asked in shock, although I really shouldn’t have been surprised, he seemed to know everything.

“No.” He chuckled shaking his head. “It’s actually not called Gypsy. They speak Romanian or the older language Romani but they always say thank you and I watched as you danced with her gently moving her out of view and the kiss the two of you shared. Everything was as gentle as a feather so I have no doubt it was her gratitude towards the way you handled yourself.”

“She must have been very powerful because I’m not known for my gentleness.” I laughed.

“No, you’re not,” he agreed smirking, “but yes, I’m guessing she was very powerful.”

“Why do you think she wanted this?” Anybody else and I wouldn’t have cared but it’s not every night that you find people who want to die, let alone call for death.

“Humans could desire death for any number of reasons. There’s no scent of illness or decay so I would have to suggest a broken heart.”

We searched her belongings like we would anyone else but inside her little bag was a letter written in the same foreign language she had used before.

I skimmed the letter and found the same name repeated over and over. It was a girls name and that’s when I realized, it wasn’t the loss of just some romance that would cause this; it was the loss of a child.

“You were right about her having a broken heart.” I said as I handed Vincent the letter.

“I was, how do you know that?” he asked taking it from me.

“Sofia, is how I know, look how many times it’s written.” I explained.

Understanding immediately lit his face.

“A daughter,” was all he said and then put the letter back in the little bag that laid beside her.

Allowing myself a glance back I looked at the beautiful (now beautifully dead) Gypsy woman and wondered if they usually worked alongside vampires? And if they were ever any help to us? But I decided to save those questions for another night. So I sighed feeling slightly strange about the whole situation and turned my head away, forgetting about the girl that lay on the street. Instead I focused on enjoying her fire that now seemed to be hidden within my body.

We merged back to the street party effortlessly seeming never have missed a beat and I waited as Vincent found someone of his own to drink.

I was done with the depression of the night; I wanted to have some fun. While he was about half way through I decided to play with my new gift. I floated straight off the roof top I had been standing on and then descended in a swirling motion to join Vince in all his bloody glory.

When my feet touched the ground he simply smiled and continued to feast, sucking the life from his near dead victims neck. I gingerly grabbed one of the mans arms and slowly raised his wrist to my lips. I looked to Vincent and smiled briefly before sinking my teeth into him harshly, enjoying the texture of his skin as it broke against my teeth. I bit him 2 more times just for the fun of it and swallowed hard as his blood overflowed in to my mouth.

We let the man fall to the ground and I took Vincent's hand in mine and I pushed my body against his kissing him while forcing him to slowly walk backward while still tangled in our kiss— he was good at multitasking. Winding my fingers in his hair I tugged a bit as a sign of what I wanted.

"Here?" He asked in a shocked breath.

I smiled but shook my head from side to side. I kissed the side of his neck sensually and gave him a little bite before licking the trickle of blood off that rested there. He shivered under my touch and I couldn't help feeling a bit smug.

"Close your eyes." I whispered, nibbling his earlobe.

I could feel the broadness of his smile move the cheek that was touching mine and I returned his smile while wrapping my arms around him and raising us both up towards the sky and the rooftops.

"Here," I whispered when our feet touched the shingles. I began to kiss him again and this time he didn't hold back.

He kissed me hard while I walked him backwards until he bumped into the chimney. Not bothering with romantics I reached my hand down so I could stroke the bulge in-between his legs, making him moan with my every touch as I slid my fingers up and down. Unfastening his pants I pushed them down, taking his underclothing with me as I reached the shingles of the roof with my knees.

Taking him into my mouth I let him slide against the velvety texture of my tongue while pushing it against him in the same rhythm. Teasing him further, I began circling him with the tip with my tongue, enjoying the taste of his skin as I licked.

My body was wet with the anticipation of Vincent's touch and he didn't make me wait for it. Grabbing me up from the roof he quickly flipped me over, my hands catching on the brick of the chimney as he ripped my panties off and threw them to the other side of the roof.

I could feel his hardness as he teased me, bathing himself in the wetness between my thighs and setting my body on fire! I bit my lower lip, gripping the brick of the chimney as he finally plunged inside me.

"Mmm.." I moaned as he began to slide in deeper and deeper; moving my hips in rhythm with his.

Digging at the brick, I crumbled the corners into dust as the feeling intensified and as my eyes started to flutter. I let out a heavier moan of pleasure as Vincent sped up. Grabbing a fist full of my curls he pulled hard and sank his teeth into my neck, making our bodies tremble with passion as we both exploded from the inside out.

I had never experienced sex as a human but God how I loved my life now! I couldn't have asked for anything better at that moment. I came to the realization that Hazel was (as Angeline would have so crudely categorized) "A Fucking Idiot!"

I chuckled at the thought while I fixed my gown. It would figure that even at a moment like this Angeline still found a way into my head.

"What are you chuckling at over there?" Vincent asked as he tried to catch his breath while he fastened his pants with a smile.

"Just at how stupid Hazel was to not want this life." I left out what Angeline and I had talked about earlier and more importantly *how* Angeline talked.

"Yes, well I am pretty amazing." He said smugly.

“You’re very smug, do you know that?” I asked him wrapping my arms around his waist.

“Sometimes, but is it still considered arrogance when others agree with you?”

“Oh shut up, you weren’t that good.” I argued stepping back with a smile.

“No, then why are you still smiling?”

“I’m not.” I said through flattened out lips trying hard not to grin.

“Yes, I can see that.” He replied gesturing towards my pitiful attempt at a straight face.

The problem was, that he was that good and he knew it, the perks of a three hundred year old “husband”.

I finally broke and just laughed making him laugh in return.

I crushed my lips against his, breaking his laughter and he ran his fingers through my disheveled hair as I wrapped my arms around his neck.

“Are you ready to go home?” I whispered.

“Yes my darling, it’s been a long night; I’m sure we could both use the rest.” He answered running his finger down the bridge of my nose.

I smiled up at him mischievously and whispered back. “Who said anything about rest?”

Chapter 21.

I laid tucked away on Vincent's arm and bare chest as my eyes slowly opened the next night. It was later than usual and I was still somewhat groggy. Vincent and I had been um… awake, most of the morning so we didn't actually get to bed until noon-ish.

The softness of his breathing told me he was still in a deep sleep and last nights meal was barely a flutter in his chest. He was completely exhausted, the poor guy, I completely tuckered him out.

I used the tip of my pointer finger to softly make swirls and shapes on his face and the arm that lay over me hugging me in close to his body. I knew he would wake up to my touch but I also knew he would enjoy it.

"Mm… Good evening." he said smiling with his eyes still closed.

"Good evening, back. I said and kissed his cheek.

"Did you sleep well?" I asked still tickling his arm.

"Yes, and you?" he answered opening his eyes.

"Too well, I didn't move all afternoon."

"Neither did I, but where could I go that would be better than this?" he said as he ran a finger up my arm.

"My thoughts exactly."

His chest rumbled with laughter under my head and I chuckled along with him.

"You're in awful high spirits tonight." He mused.

"Yes, well, the love of a good man will do that to a girl." I teased back.

"Not bad for someone so smug." he bragged as he patted my shoulder.

"I stand corrected and I have to admit for once being proven wrong was nice." I said giving him lifted eyebrows.

"It's about time you give me my appropriate appraisal."

"Mm… any time." I said kissing his neck just under his ear.

"You keep that up and we'll never get out of bed."

"And what's wrong with that? We're supposed to be married right?"

"Yes, it's certainly an easier explanation."

"Well this can be the honeymoon. I said proudly and went to nibbling instead of kissing.

"Is there food on this honeymoon?"

"I have all u can eat right here." I said in-between nibbling and licking his neck and earlobe.

Vincent laughed and then flipped me over pinning me underneath him. "Mm… I bet you do." He smiled and pressed his lips to mine and began massaging his tongue against mine.

I arched my back pressing my body against his in anticipation as he ran his hand up my thigh, stopping and running just one of his fingers up my slit he tapped me once and got up. "But first we eat."

"Tease!" I yelled and used my elbows to prop myself up so I could glare at him from the bed.

He gave me his mischievous grin and said "The sooner we leave the sooner we can come back."

I didn't move at first I just continued to glare to show him my unappreciation for this little stunt.

"If you remember correctly," he said grabbing a pair of under shorts form the drawer. "I didn't eat that much last night and then I got held captive and made to work for hours and hours until after daybreak." he said in an exaggerated tone.

"Oh? Well I can make sure that you're never made to work again… if it was that much of an inconvenience to you?"

"Hold on Delilah, I never said I was inconvenienced. No need to go to extremes here. I just want some food. Then I'm all yours to do with me what you will. I live to serve."

That's what I thought! Instead of saying that, I smiled and then in a flash I had my naked body back up against his bare chest with my legs wrapped around his now clothed waist. His arms instinctively held me up which left him defenseless. "Anything I want if you get food?" I asked smiling up at him. Before he had a chance to answer I pressed my lips back to his fiercely.

"Anything." He agreed breathlessly when we pulled apart.

"Alright!" I said hopping down.

At first he just stood there, and I could tell he was fighting with himself over whether food was really worth the sacrifice or not. Until finally he said "Yes, food first but then you better be aware, my sweet Delilah."

I giggled with anticipation and then we both rushed to get dressed because he was right. The sooner we got out of our room, the sooner we could come back.

* * *

We stood in front of a little place that was so crowded with people that the party spilled out onto the street. People dancing and couples gyrating to the beat of the jazz that surrounded them.

It was nice to just have a good time and it seemed that New Orleans knew exactly how to do that, which suited me just fine.

"I thought everybody was on Lent?" I asked Vincent as I looked around at all the party goers.

"Not yet. Mardi Gras has parades and parties going on basically all month before Lent.." He answered.

"Works for me. It makes shadowing that much easier."

"I agree."

"So Mr. Vanhorne, what cha in the mood for? We've got tourist, native, young, old, male *and* female." I teased.

"Well, Mrs. Vanhorne, I think I'll browse for a while before I make my selection, if you don't mind?"

"Why sir, take your time. Down hea in New Orleans, we have some of the finest food available." I said using a very New Orleans accent.

"Why thank you, I think I will." He teased back.

"Any time, any time. Shall we walk then?" I asked looping my arm through his.

"Why yes, I think that would be just fine, just fine indeed."

We strolled through the city spotting party after party until we decided to join the fun. We stopped in at a little restaurant by the river. It had petite round tables covered in white linens and a little stage sat in the front so every eye could see the band that filled the air with more jazz.

The tables were set far enough away so that there was room to dance and I could see that there were already couples on the floor swinging and swaying to the horns that filled the room with music.

I was excited to join in on the fun so I grabbed Vincent by the hand and drug him into the middle of the crowd.

We danced and he swung me all over that floor while secretly seeking out someone we could eat.

"What about that blonde one over there?" I asked as he brought me into him.

"No champagne tonight, I think maybe something a bit darker."

Hmm… I kept searching the crowd for something darker that might spike his interest. I scanned the dancing crowd with each spin and twirl through blonde and brunette, until I spotted her. She was a taller, thinner woman with short black hair and caramel colored skin. She was dancing with another woman that was around the same height but she was thicker than her friend and she had longer auburn hair and fair skin.

"Dip me and look over me when you do." I whispered in his ear.

He dipped me low and glanced at the dancing girls before pulling me back up.

"Aren't they perfect?" I asked before he twirled me back out.

"I believe they are." He said with a grin and began spinning me towards the two girls.

"Isn't this band just the bees knees?" I asked when I was close enough so they could hear me.

"They sure are!" The one with auburn hair agreed.

"Say big daddy have you got a cigarette?" The black haired one asked.

"Unfortunately not, but we were on our way out to pick some up. If you ladies would like to join my wife and I, we could get some for you as well?" Vincent offered with a smile.

I smiled at his conniving nature as he baited the girls. He really was a creative little devil sometimes.

"That sounds swell. I'm Casey and this is my cousin Kate," the auburn haired one introduced.

"Nice to meet you, I'm Delilah and this is Vincent." I replied. We led the girls off the floor and back out to the street so we could "go get their cigarettes."

“So what brings you two to New Orleans?” Casey asked as we walked.

“Honeymooning.” I answered with a bashful smile and looped my arm through Vincent’s.

“Newlyweds, how swell.” Kate mused with a smile. “I always wanted to get married but I just neva found the right guy.”

“I never did either; he found me.” I answered leaning my head against Vincent’s arm and rubbing it affectionately.

“You’re just a regular cake eata aint cha?” Kate teased smiling at Vincent.

He just laughed in response —like you are going to think cake eater while I am eating you.— I smiled with him, guessing his thoughts.

“Couldn’t we have bought cigarettes in the restaurant?” Casey asked as we walked.

“I asked the cigarette girl shortly before you asked my husband but she had run out.” I answered. “The store is right over there though, then we can go back.”

I looked at Vincent with a playful expression letting my eyes glisten with the thought that our game was about to get much more interesting.

“I should have known betta then to where my new shoes to go out dancin. My feet are killin me.” Casey complained.

Ah, opportunity, I thought.

“Then why don’t I stay here with you? Vincent and Kate can go get our cigarettes and meet us back here. That will give your feet time to rest." I so casually suggested.

"Sounds swell." Casey chimed in.

Sooo easy!

"Are you sure?" Kate asked looking worried.

"I've got blistas on my feet the size of my thumb." Casey answered holding out her thumb for emphasis. "I'm sure."

"The store his just around that corner." Vincent said pointing, "We'll be back within a few minutes."

"I'll look after her, don't worry. We'll just go sit over there and wait for you." I said pointing to the little secluded area off the main street.

I could see Vincent's eyes dance in the moonlight as I spoke.

"Alright then, we'll be back in a flash." Kate hesitantly agreed.

I kissed Vincent and whispered "Enjoy your meal she looks good," in his ear to low for either of the girls to hear me.

"You too my darling," he whispered back before we pulled apart.

"We'll just be over there when you come back." I called as they started to walk. More for Vincent's sake because it wouldn't matter in a minute for Kate.

"Alright," he answered as they continued to walk.

I sighed watching him turn the corner and disappear.

"How long have you two been married?" Casey asked me as we walked.

"Since November." I answered smiling to myself.

"He sure is handsome." Casey mused.

"Yeah, he sure is," I agreed, leading her away from the lights and sounds of the busy city.

When we got far enough away from prying eyes I added "and just as deadly too." and smiled at her showing off my long white fangs.

Her face drained of all its color as she stood frozen with fear. I loved this part!

She started to scream but I choked it off by lifting her off the ground one handed by her throat. She gurgled and kicked, her shoes falling to the ground below her, while her eyes started to bulge under the pressure. I laughed as I slowly began to ascend still holding her by one hand.

Her hands were clutched around my wrist digging her nails into my skin as she struggled and gasped for air. I slid my other arm around her waist and tilted her head to the side so I could sink my teeth into the throbbing vein in her neck.

I drank her in thinking about how feisty this one was and wondered if Kate was any kind of challenge for Vince while we moved closer to the water. I sucked out all of her warmth and soon her struggles seized leaving me able to gnaw at her flesh in different spots to make sure I got every last drop of her.

I lifted away once she was bone dry and tilted her face up to caress her long auburn hair. Her green eyes that had shinned like emeralds were now glazed over like the eyes on a dead fish.

I kissed her on the cheek and took one last look at her pale but still beautiful face before I released my hold of her body and let her plummet into the awaiting water.

Slowly I descended back to the ground and found Vincent patiently waiting for me.

"You seem to have taken quite a calling to your new gift."

"Yes, and now that I'm learning how to use it better it's a lot of fun. How was your dinner?"

"Delightful, and yours?"

"Surprisingly spicy, and tender." I answered letting myself become wrapped in the memory of how soft her skin was and that amazing feeling when my teeth broke through it.

Then a smile suddenly lit up my face as I recalled our little deal "You did say anything?" I said teasing his chest with my fingertip. "Didn't you?"

He smirked back. "Now that you mention it. I do recall saying something to that nature. Yes." He kissed me hungrily and I felt his heartbeat quicken against my body sending my heart to race with his. Our senses were on high now and the thought that his touch was only minutes away drove me to do what I hadn't tried yet. I wrapped my arms tighter around his waist and shot us both into the midnight sky. Lost in our kiss I trusted my instincts to direct me back to our house and back to the bed that awaited us there.

Chapter 22.

I felt his weight beside me on the bed before he whispered "Happy Anniversary my Darling." Kissing my forehead to wake me up, I smiled and wrapped my arms around him, squishing him to my body and flipping him over so I was on top. As I opened my eyes he smiled making my heart melt. It was hard to believe we had been together for a whole year now.

"You have to get dressed, I have a surprise waiting for you down stairs."

"What kind of surprise?" I asked kissing his jaw line. I loved his surprises they were always something good and usually in a big box.

"I can't tell you. It will ruin all my hard work." He grinned. "The first part is waiting for you on your vanity bench just over your shoulder. Are you going to get up?"

"Are you really sure you want me to get up?" I asked as I lightly ran my nails down his chest over his white dress shirt. "We could always stay in bed?"

"Mmm… So tempting." he replied twirling one of my curls in between his fingers. But he stood up, taking me with him, kissed me on my nose and set me on the floor.

"Well considering I'm standing now, I guess I'll get up." I laughed.

"I thought you might be a little more excited but if you would rather sleep I can always return things?" He casually suggested.

"No, after you went through so much trouble. It would be rude of me to waste it." I couldn't help my smile.

"Yes it would. Come." He grabbed me by the waist and pulled me towards the vanity bench. "To start the evening." He gestured to the white box.

I opened the lid and in between the white tissue paper sat a cobalt blue gown. It was sleeveless with a V neckline and long as I pulled it from the box. I looked to Vincent and he was beaming. I think he liked giving me presents as much as I liked getting them! I loved his taste. Everything was always the finest and most elegant anyone could buy.

Also in the box were black nylon stockings,garters and long white, satin gloves. Under the bench sat black heals with straps.

"I don't know what to say." I admitted looking at everything; my eyes welling up with red tears.

"Don't cry my love. This is a happy occasion." He said using his thumbs to wipe under my eyes.

"Thank you." I whispered and kissed his lips.

"You are most welcome. Now, no more tears. I have a few more things to arrange. Meet me down stairs in an hour?"

"Okay." I answered and smiled.

"Good. I shall see you soon then." He kissed me again on the cheek and headed for the door.

I dressed quickly so I could spend a little more time on my hair. I knew Vincent didn't want me to cut it short but that didn't mean I couldn't pin it up! I brushed and molded my ruby locks pinning it under as I went to create the perfect faux bob. I stood putting my leg on the bench to put my nylons on followed by my strappy heels.

Afterwards I walked while sliding on my gloves to the full length mirror to take a peek before I went down stairs. I stopped sudden. I didn't know what to do. I had never looked this modern, ever. The dress, the hair, the gloves, all of it was new. I felt my hair and checked the back just to make sure it wasn't going anywhere and smiled. I hoped he liked it but there was only one way to know for sure. I turned away from my reflection and headed for the door.

When I reached the bottom of the stairs Vincent was talking with Red. I smiled when I watched him double take when he saw me. It looked like he stopped breathing let alone talking. Red also turned around because Vincent was a statue.

"You boys look like you've seen a ghost?"

Vince shook his head "An angel." he replied walking towards me. He looked as beautiful as usual. He wore a tailored blue suit, and jacket with a white shirt, black tie and polished wingtip shoes.

"Fallen maybe?" I suggested as Vincent took my arm and both the guys laughed.

"You two enjoy your evening." Red said with a nod.

“Thank you Red. You too.” I offered and winked at him when Vincent wasn’t looking.

“Yes, Thank you for all your help to make this night special.” Vincent said and clapped him on the shoulder.

“So where to now?” I asked.

“Not far, just to the dinning room.”

“What for? We don’t eat, remember?”

“You’ll see.”

He led me through the house to the dinning room where there were white candlesticks lit all around, a white lace table cloth covered the long rectangular table. Crystal wine glasses sat at the head of the table and the seat to the right as well and a crystal vase sat in the center holding a huge bouquet of white roses.

“This, is beautiful.” I was in awe. Everything looked amazing.

“Come, sit.”

He held out my chair for me making sure I was properly seated before he sat down.

“Are you hungry?” he asked

“Starving, bu—”

He held out his hand to stop me. He then snapped his fingers and two people, a man and a woman, came out from the kitchen. The woman stood to his right and the man stood to my right. Both were young and attractive, dressed in evening wear and also blonde.

I looked to them and back to Vincent not quite understanding what was happening here. He winked at me then began to explain.

"Remember Ezra telling you about what he called "Taps?"

I thought back to the night of the Ball and Ezra explaining that some vampires kept humans for feeding purposes because they could erase the memory of it later.

I nodded. "Yes, I remember but how did you do it?"

"I called in a favor from a friend. I thought you might like an old fashioned sit down dinner."

"I'm impressed." I admitted. "So how does this work?"

"Quite Simply. Susanna, would you be a doll and hand me your wrist please?"

I watched as Susanna smiled and replied "Of course." and offered him her arm without hesitation. Vincent grabbed a hold of her arm and also the wine glass in front of him. He bit into Susanna's wrist and she sighed almost half moaned in response then held it over the glass until it was half full. He handed her a napkin "Thank you Susanna, dress your wound."

She nodded and held the napkin to her wrist to stop the bleeding and took a step back.

"Your turn. Your vessels name is Samuel. If you haven't noticed they do look quite a bit alike. Not only are they related but they are twins!" he smiled.

This was definitely unusual. I had never made eating so personal before. I didn't get this close to my food but he did go through a lot of trouble to make tonight special so I thought, why not?.

"Samuel, could you give me your wrist please?" I did notice Vincent was polite so I figured I would also be nice. I'm sure they were to be returned later. He did as he was asked and he too looked pleased when I sank my teeth into his skin. I filled my glass in the same manner as Vincent and handed Samuel a napkin. "Thank you Samuel." I added as he stepped back out of view.

I lifted my glass. "I would like to make a toast." Vincent cocked his head to the side in surprise and gestured toward me for me to continue. I took a deep breath and opened my heart up to tell him the things I rarely said out loud.

"I haven't been immortal long enough to imagine eternity being a reality but if I'm going to live forever I can't think of a better person to share it with. My loving Vincent you are patient, understanding, smart, talented and… breathtakingly beautiful." I smiled at him and continued. "You came into my life suddenly and changed everything I thought I knew about the world and most importantly, you changed what I thought I knew about myself." I was starting to get chocked up but was doing my best to keep the tears from ruining my face and dress. "It has only been a year but I'm so excited and curious to see what other amazing things this life, this unbelievable gift, will bring the two of us in the many years to come." I held up my glass and Vincent did the same "I love you." I said

"And I love you my darling Delilah." We both clanked our glasses softly and drank.

After we sat our glasses down Vincent grabbed my hands in his. "That toast was an unexpected surprise and delight! You are so unbelievably amazing and every night I never think I can love you more and every night you surprise me and prove me wrong. My life has been long but never fulfilled until I met you. You make my heart whole and my life complete."

Wow, I sat in amazement while he spoke. He had such a way with words but I never thought I meant as much to him as he did to me. "It has been an amazing year huh?" I smiled and so did he both of us with red tears threatening to spill on to our cheeks.

"It has indeed." he agreed. "I love you." He leaned down and kissed my hands. He really was so loving, I was a lucky woman.

"I have something I would like to give you as well." I said standing up. "Stay here and I'll be back in a jiffy."

I didn't get him presents like he did me but I did ask Red to help me a couple weeks ago to get him something nice to surprise him. I had no idea he was planning all of this but I did remember the date so I thought it would be nice to get him a thank you gift.

I quickly headed for our room to get it from my top drawer and came back down stairs with the small box in my hands. I couldn't help but smile when I set it on the table in front of him. I hadn't been able to give him anything like this before.

"What's this?" He asked

"A thank you gift." I said simply and sat down to take another drink from my glass.

He slowly grabbed the box and opened the lid and I tried to sit still. I was excited to see his reaction and could now understand why he always looked happier than me when he gave me things. I really hoped he liked it.

"Oh, wow…" He said "What beautiful cuff links."

"I had them made special so they would match the necklace you gave me on the bridge." I explained

"With a little extra flare I see."

"Well, who doesn't love a little sparkle?" I winked at him. Not only were they tear shaped rubies but I had each one surrounded by small diamonds for a little extra pizzazz!

"Do you like them?"

"I love them! They are stunning, and very thoughtful Delilah. Thank you."

I know my smile had to be huge. He liked them! "You are most welcome." I answered.

"Will you help me with them?" He asked, surprising me.

"Are you sure? They don't match the suit you're wearing tonight. It won't hurt my feelings if you wait."

"That's absurd, I'm pretty sure rubies and diamonds can go with anything." he laughed.

"If you insist." I took his wrist and undid his other cufflink and set it on the table and he handed me the new one and I fastened it. When both were in place he looked at them again admiringly. He leaned over and kissed me.

"Thank you." He whispered and sat back down.

"You are most welcome." I answered. I thought I would lighten the mood a little bit. I sat back in my chair and grabbed my glass "So what are the rules for our dinner tonight?" I asked then taking a sip.

"The rules?"

"Yes, I'm assuming they're borrowed. What can or can't we do with them?"

"I see, I suppose yes, they are borrowed. I was asked not to kill them."

"That's it?"

"Yes."

"I noticed they seem to like being bit. That's part of the illusion right?"

"Yes, it is done so there is no resistance. It keeps both parties satisfied and able to keep an ongoing arrangement."

"Will they remember this afterwards?"

"Probably not. I suppose it depends on what happens tonight." He looked at me with a smirk.

"I'll behave myself. I promise." I reassured. He knew me well. I'm sure he was suspicious with every question.

I downed the last of my glass and called out to Samuel "I think I'll drink straight from the source…

If that's okay?" I looked from Samuel to Vincent for the go ahead.

"Yes of course, you know the one rule." He seemed genuinely unconcerned so I continued.

I stood and lightly placed my hand on the side of Samuel's head "Could you tilt your head a bit for me please?"

"With pleasure." he replied and tilted for me.

I bit down softly and drank in the heat I was looking for. A glass looked nicer but nothing beat the taste of a straight vein. After a couple pulls I stopped to look up at Vincent, "Join me for a drink?" I smiled a blood stained smile and he laughed and shook his head. "You're really something. A small drink." He clarified. "Too much and I break my word to a very old friend."

"Samuel, please give Vince your un-bitten wrist." He did so without complaint and Vincent took a hold of his arm with both hands. "Cheers." I said with a smirk and we both bit down together. This time Samuel did moan which was a new reaction for me but I liked it. It was almost sexual and kind of arousing. Here we were drinking from the same person but not allowed to kill him. What would happen if we did? The thought of breaking our only rule was intriguing so that made it exciting! I pulled a few more times but I let go. I didn't want to jeopardize Vincent's friendship, he went through a lot of trouble to make this night special and I would respect his one condition.

When I lifted up Vincent was looking at me and he smiled and started to sit.

“Samuel, you can go see Red. We won’t be needing you again tonight.” I Thought I would dismiss him now before I broke my promise.

“You handled that nicely.”

“I’m a woman of my word.” I said as I wiped my mouth with the napkin, sitting.

“So I see.”

“This is nice.”

“But?”

“But what?” I asked

“You’re bored aren’t you?”

“No, not at all. We’ve never ate in the dining room. It’s a nice change and quiet.”

“And boring.”

“I didn’t say that. This is very considerate.”

He just glared at me. I didn’t want to hurt his feelings but I was used to going out at night. It was exciting and sometimes we went dancing and I loved to dance!

“Okay, I’m bored! I’m sorry. I do really appreciate this. It’s beautiful and elegant and thought—…”

He held out his hand to stop me. “Delilah stop, I figured this would happen.” He laughed. “We can go out.”

“Really?” I was a little shocked but also hopeful.

“Of course. Let’s go.”

I stood up and pushed in my chair. “What about Susanna?” I asked.

“She’ll be fine. Red will take them both to a guest room. We’re free to leave whenever you’d like.”

“Then let’s go!” I was excited!

After leaving the house I convinced Vincent to go dancing. We both looked so good I couldn’t see wasting it. We really let loose, we danced and laughed and really enjoyed the night.

As we headed out to walk around for a little while before we headed back I laced my fingers through Vince’s and put my head on his arm I was happy, really happy—until I started to disappear that is.

“Vince!” I said looking down at my hand —or rather looking *through* my hand. The only thing that was there was a wrist and a lingering trail of smoke. I moved my arm and the smoke followed.

I glanced down at the other hand to see if it was still there, nope just more smoke.

I looked up at Vincent confused and scared, to see that his face was completely calm and he was smiling.

“How can you be so calm at a time like this?” I yelled. “I’m disappearing!”

“Because it is your birthday Delilah. Your *one year* birthday. He answered calmly.

I started to yell at him and tell him who cares about my stupid birthday, I’m disappearing! Until his words really caught up with me. My one year birthday. On our first year anniversary we get our defensive gift.

I'm guessing Vincent saw realization light up my eyes because he gripped me up, spinning me around and smothered me with kisses and laughter.

"My gift?" I said through a smile looking up at Vince's sparkling eyes.

"Your gift," he agreed brushing a fallen curl away from my face.

"But how do I get my hands to come back?" I asked curiously.

"The same way you do everything else. Our gifts are tied to our emotions. Think about what it is you want to do, and do it." He answered in his matter of fact way.

"I don't know why I even ask you; you're never any help." I grumped.

"Sure I am." He laughed.

I just looked at his cocky grin and shook my head in disapproval.

All right then. Just think about what I want to do, and do it. Just think about what I want to do, and do it. I mentally coached myself over and over. But what did I want? You want your hands to come back of course. I yelled at myself. Didn't I? But what if I could do this to my entire body? What if I could disappear completely? Wasn't it worth at least testing it out? Answer? Of course it was. After all, it was late and most of the late night crowd had already settled in for the night. So with my eyes closed I thought about what I wanted, and that was to let the dark smoke consume my entire body.

“Delilah darling, I think you’re going in the wrong direction.” Vincent’s voice broke through my concentration.

I opened my eyes to see that all of my lower body was nothing but black lingering smoke.

I gave Vincent an excited grin and breathed in deeply before concentrating (with my eyes open this time) on disappearing.

I watched his eyes glisten as the rest of me vanished. It was a strange feeling to see everything so clearly but not see myself.

I had gotten used to rising so to feel the wind against me wasn’t an unusual feeling. But this was different;   I was part of the wind. I could feel every current flow through me like a soft feather tickling my insides.

I used both of my abilities to swirl myself around Vincent and let out a soft giggle as his body brushed against mine, tickling me in that strange new way.

This I could get used to, I thought swaying in the wind. It was odd that even my clothes and jewelry vanished. But I guess they were an extension of myself so why wouldn’t they? All well, I sighed, for whatever reason, it worked, and for that I was grateful. I mean how awful would it be for me to have to get naked then tote my clothes around with me? Yes, this was much better.

After playing with Vince I decided it was time to have a body again, so I stopped swirling around and started to wish I was whole.

Soon I stopped feeling the wind blow through me and it didn't take long for me to feel a solid shell enclose my misty form.

Vincent took my hands in his as I opened my eyes.

"Nice to see you again." He said and pressed his soft lips to mine.

"Mm… yes," I sighed. "It is good to be seen too." I agreed when we broke apart.

"Shall we go home now? I still have 1 more thing I want to give you before this night ends." He said giving me a lifted eyebrow for emphasis.

"Why Mr. Vanhorne I'm shocked!" I said with a devious grin.

"Just wait until we get home."

I giggled in anticipation looping my arm in his as we raced back to our house.

Mist:

The air blows right through me and I'm out of sight. I'm free, no form to encase me, I'm now one with the night. Swirling and soaring, loving all this. I'm death rolling through, as the ebony mist.

Delilah Vanhorne- 1930

Chapter 23.

After nights of trying to get my new gift under control I learned that being able to turn myself into black smoke was pretty swell.

Vincent and I had started experimenting with the possibilities one night at home. He casually suggested I try to be inhaled. Of course I thought the idea was crazy.

“Have you ever heard of anyone doing this?” I asked skeptically.

“No, in fact you constantly surprise and amaze me.”

“Well, I am pretty amazing.” I teased back. “So, how do I do this then?”

“First see if you can thin out your form?” He suggested.

“And what exactly is wrong with my form?!” I mocked outrage.

“I apologize, your smoke, thin out your smoke to make you lighter and easier to inhale.” he smiled.

“Now you wish I were lighter?”

“Are you done?”

“Maybe.” I smiled. I loved to frustrate him.

He just glared at me from one of the chairs in the Parlor.

“Okay, I’ll behave myself, I promise.”

"Good. Now, do as usual to become your smoky form."

I closed my eyes and within seconds I was whirling around him.

"Excellent! Now, concentrate on the feeling of spreading yourself out."

"Like a hug?" I asked.

"I suppose, but bigger."

I thought for a minute on how I was supposed to do that? Strangely I remembered the summers in Detroit. It got so hot in my room I would stretch myself out as far as I could go on my bed, trying to keep anything from touching (and sticking) to anything else. Maybe that would work?

I spread out my arms and legs as far as they could go.

"Is that any better?" I asked.

"You do look wider."

"Watch it." I warned.

"Dear God help me." He said shaking his head. "Your SMOKE looks much wider Darling. But THE SMOKE doesn't look any thinner."

I giggled. "Okay, maybe it's internal?" I suggested.

"Perhaps, do what you feel."

If my physical actions dictated my shape, maybe my subconscious would change its consistency? I simply thought about being thinner (I would never tell Vince that) and hoped that worked.

I even thought about the color and lightened it in my head to white and as invisible as possible.

"Amazing." was all I heard.

I looked to what should have been my arms but it was so light I could barely see anything.

"I did it! Now what?" I asked excited.

"Hang on, I'll be right back."

He darted out of the room and came back holding a big jug, a vase, and a decanter.

"What are those for?" I asked looking at them.

"To see if you can fit yourself inside, of course."

"Oh, of course." I agreed sarcastically.

"Try the jug first, it's larger."

"Just smash myself in there? What if I get stuck?"

"It's a clay jug Delilah, I can get you out… Rather I will or not is another matter." He smiled deviously.

"Ha Ha… Very funny."

"Oh, come on. If you think you're stuck just solidify your form and it will break."

Seriously, why didn't I think of that?

"All right. Here I go. No funny business though." I warned, just in case.

He put one hand in the air. "You have my word."

I moved over to the jug, it had a smaller opening then the vase but the bottom was a lot larger. I wasn't sure about this at all but I thought about shrinking down and diving in, like swimming.

It was dark inside and cool and honestly it still smelled like earth but I didn't feel smashed or cramped, it really was like swimming in cool water!

"Everything alright?" I heard from outside the jug.

"Actually, yes! It's just fine." I answered back. This was so neat!

"Can you get out?"

I looked up to the hole at the top and it looked a lot bigger from this angle meaning I was a lot smaller than I thought.

"Yes, definitely."

I headed for the light at the top and before I knew it I was lingering around in front of Vincent again.

I was getting tired though so I thought about being whole again.

"How was it, did you have enough room?" He asked smiling.

"Amazing. I could even swirl around inside!"

"Unbelievable. Can you imagine the possibilities? Who knows what this new ability could be used for?"

"Well, not tonight, I'm tired. I think I'll have to practice more before it comes in handy." I yawned and stretched.

"We have plenty of time my love." He put his arms around me and kissed the top of my head.

* * *

I got good in the following months. It started out slow but I wanted to be useful so I pushed myself hard every night. I wanted to have an edge on our enemy so I toyed and played with my victims.

Vincent had been right about being inhaled. I could seep into their bodies through their mouth or their nose but I took it another step further once I accomplished that. I found that I could attach myself to their heart like a leach and suck them dry from the inside or just smother them, letting them drown in smoke.

Night after night I went out and I hunted, trying new things and as the decades passed I added to my collections of murderous qualifications.

Now I had Smoking, Rising and of course Somnolence. I had to admit I was doing pretty well. What I couldn't rise above I could just smoke and go through.

With all of my abilities perfected I couldn't understand why I was still arguing with Vincent over the human ordeal.

"And why exactly can't we start going after them?" I argued. "It's been two decades since Ramiel and Fidelia's slaughters and we still haven't done anything about it!"

"That very reason is why we have yet to see any of the Rising Sons in so long Delilah. If we give ourselves away they won't simply sit by and watch; they'll retaliate with forces unimaginable."

"With what the Elders can do alone we can over power them, plus the gifts each of us have. I know others will stand with us. Angeline and Ezra will; I know for sure, and with Angeline's ability to force thoughts they don't stand a chance."

“Maybe, but I still won’t risk those lives unnecessarily right now when there’s no danger.”

“You know very well that just because there’s no danger here doesn’t mean that there is no danger. You’ve heard the news about the attacks; maybe more so then me. Vampires are still dropping like flies somewhere else.” I fought back.

“Yes, I have heard the stories but you are my only concern, and as long as you are safe then I will not willingly bring them to our doorstep.”

“Fine! But I shouldn‘t be your only concern, think about the countless other vampires that you once considered friends. Think about Nariyoll and what they did to him?” I shot back annoyed.

“I am sorry for all of them but we both know that Nariyoll went looking for death after the Hazel incident and getting ourselves slaughtered will not bring him, or any of the others back.”

Of course I knew that, every vampire knew the story of how depression tugged at Nariyoll after Hazel refused this life. Unfortunately he never got out, The Rising Sons picked him off just a few short months after her death. Most believe he went searching for them but no one truly knows for sure what happened that night. Just another tragic ending for one more of our kind.

“I can’t believe you sometimes?!” I yelled aloud as I stalked through the double doors to the balcony of our newest house. I had to get some fresh air.

I glided up to the top of our roof and sat in my usual place just above the attic window of the modest white house.

I started to sit up there in the summer months when we first moved here and I wanted some time to think. Vincent was always his polite self and gave me as much time as I needed. And why was I mad at him anyway? It wasn't his fault vampires were dying; it was their fault! The thought just made me angrier and I was getting hot at the thought. I took a deep breath to cool down and told myself that's not why I was up here. I was supposed to be calming down.

Of course Vincent didn't want to fight if he didn't have too. Shouldn't I want the same thing? We were safe as far as we knew. It had been many years since that horrible night in Chicago. We could stay here forever (literally) and never see them again for all we knew; shouldn't that be good news? My head was screaming, yes of course it is! But there was just something in my gut that was screaming back, they're getting closer and you know it! And that's the part I couldn't get to shut up and that's also the part that I couldn't get anyone to believe.

I continued to sit up there for a little while trying to make something out of this overwhelming feeling I had.

Did vampires have intuition? Of course we did when it came to hunting but there was still a lot of things that I didn't understand about this life (as Vincent kept reminding me) and if we do then why am I the only one feeling like this?

I looked to the sky for help. The moon always seemed to comfort me when I needed it but tonight the sky was black. There would be no comfort from the moon tonight. “Figures,” I huffed at the absence of the moon.

“So what now?” I asked myself aloud. “I have no idea.” I answered in disgust shaking my head, sitting alone on the roof of my house.

But either way I didn't want to sit up there all night. Honestly I wasn't getting anywhere with my mood, I went from frustrated to aggravated. Great!

I sighed and tried to shake off the rest of my bad mood before I dropped off the roof landing softly on the grass in front of the house.

“Feeling better?” Vincent asked with a smile.

“No!” I shot back making his smile grow even bigger.

“Yes, I can see that the moon was of no help tonight.” He said gesturing toward the black sky.

“No, she wasn't. I guess I will just have to figure it out on my own.” I said with a sigh.

“If things are still bothering you tomorrow night I'm sure you'll be able to seek guidance from her then?”

“I hope so. I could have used her tonight for sure.”

“Well you could try asking me, maybe I could substitute?” He offered.

“I did try talking to you. You're the reason I'm out here talking to the moon!” I answered gesturing to the empty sky.

“No, that wasn’t a conversation between two people, that was a trial. You were clearly trying to plead your case to me.”

“Either way it didn’t work.”

“Why are you so obsessed with this?” he asked frustrated.

“I’m not obsessed. I just know there is something already coming. I can’t explain how I know. I just know.”

“The Rising Sons?” he asked his expression changing to worry.

“Just danger, but I’m pretty sure it’s them. I can feel it. And we’re not going to have to give ourselves away, they already know where we are.”

“You can feel it that strongly?” he asked in wonder.

“Yes.”

“We should leave then. Maybe if we keep moving it will make it difficult to track us.”

I knew he was just adding me into his thought process as he spoke but I —like usual— spoke up anyway.

“Running isn’t the answer Vincent.” I said taking his hand in mine to stop his pacing.

“I won’t let them harm you Delilah, even if it means running forever. As long as you are safe and I can still tuck you away every dawn in my arms then I’m a satisfied man.” He finished by pulling me in to him and kissing me sweetly on the top of my head.

"I never realized that I was worth that many." I said bitterly looking up at him. I couldn't help how cold it came out.

Instead of him getting angry he simply looked down at me with red tears rimming his eyes and said. "A million of them couldn't replace you, I thought you knew that." and let me go then walked into the house.

I just stood there on the verge of tears myself thinking about the situation we were facing.

If we continued to do nothing, more would die. If we did do something it was possible that Vincent or I might die. Either way someone would be lost and no matter what someone would suffer from either decision we made.

I reluctantly followed him into the house to find him sitting in the dark living room in one of the corner chairs we rarely used.

"I'm sorry." I said standing in the door way.

"I understand that you don't want anything to happen to me Vince. Don't you think I feel the same way about you? I don't know what I would do if I lost you. I only want us to be ready because the time is coming and we're going to have to defend ourselves. They're not going to give us the opportunity to run away next time."

"I know." He answered from the darkness. "Just understand that I will not intentionally put you in harms way. If they come, then we will do what we must."

"I understand that, but it won't be much longer; I'm telling you they're on the way here."

"And we'll be waiting." He answered coldly.

I walked to the chair where he sat and kissed the top of his head. "I love you, you know?" I whispered playing with his hair.

"I do," He agreed right before pulling me into his lap leaving my feet to hang over the arm of the chair. "And I love you back." I could hear the smile in his voice as he told me he loved me and I couldn't help a smile of my own in response.

"And always remember that I'll love you for all eternity." He whispered running his finger down the bridge of my nose.

"Eternity." I agreed before kissing him and snuggling even closer into his strong but loving arms.

Chapter 24.

March was once again upon us so we traveled to this year's secret location. The Ball was held at a beautiful old theater in Germany. Vincent said it had been completely destroyed in the war but they started rebuilding as soon as Hitler was gone. So far half was finished and we were given permission to use that half.

The entrance into the Ballroom was big with red carpeted floors and two sets of golden double doors that were being held open for us by good looking male vampires in black tuxedos.

When we entered the main area there was a huge domed ceiling made of glass so you could see the twinkling stars in the night time sky. All around the room held sculptures carved out of the creamy marble walls of women and men. Some were wrapped in each others arms, others were alone holding their arms and hands in different poses. Some were mostly naked, wearing sculpted draping material and others wore nothing at all.

Soft light filled the room from the brass and crystal sconces that hung on the walls. The seats hadn't been added yet leaving a huge dance floor and in front of the stage sat the five matching chairs awaiting each Elder.

On the side of the room sat round tables covered in red linens that held two lighted white candlesticks in crystal holders to add more glow to the area. Then to accompany the tables edge sat dark wooden chairs with matching red velvet cushions.

I had gone to two previous Balls but this was by far the prettiest venue I had seen yet and I thought maybe it was because everything was new.

Waiters carried trays of spiked red champagne flutes like usual, to offer to each guest as they arrived. I stopped and took one from the tray before continuing to walk down the three steps to the floor where the tables sat.

Starting a little early aren't we? I heard in my head.

I just shrugged before turning to see my best friend Angeline coming through the crowd. I smiled seeing her face again and I hadn't realized how much I'd missed her until that moment.

"I've missed you too." She said smiling. And like always, answering my unspoken thoughts.

I hugged her as soon as she was close enough for me to get my arms around her and she laughed.

"What's going on Delilah?" she asked breathlessly as I released her.

"I'm just so happy you're here. I answered. "And you too Ezra, "it's nice to see you both."

"Well where's my hug then? I see how it is, but I understand, sometimes it's hard for me to keep my hands off of her too." Ezra teased with a grin.

"Oh, come here you!" I said smiling hugging him in close.

“What’s this? I leave you alone for a minute and Ezra’s already moving in?” I heard Vincent’s bantering voice over my shoulder.

“That’s what happens when you leave a beautiful woman alone at a party.” He teased back when we broke apart.

“Next time you’ll know better won’t you?”

“Know better than to leave her near you!” Vincent answered sarcastically.

“Hey man, better I teach you then one of these other guys.” Ezra nodded in the direction of a group of attractive men standing by the entrance. “You might not get her back from one of them.”

“Now now boys, let’s not get feisty. We all know what a catch Delilah is but there’s no need for you two to fight over her.” Angeline broke in.

“Of course there isn’t” I said taking her lead. “There’s enough of me to go around. How’s alternate weekends sound to you boys?” I asked trying not to laugh.

“I think that’s a wonderful idea!” Angeline agreed.

“Sounds good to me.” Ezra added.

We all looked at Vincent waiting for him to speak.

“Hilarious,” he said looking at Angeline and Ezra. “And I’ll deal with you later.” He added in a low tone staring at me.

“Promise?” I asked giving him a suggestive look, and we all started laughing (including Vincent.)

“So, where are you two staying now? You’re not still in New York are you?” Angeline asked tilting her glass to her lips.

“No. Pennsylvania now. I thought I should brush Delilah up on her German and a lot of German immigrants live through there.”

“How’s that going?” she asked sarcastically.

“Wonderful!” Vincent replied.

“Really?” I knew she didn’t buy it by the eyes she gave me over her glass.

“I wouldn’t actually use the word wonderful to describe it.” I answered.

Train wreck about sum it up? my head asked.

I shrugged and nodded in response. Then played back the sentence Vincent was trying to teach me, and what I said instead.

She looked at me with those eyes again and I shrugged once more and we both burst into laughter.

“They’re at it again.” Ezra said looking over at Vincent. “What’s so funny?”

“Delilah’s German.” Angeline answered chuckling. Then she repeated in German what I had said.

Ezra looked confused as she spoke then when she finished he looked to me and again I shrugged and this time the boys joined in laughing at me.

“She really is catching on quite quickly; that was in the beginning, she’s pretty fluent now in fact.” Vincent offered my defense.

“I hope so.” Ezra laughed.

"Sorry to break up your little party, but look." I broke in nodding to the stage.

The five Elders stood confidently in front of each of their chairs. The four men were debonair in white tuxedos with black bow ties and Zariah was draped at the top in black sheer that twisted and hugged her curves, letting her chocolaty skin show through before flowing out at her hips into a beautifully gathered, black silk skirt that stopped at the floor.

All of them looked stunning and regal, standing on stage about to take their seats.

Carlus stood in the middle like always. His black hair was a little longer in the front now and slicked back on both sides and his big brown eyes gleamed even more in contrast to the white tux.

Ian, I noticed had been trying something new with his hair. Instead of just black he had put brown through it, taking some of the focus off his glossy black eyes.

Julius' dirty blonde waves were slightly longer too. He had it flipped over in the front to the left side.

And Nathaniel hadn't changed at all. Even after all these years he looked the same. Same muscular build, same disheveled brown hair, same cocky smile and the same unbelievable limpid eyes.

I smiled looking up at them. The beautiful of the beautiful. The first five and all our history, elegantly placed for all to see.

Unfortunately all of us were looking up at them and not the surrounding exits. Cause that's where they came in from.

Chapter 25.

Vincent had been right about their forces being unimaginable. When they hit us they came from all angles; there were tons of them. Big men, running with swords, and scythes, the men in front were carrying odd looking guns that had round jagged blades strapped to it. Others had wooden steaks and crosses. Some even had bibles. Like that would help, we had been cursed by God. He knew all about us and was the reason we were here.

The few of us that had been further toward the middle had more time to react and fought back, having some sort of plan, but for the others; they never even seen it coming. There were heads flying through the air left and right. Fresh blood poured on to the white marble floor, human and vampire alike.

I wasn't sure what happened to the Elders. At first I thought they ran too until I started to see some people go up in flames and others start to gush blood from every orifice. Some took their weapons and started attacking themselves or others on their own side. Others were mysteriously stuck with their steaks or had a head one second and didn't the next.

But no matter how many we slaughtered, more started to come in and soon they were everywhere. The enemy cornered groups at a time while others fought one on one; both sides maneuvering to dodge each others attacks.

Our hope started to dwindle and most ran when they were able, including the Elders. Someone had finally got them out and back to safety. But there was a few of us that stayed to fight. Sevelin and his new mate were among those who fought, as well as Vincent, myself, Angeline and Ezra. The majority of the Rising Sons that were left fell victim to hallucinations of drowning before really drowning in a gust of smoke.

The situation looked mostly under control so I left the others to see what information I could get. It seems Vincent's German lessons might come in handy after all.

I drifted down and grabbed a man that was trying to escape. "Und wo gehst du hin?" I asked grabbing him by the throat to stop him. " Ich denke, du und Ich werden unsein wenig unterhalten." I grabbed him on both sides of his shoulders and we rose up to the big dome ceiling.

"Das ist besser, würdest du nicht zustimmen?" I continued in German looking down the fifty plus feet to the floor.

"Whatever it is you want Demon I won't give it to you." The man said breathlessly, in English.

"Demon? I asked calmly. "Now is that any way to speak to a lady?"

"Lady?" He laughed. "You're no more a lady then I am."

"Alright maybe lady is a stretch, I agreed tilting my head a little at the thought. "But I'm certainly no demon." I shot back.

"Do not poison me with your lies. You are a demon, and I repel you. Get behind thee Satan! Though I walk through the valley of the shadow of death, I shall fear no ev—

"You know you're really starting to piss me off! Shut up or can't you see that's not doing you any good?" I interrupted.

"I guess we'll just have to do this the hard way." I sighed letting go of one of his arms so he was left dangling.

"Now will you listen, or will I have to let you splat like the roach you are?"

"I don't fear death Demon. God has prepared a place for me in his kingdom." he announced like he had won something.

"Oh, no? How about I give you eternal life then? We'll see how much God welcomes you into his kingdom after that!" (After all he didn't know I couldn't do it.)

His eyes widened with fear, a look I had seen once, a long time ago on Hazel. He clearly would rather die first.

"Ah, that got your attention didn't it? Now if you answer my questions I'll kill you quickly, if not, you'll become what you despise most. Do we have a deal?" I asked smiling down at him.

He thought about it before answering. "Ask your question, Demon."

"For one it would be nice if you would stop calling me Demon. I'm Delilah." (There really was no harm in his knowing my name; he was, after all, about to die.)

"Now for my questions. Is this all of you or are there more out there?"

He paused in hesitation so I smiled a big fangy smile at him for encouragement. "No." He said through gritted teeth.

"Well which one is it? No there's not or no there is?"

"No, they'll be more. We'll never stop, not until you're all dead!"

"Well that's unfortunate," I sighed. "Here I was hoping we could come to some sort of arrangement or understanding."

"Where do you stay? If there are a lot of you I'm sure you are stationed all over right?"

This he didn't answer he just stared at me with the same disgust plastered on his face.

"All right then, why us? Shouldn't you be concentrating on something else, something worse?"

"What's worse than you?!" He asked outraged. "You demons lurk in the night killing innocent people and snatching women and children from their beds. There isn't anything out there worse than you."

"Wait just a minute. How many people has your kind killed? I'm sure plenty of women and children were killed in World War 2 and now a new war just started! More death on the way delivered from your own kind. At least we kill to eat, what's your excuse?" I shouldn't be arguing with him but come on! Humans just couldn't stop killing each other… for nothing.

"It doesn't matter, war or no war we won't stop and even if it takes the next thousand years we will hunt every last one of you blood sucking whores of Satan down! We won't stop until every one of you burn!" He ended with a sadistic smile of which I returned before pulling him close enough to whisper.

"You won't." and I let him go, plummeting and screaming through the air to hit the hard marble floor with a thud.

"Not so arrogant now are you?" I shouted down to the twitching corpse on the floor. "Ha!" I said as I brushed my hands together. Now that's done I thought to myself as I immediately started searching the area for Vincent.

I spotted his fight from the air. He was fighting a man twice his size but compared to Vincent's speed every blow the man made with the scythe moved in slow motion. The other man didn't give up though. He struck out at Vince over and over before Vincent finally got a clear opening and took it. Placing a beautifully sculpted hand on each ear he simply twisted and his enemies head came off in his hands.

He noticed me watching from the air; our gazes locked on to each other and he smiled this megawatt smile at me as he carelessly tossed the head behind him.

I chuckled and rolled my eyes at his usual cockiness. He was such a ham.

He continued a few more steps towards me until suddenly he froze in mid stride. His smile fading.

"Vince?" I looked at him curiously, as my feet touched back down to the floor. I didn't understand his strange reaction.

My eyes followed his as he looked down in shock to find a silver ring of pointy, metal shards, sticking out of his chest.

Blood began to seep from the circular wound, like red syrup, slowly spreading over his white shirt.

"No…" I gasp as understanding hit me like a lightning bolt; he had been shot.

Everything slowed down to a crawl at that moment. The clanging of weapons and the battle cries of both sides at war went silent leaving just the ringing in my ears and the sound of each breath I took as I ran towards him. I felt every heartbeat slam into my ribcage like a sledge hammer as panic started to settle into my chest.

"Run!…" he urged in a heavy breath as he staggered. I barely caught him as he collapsed; forcing us both to the cold hard floor. "Get out of here!"

"I'm not going anywhere, so you can stop that right now. I'm going to pull this thing out."

I slightly turned his body towards me and felt around his back for something, anything to grab a hold of. I couldn't see where I was grabbing but a smooth, cool metal plate met my fingertips as I searched; it was wet with blood and there were no edges.

"There's nothing to grab a hold of."

I realized I was talking out loud and quickly added."But don't worry. I, will figure something out." I didn't want to upset him any more than I had to.

I turned him back to face me and he was pale, paler than I had ever seen him.

I looked to his chest and it was soaked, each beat of his heart pushed out more blood, soaking us both. I didn't know what to do!

"I'm going to push it back through." I announced, amazed that I sounded so confidant.

I placed my right hand on the shards of metal "Hang on." I said and pushed with all I had. I felt the sting in my palm as the shards pierced through the flesh of my hand but I didn't care about me. I had to save him.

He screamed out and I felt the piece move! My heart raced with excitement. I could do this! I pushed a little more and this time we both cried out but the ring stopped.

"I think it's stuck!" I yelled. But I kept pushing! I was so close, just a little farther and I was sure I could grab it from the plate in the back. If I could just get it out he could heal. I could give him my blood and he would heal.

I gritted my teeth and pushed through the pain. This had to work!

"Delilah, Sto…p." I heard him rasp. Snapping me back to him from my mental frenzy.

"What?" I froze. He was gray.

"You're hurting yourself."

"No, I can do this. It's working!" I pushed more and the shards bit deeper into my hand.

"Delilah, stop." His voice was barely a whisper.

"I can't just sit here and let you die." I pleaded with tears streaming down my face.

He shook his head and grinned. "So stubborn." He gasp rising as far up off the floor as he could in search for air but he started to choke, blood spraying from his mouth and nose.

"I'm sorry." I whispered. This was all my fault.

"No." he answered. His eyes were kind even though there were tears sliding from the outer corners.

"E...ter…nit…y." he gurgled as more blood spilled from his mouth, soaking his face.

"Eternity." I agreed, crying.

He gave me what he could of a smile and then his face fell slack. There was no movement, no heartbeat, there was… nothing.

"No, no no no.." I pushed at the ring again and again. My blood mixed with his as the shards continued to rip through my palm.

"God damn it!.. You promised me. I need you to get up!" I screamed, pushing as his big body covered mine. He didn't move. He didn't scream out. He didn't do anything; and he wasn't going to.

I gave up.

I kissed his face and then I slowly lowered him to the floor and pulled my hand from the metal. I didn't even feel it rip away.

Leaning my head down I put it on his chest. Laying on the floor I stared off into the distance. Red tears fell in silence down my face and I whispered,"What do I do now?"

Chapter 26.

"How sweet…" I heard come from in front of us. I looked up to see a dark haired man holding a homemade wooden gun that looked like a crossbow, only used to shoot something besides arrows.

"You know?" he said thoughtfully. "They're supposed to remove the heart all together, but I guess this works too." he added sadistically, hand gesturing towards the blood that stained Vincent's shirt.

I looked from him to Vincent's bloody body and back again.

"That's right sweetheart, I'm the one you want." He antagonized, wiggling his fingers in a -come here- manner, smiling.

I kissed Vincent's forehead, then while staring at this dark haired executioner I slowly got up from lying on his body. I left my beloved Vince on the blood soaked floor so I could stand before my enemy.

I could imagine the view of this man. My white silk gown covered in blood to the point you might not have guessed its original color. A tangle of untamed red curls reaching out like wild flames, sticky with blood and eyes of emerald directed solely at him.

I knew this game; I had already seen it with Fidelia many years ago. As soon as she went for the man in front of her she was grabbed from both sides. But little did they know I had a trick of my own up my sleeve.

I shot up, hovering just above the height of a man, and began to laugh. This wasn't the laugh that I had shared with my friends earlier in the night. This wasn't the laugh that I had shared so many times with my love that was now lying lifeless on the floor.

This was the laugh of a woman that didn't have anything left to lose. The laugh of a vengeful murderess who's greatest talent was dealing death.

I laughed as I hung in the air and the more I laughed the hotter I got. My skin was redder than I had ever seen it and soon my blood soaked white gown started to cinder and ash, falling away from my body to the floor beneath me.

The wind started to flow through me like it had done for so many years but I had not turned into smooth, black smoke; I was something else entirely. I was now uncontrollable, raging, red flame.

I touched back down to the floor in front of the dark haired man and stared at the figure that reflected off his frozen brown eyes. My naked flaming silhouette and raging red locks were nothing compared to my glowing green eyes and I was coming straight for him. I was coming for them all!

I moved like the wind as I placed a hand on both sides of his head. Breathing in the odor of his scorching flesh he screamed out in agony before I easily twisted and ripped his head clean off.

"Catch!" I chuckled, tossing the flaming head at one of the others that were now cautiously stepping backwards to get away from me. He dodged it before the burning head caught his clothes on fire and he started to run for the doors.

"Leaving so soon?" I asked, tilting my head to the side. "But we're just getting… started!" I yelled pushing a gust of fire from my body with my hands and setting him ablaze.

"Isn't this fun?!" I shouted as I walked and set more running, screaming, people on fire. I laughed as I watched them panic and scatter like frightened mice, bumping into walls and one another, setting the room on fire as well.

"RUN!" I screamed as I lifted my arms to raise the flames higher creating an inferno all around me.

Soon their screams were no more than gurgles but I stayed alert and ready for an attack to come at any minute. That's how they work right? They wait until we're vulnerable. Then when we're at our weakest they come in large numbers to finish us off? Well they would have to wait a long time if they were waiting for m—.

"Delilah! We have to go." Someone screamed from below me. I hadn't even noticed I was rising until I looked down and saw Angeline and Ezra standing on the once beautiful tile floor.

"I'm not going anywhere. They'll come back and they have to pay for what they've done! I said cracking, through blurry eyes.

"They're dead! Honey, they're all dead. Look around you."

I followed her gesture to the room full of burning bodies. And she was right, I had killed them all. In some places there was nothing left but bones and ash.

"Vincent." I gasp. I had to find him. I couldn't leave him here in here with all this trash; he was better than that. I had to take him with me.

I scanned the room, frantic to find his body, and there he was, lying there on the floor right where I had left him.

"I can't touch him." I realized aloud.

"You have to come down sweetie, you got them. Everyone's gone. Come down Delilah." Angeline coaxed.

I continued to stare blankly until I realized that Ezra had Vincent cradled in his arms. How I longed to touch him, to hold him and I couldn't do that if I was an inferno.

Slowly I started to pull myself together again, letting go of my hate and rage towards those who were already dead. I started towards the floor, my body only lightly glowing from the fire until my toes touched down with a sss… as they made contact with one of the many puddles of blood that covered the tile.

I might not have been burning anymore but my skin was still so hot that it would set Vincent's clothes on fire like it had my dress.

"Let's go Delilah, not all of us are fire proof and this building won't last long." Ezra warned.

I took another look around at the falling building and piles of ash that were scattered around the floor while Ezra held Vincent's body in his arms.

Amazingly there was one red velvet table cloth left that was only partly burned.

"Angeline?"

"I got it." she said with compassion then flashed to the table.

As we walked towards the door I seemed to cool off almost as quickly as I had heated up. By the time we reached the foyer Angeline was able to stand near me again, so I took the tablecloth and wrapped it around my body tucking it under my arms. Then with grieving hearts we all walked out of the building together, letting it burn to the ground in the distance behind us.

Chapter 27.

I knelt down still wrapped in my table cloth holding Vincent's upper body in my arms as the stars shone down on the four of us. The night was beautiful and the moon was his favorite, a perfect crescent.

I stared at his beautiful face just like I had done so many times as he slept peacefully in our bed. I ripped off a piece of the table cloth and slowly began to wipe the blood away from his mouth as tears began to stream down my face.

"I love you. I'm sorry. I'm so very sorry." I wept, leaning my face in close to nuzzle his. I wanted to hold him in my arms forever. I wanted to rewind time.

To go back to the first time I seen him and his megawatt smile at the Bakery.

I smiled thinking about our first fight when I beat him all over with the roses.

The way he would read to me.

The way he kissed me and how many times he left me spinning while my feet were safely on the ground.

When we made love through the morning...

The pain and anguish consumed me, heating me up from the core of my body until my outsides matched my insides.

My arms started to singe his clothes. The smoke trailing into my nose as they ignited.

The flames licked at his luscious black hair; first turning to cinder and then blowing away.

The flames crept up slowly, beginning to take away his face; the beautiful face that I fell in love with as a girl and had been looking at every night since for the past 20 years…

I couldn't do this, I couldn't watch him slowly burn! I screamed out not being able to hold in the agony of slowly watching him fade away and a beam of raw flame burst out of my chest, instantly turning the rest of his body to black ash in my arms.

Then everything went black.

Chapter 28.

There was nothing. No color, no life… no sound. I was surrounded by blackness where I was safe. I looked for Vincent but he wasn't there. If I were dead surely he would be there waiting for me? Wouldn't he? But what if this was my version of Hell? Stuck forever in black nothingness without Vincent, without anything?

I started to hyperventilate as I walked in the pitch black abyss. Was this it? Was this all I would do for the rest of eternity? Wander around on an endless search? A search for what though? How was I supposed to find what I didn't know to look for? I decided to sit. Maybe if I sat for a while the reason I was stuck here would come to me.

So I sat…. and sat…. and. sat……… Until I heard it. First a whisper.

"What? I can't understand you." I yelled at the nothingness.

__________"Find."

"Find who? Vincent?" I asked standing up so maybe I could follow the sound. "I tried to find him but it's dark. Where can I find him?"

"You have to find THEM!"

"Who?" I asked annoyed.

"T–

“Delilah?”

“What? You broke of.” I called out.

“Delilah!”

“What?” I asked confused with Angeline’s face an inch from mine.

“Finally! You passed out. I think the trauma was too much for you.”

“Trauma?” I asked blinking hard to remember.

Angeline and Ezra just looked at each other and then back to me.

“Honey, don’t you remember what happened?” Ezra asked touching the bed sheet covering my shoulder.

I sat for a minute trying to remember but I didn’t even recognize where I was. I didn’t live here?

“Where am I?” I thought I would start with the basic questions.

“You’re at a Hostel in Germany. You collapsed in an alley two nights ago so we brought you here so you could rest.”

“Do you remember why you passed out?” Angeline asked.

I thought about it for a minute, letting the shock ware off about where I was and the fact that I had passed out at all. That was so unlike me, even Vince wou—

“Oh… He’s dead. Vincent’s dead.” I realized as everything suddenly drained out of my body.

“And I did it. I killed him.”

“What happened is not your fault, Delilah.” Angeline said leaning and putting her hand on my leg to comfort me.

“Isn’t it?” I answered rising up to look at her. “He never wanted this, Angeline. He warned me a long time ago that we would lose if it came to a fight, but I didn’t listen. In fact I argued that it was worth it to go after them.”

“Yes, that’s because you knew what happened was inevitable. It never mattered if we stayed concealed. They were coming regardless. He knew that too. We all knew that.”

“Then why did this happen?” I wanted so badly for her or anybody to give me some kind of reason why it wasn’t my fault that Vincent was gone. He was looking at me instead of what was going on around him when he was shot. It was absolutely my fault.

“I don’t know. I wish I had an answer for you.” I could tell she wanted to cry as she sat, staring at my desperate face.

“I don’t guess it matters anymore anyways. Vincent’s gone now, and I have nothing left.”

“He might be gone but that doesn’t mean you can stop living. He wouldn’t want that and you know it.” She said giving me her usual set of eyebrows.

I thought back to one of the more recent arguments we had about revenge for those who had fallen at the hands of the Rising Sons and Vincent said us dying would not bring them back. And he was right; both of them were right.

“You’re right.” I said wiping the blood from my face with my hand. “And I can’t stay here any longer either." I said as I started to move forward off the bed.

"Are you sure you can do this? Ezra asked sympathetically.

I took a deep breath before answering. "Yes, I have to."

"Is there anything else I can put on besides this?" I asked pulling at the sheet.

"Yes, we got you a pair of tan slacks, a black blouse and some flat shoes. They're over there in the bathroom along with a clean towel and a toothbrush." Ezra answered pointing towards the bathroom door.

"Thank you both." I said before I closed the door.

The hot water was amazing on my cold skin. I couldn't even remember the last time I ate. And I was sure to stay away from the little mirror because the condition my skin was in was probably not flattering at all, and who needed that at a time like this?

So I watched the water change colors while I washed my hair and body, going from black to gray and red then finally to clear. It's amazing how much grime you can get off of one person with soap and water.

When I was finished with towel drying my body I started to dress myself in the clothes they bought me.

"Where's Vincent?" I asked threw the door as I slid on the tan slacks.

“We have him; I found a vase big enough to hold him so I sent Ezra back for him once we got you here.”

“Good.” I said opening the door with a gust of raging steam behind me.

Ezra handed me the vase as I stepped out into the room. I looked inside to find nothing but black ash.

“Thank you both for everything, I couldn’t ask for better friends.” I said smiling as my eyes started to fill up again.

“No problem, sweetie. I’m sorry about Vincent; he was one of my best friends. Angeline cried as she hugged me. And as I held on to her with tears streaming down both our faces I looked down to the ashes of my beloved Vincent. At that moment I made a silent vow that no matter how long it took me, rather it be one year or a hundred that I would hunt down every last member of the Rising Sons. They would pay for what they had done. No matter what, one by one, they would all die!

About the Author

C.R. HANOVER is a Detroit based, 1st place poetry contest winner, Writer and Author with a deep rooted love for Horror movies, Paranormal Romance novels and all things Vampire!

She admits to being a little obsessed and says it started when she was a young child, dressing up as Dracula to put on plays at her house.

Things that make her happy include: Tacos! Tattoos, Piercings, Bright hair colors, GLITTER, Thrift Store shopping and her 3 furbabies, Hades, Andromeda and Layla.

Her goals are to write amazing books, eat delicious food and see beautiful things.